The HOLIDAY WHOOPIE

SARA L. HUDSON

Copyright © 2025 by Sara L Hudson

Cover Design: Yummy Book Covers

Editor: Kasi Alexander

All rights reserved.

No part of this book may be reproduced in any form or by any electronic or mechanical means, including information storage and retrieval systems, without written permission from the author, except for the use of brief quotations in a book review.

Without in any way limiting the author's exclusive rights under copyright, any use of this publication to 'train' generative artificial intelligence (AI) technologies to generate text is expressly prohibited. The author reserves all rights to license uses of this work for generative AI training and development of machine learning language models.

This is a work of fiction, created without the use of AI technology. Any names, characters, places, and incidents are the products of the author's imagination and used in a fictitious manner. Any resemblance to any actual people, living or dead, events, or locales is entirely coincidental.

"The author acknowledges the trademarked status and trademark owners of various products referenced in this work of fiction, which have been used without permission. The publication/use of these trademarks is not authorized, associated with, or sponsored by the trademark owner.

Welcome to

HIDEAWAY HARBOR

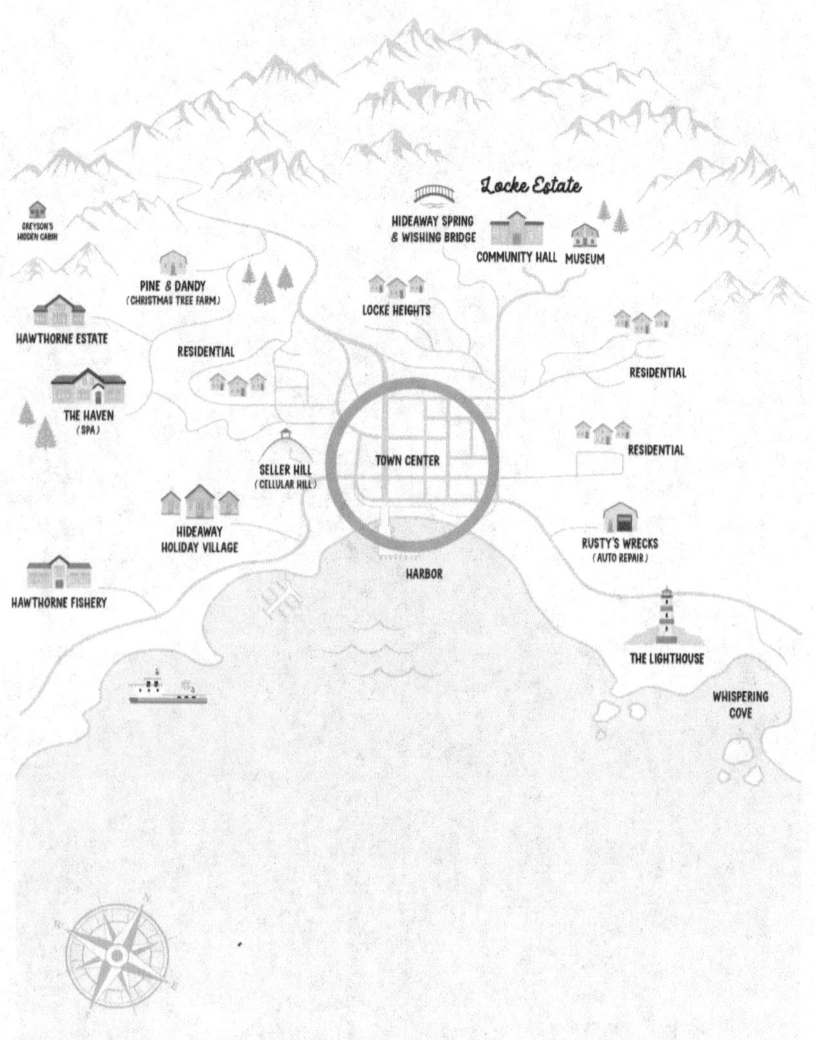

HIDEAWAY HARBOR

The town center

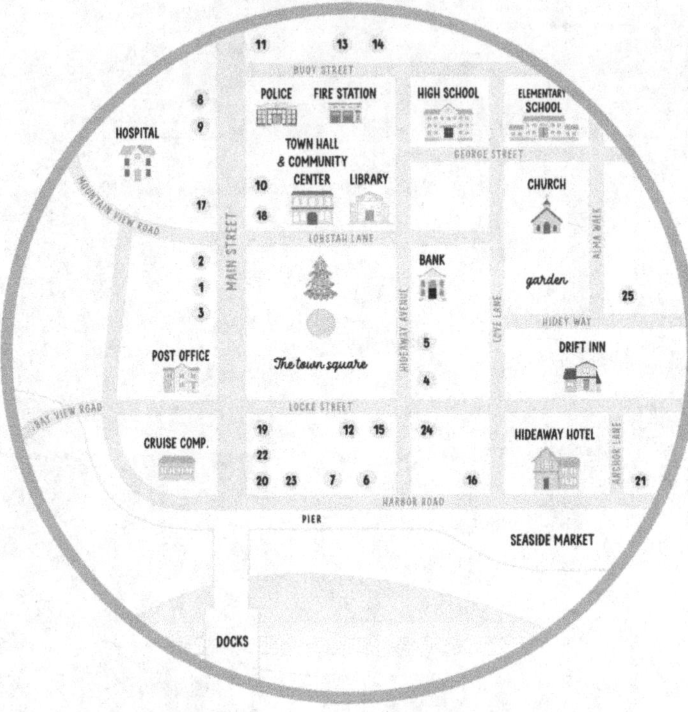

1 LOVE AT FIRST SIP (CAFE)
2 HIDDEN ITALY (RESTAURANT)
3 MAKING WHOOPIE (BAKERY)
4 HARD TO FIND (BOOKSTORE)
5 CHRISTMAS WONDERLAND (POP-UP STORE)
6 HOOK, LINE AND SINKER (RESTAURANT)
7 THE SHORE THING (BAR/RESTAURANT)
8 THE PERFECT PACKAGE (ADULT TOY STORE)
9 SCENTS AND SENSIBILITY (PERFUME SHOP)
10 THE WILDE KETTLE (TEA SHOP)
11 HIDEAWAY GROCER (GENERAL STORE)
12 PAPER MOON (OFFICE SUPPLIES)
13 LOBSTAH LIFTS (GYM)
14 HIDEAWAY CLINIC
15 HIDEAWAY TREASURES (GIFT SHOP)
16 THE CHOWDER HOUSE RULES (RESTAURANT)
17 ALMANAC (TOWN PAPER)
18 KIPPIS (SMALL BAR)
19 THE SWEETEST THING (CANDY STORE)
20 BEAUTY PARLOR
21 SALT & EMBER (RESTAURANT)
22 HOUSE OF PEARL (CLOTHING BOUTIQUE)
23 THE MASTER BAITERS (BAIT & TACKLE SHOP)
24 HAMMERTIME HARDWARE
25 OFF THE BEATEN PATH (ADVENTURE COMPANY)

PRE-HEAT

Jack

I'm freezing my balls off for whoopie.

I—a steadfast southern Californian—am burrowing into my newly purchased Tom Ford cashmere scarf as the cold from the cobblestone sidewalk seeps into my leather Cole Haan loafers and my testicles stage a full retreat.

And all because of a Freudian-named pastry sold in an innuendo-laden bakery called Making Whoopie.

"Isn't this fantastic?" Amanda Willis, actress, celebrity, and the reason I'm standing outside a bakery in a fishing village at the ass-end of Maine, clasps her mittened hands together and inhales like the air itself is cinnamon-sugar flavored.

I scan the scene—Main Street, Hideaway Harbor. No palm trees. No women in bikinis. Just a ridiculous number of Fraser firs and townspeople wearing enough buffalo plaid to start a lumberjack militia. "'Fantastic' is not the word that comes to mind."

Amanda's been riding a high since we crested the hill and rolled into town this morning. We flew a red-eye from LA to Bangor, rented a car, drove through a postcard, and landed in a town that looks like a Hallmark movie exploded only to spend what was supposed to be a scenic one-hour drive from Bangor white-knuckling the steering wheel, dodging snowbanks while the GPS glitched—all as Amanda waxed poetic about the storybook scenery and holiday charm.

Stamping my feet, I knock snow off my shoes. "What even *is* a whoopie pie?"

Amanda hugs her coat tighter. "Two soft cookie-sized cakes—chocolate, pumpkin, red velvet, you name it—sandwiched around a fluffy cream filling. They're Maine's state dessert."

I arch a brow, not having realized states had their own official desserts. "And you think that's worth frostbite?"

She tips her head, eyes glittering. "Well, it's also a long-standing euphemism for sex. *Making whoopie.* So technically, we're freezing for dessert and innuendo."

The cold catches my exhale, turning my exaggerated sigh into one giant puff of smoke. "Figures you'd drag me across the country for pastry foreplay."

Amanda just laughs. I glower.

It's during times like this that I remember the psych survey I took for extra credit in college—the one that declared I had "high responsibility" as my top personality strengths.

Other times include when I left corporate law for entertainment law after Felix decided to become an actor. Or when I took on Amanda after her coming out scandal during that movie she and Felix shot last year—even though I'd already started thinking about a career change.

"I read all about this place online." Amanda pivots in her sheepskin-lined boots and nods toward the large bakery window, where the lucky early birds are inside, warm and content, selecting their sweets under the glow of central heating.

With her shearling-collared red plaid coat and matching ear-flapped hat, my friend, nee client, looks less like the Oscar-winning actress she is and more like the Grand Axewoman of the aforementioned militia.

"Today's the first day Making Whoopie rolls out their holiday-themed whoopie pies." She's practically vibrating. "That's why it's so packed."

I'd chalk up her excitement to how different the colonial Northeast coastal holiday culture is from her everyday West Coast Hollywood-hippie lifestyle, but as we're *both* Californians and *I* feel nothing close to her level of enthusiasm by my surroundings, I don't.

"I can't feel my toes." Chin tucked, my lips move against my too-thin scarf. "Amongst other things."

"What was that?" Amanda eyes me sideways, her expression equal parts feigned innocence and amusement.

The bell above the door chimes as one happy pie-holding customer leaves, holding the door open so the person at the front of the line can slip in.

"Nothing," I grumble, herding her forward in line.

She rolls her eyes before facing the window, nearly pressing her nose against the glass trying to see the whoopie pies past the crowd inside. "If you hate the cold so much, why did you follow me to Maine for the holidays?" Her breath fogs the window in front of her.

I'm about to blame it on my impulsive sense of duty but stop myself. It's not the truth. Because while I may skirt around honesty with legalese and vague Hollywood agent-speak, I make it a point not to lie to my friends. And a year in to taking on Amanda as my client after her "scandal," that's exactly what she's become. A friend.

So instead of telling the truth, I lean into the Scrooge aesthetic and glare at the tinsel-covered storefronts.

"Men in flannel. Environmentally questionable vintage trucks. Axe throwing as a viable dating activity." I shrug. A gust of wind slips between my scarf and my double-breasted Burberry. "I was curious."

"You were bored." Amanda smirks, shuffling backward as the line creeps forward. "And maybe a little lonely." She nudges my shoe with her boot. "Admit it."

She's not wrong. But it's more than that.

Disregarding the lack of sleep and the unfamiliar weather, there's something about Hideaway Harbor that scrapes up old memories like frost off a windshield—memories from my early childhood. Before my parents died.

The smell of pine. The crunch of salt underfoot. People hustling down the street, bundled up, arms full of Christmas purchases. Small-town stuff I remember from a time I've spent most of my life trying to forget.

Thanks to Felix's mom Sofia taking me in when I was ten, I got to rewrite the script. Make new memories. New traditions.

Californian memories like faux Christmas trees that may not smell but never die and women rollerblading by the beach in red bikinis trimmed in white fur. And Portuguese traditions like Sofia's honey-spiced cookies served with warm cinnamon milk.

Except this year, Sofia and Felix are spending the holidays with Elizabeth's family.

Elizabeth—Felix's fiancée, and the best thing that's ever happened to him.

Worst thing that's ever happened to me, though.

I shake off the churlish thought, blow on my hands, and pretend it helps. Then, like I'm not actively plotting my escape to the nearest heat source, I deadpan into Amanda's heartfelt gaze, "I admit nothing. Except early-stage frostbite."

AUDREY

THE SCENT of sugar and cocoa wraps around me like an old friend as I pace behind the counter, trying to pretend I have full control over my bakery right now.

—"She's so down-to-earth looking."

—"If she's had work done, you can't tell."

—"I can't believe Hideaway has an Oscar winner in town for the holidays!"

My customers are in full gossip mode, huddled like kids plotting their Christmas lists, buzzing with excitement and completely oblivious to the rising panic crawling up the back of my neck.

"I can't believe it's really her."

Mia Keye, photographer for the local paper, *The Almanac*, has her eyes glued to what she can see of movie star Amanda Willis through the window display—past the carefully arranged tower of whoopie pies and the garland-tangled reindeer I spent all night positioning for today's holiday flavor launch.

She glances down at her hands—latte in one, whoopie pie in the other—like she's cursing herself for not bringing her camera, seeing as this is the biggest celebrity scoop Hideaway's had all year.

"She's even prettier in person," Hudson Locke, fireman and frequent public nuisance, mumbles around a mouthful of whoopie pie. A whoopie pie from the order he just purchased —and is still standing here eating and gawking. He's large enough to block the counter for two people, and until he leaves, I can't let in the next round of customers, celebrity or not.

I shake off the thought that an assistant would be nice and keep alternating between counter service and bakery work. This past fall, looking over the numbers, I convinced myself I could handle the holiday season alone. That I didn't need extra help. By saving money on staff, I could afford more advertising. And more advertising meant more reach. More reach meant more success.

Success I'd very much like my number-driven mother to notice so she can finally stop sighing dramatically whenever someone mentions my "little bakery" in "that little town" I moved to two years ago. Because once I ensure Making Whoopie's success, I can stop feeling guilty about why I really left my near celebrity-level status as New York City Ritz Carlton's foremost pastry chef for small-town entrepreneurship in Hideaway.

Mia snorts. "Amanda Willis wouldn't be interested in any of your equipment, Hudson." She gestures at his pants with her pie hand. "She came out as gay last year."

Hudson shrugs, unfazed. "Then who's the guy with her?"

Every head swivels toward the window like it's choreographed.

"That's her lawyer." Mia lowers her voice. "I heard from the mayor he'd be coming with her."

A hush falls over the bakery. Not the good kind. The kind people usually reserve for car crashes or funerals.

Hideaway Harbor prides itself on welcoming outsiders with mittens and maple syrup—but if there's one group this town collectively mistrusts, it's lawyers. No one says it out loud, but everyone knows we take more pride in not having one than we do in winning the sock-running championship.

And it doesn't help that the guy standing stiffly next to Amanda in his designer coat has a whole "I don't belong here" vibe.

I give up on trying to serve the next customer—everyone's too focused on the sidewalk—and move to pull a tray of fresh pies off the trolley to restock the display.

"Poor girl," Alice Cassidy, local librarian, murmurs from her spot near the door. "Amanda probably brought him to fend off paparazzi. She doesn't know we'd never do anything invasive."

Hudson glances at Mia, who's now digging in her coat pocket and coming out with her phone. "Exactly." He plucks it out of her hand just as she swipes the camera app open. "We don't want to run her out of town."

Mia's glare promises vengeance.

A few customers chuckle, the tension softening, until Eileen Burrows—town matchmaker and owner of next door's Love at First Sip—claps her hands like she's just been handed a Hallmark Christmas plot on a silver tray.

"Instead of a lawyer, I could help find her a lady friend instead."

Alice groans. "Eileen."

"What?" Eileen shrugs. "It's the season of giving. And frankly, those Hollywood types would be lucky to link up with a Hideaway local." She eyes me over the top of her latte like I'm a box of cookies she just remembered she left on the shelf. "Bring them down to earth to what really matters."

"I'm not gay." I slide the back of the display case closed on a sigh.

Part of me is flattered—being referred to as a local means more than I want to admit. But another part is irked it's taken Eileen two whole years to include me in her matchmaking mayhem.

At first, I assumed her lack of interest in my dating life was because I was new to town. But then as months turned into years, I worried it was something else.

Like maybe she thought I was too prickly. Too controlling. Too... something that had my love life just as stagnant as it had been in New York City.

Now I'm wondering what I could've said—or done—that made her think I'm not in the market. Or at least, not in the market for *a man*.

Eileen just smiles, cat-who-got-the-canary style. "I know."

Before I can press her on that, the front bell chimes again, the warm scent of cinnamon and cocoa colliding with a gust of cold air as another customer squeezes inside before anyone has left.

I close my eyes for a second and breathe it all in. Holiday Whoopie Day. My busiest, most chaotic, most profitable day of the year.

If I can keep the line moving.

If I can turn over customers before they freeze to death outside and give up.

If a movie star and her fancy lawyer don't walk inside and blow the whole system to hell.

Mia whispers something about helping Amanda skip the line. Hudson's talking about running interference. Eileen's leaning toward the window like she's already planning matching flannel pajamas.

Nope. Not happening.

If Amanda Willis walks into this bakery, she'll be swarmed.

Which means chaos.

Which means delays.

Which means a full-on holiday meltdown.

Time to save us all.

I grab a fresh box, fill it with an assortment of crowd favorites—Hot Cocoa & Chill, Jingle My Berries, Fa-La-La-La-Filled—and head for the door.

MISTRIAL

Jack

I'm about to call off the baked-goods excursion in the name of testicle safety when the guy at the front of the line sneaks inside without waiting for someone to exit.

The door doesn't fully close behind him, his puffer jacket sticking out over the threshold.

Something I'm sure the owner—who's probably paying astronomical prices to heat the place—wouldn't be too pleased about. But I am. The blast of heat is the first welcome bit of ambiance this town has given me.

If I hadn't listened to that pesky little voice inside my head that keeps telling me not to take on more clients, I'd be basking in California sunshine and having sushi and sake lunch meetings.

Okay. Maybe not basking. I don't remember ever having

basked before. But I'd be working, and that's as basking as I get. And the new client would be a great challenge. He's a good actor. Has loads of potential. And his current agent was the one who reached out wanting to offer him up. Unusual in my line of business, but his agent is relatively new and doesn't think she has the resources and connections to do her client justice. Got to respect that.

"Oh. My. God." Amanda elbows me hard in the ribs. "Look." She points toward the other side of the door, where the wall of customers in front of us had been blocking the view.

"Is that a dog?"

It's a rhetorical question—anyone can see the lump of fur is indeed a dog—but I'm confused as to why it's lying in a snowbank directly in front of a bakery entrance and no one in line before us mentioned it. "Is it dead?"

Just then, the large animal lifts its head, looks at me, and, as if finding me just as unappealing as I find this small-town Christmas-time excursion, flops back down onto its snow pillow.

Amanda rolls her eyes. "I was talking about *that*." She jabs her finger again, this time clearly pointing at a foldable chalkboard sign sitting behind the dog. "Isn't that the most amazing thing you've ever seen?"

Fearing another jab, I move out of elbow range—and closer to the warm air escaping the bakery—and read the handwritten menu, festooned with doodled ornaments and candy canes.

Hot Cocoa & Chill: Decadent chocolate cakes wrapped

AROUND MARSHMALLOW FLUFF AND TINY CHOCOLATE BITS. *Pairs well with a snuggle and absolutely nothing else on.*

Stuff My Stocking: Gingerbread cakes filled with silky eggnog cream and a cinnamon kick. This one finishes fast. *Better go for round two.*

Jingle My Berries: Spiced vanilla cake with cranberry-orange cream cheese filling. *Tangy, tingly, and totally unexpected—like a holiday hookup with an ex.*

Dasher's Midnight Ride: Espresso-dark chocolate cake + mocha cream with a peppermint finish. *Stays up late. Rides hard. Leaves you breathless.*

Kiss Me Under the Whoopie: White chocolate cakes hugging raspberry mascarpone cream. *One bite and you'll be puckered up and emotionally compromised.*

Fireside Fling: Toasted s'mores whoopie with graham cracker cake and gooey marshmallow-chocolate swirl. *Just the right amount of sticky.*

Unwrap Me Slowly: Chocolate cake with hazelnut crème, dipped in gold luster dust. *Looks classy. Tastes filthy.*

The sign and menu are pure Christmas: quaint, clever, and hilariously perverse. Much like the bakery's name.

The branding is on point.

And if I wasn't exhausted, grumpy, and—as my whoopie pie-loving client claims—*lonely*, I'd agree with her that it's amazing.

But I *am* all of those things. So I do not agree.

Instead, rubbing my sore ribs, I lean back against the painted shingle siding, inhale the warm air that smells like sugar, vanilla, and something dangerously nostalgic, and embrace my inner petulant child.

"If you think a baker who's mistaken a perverted sense of humor for originality is *amazing,* then yeah. Sure. It's amazing." I nearly give myself a migraine from the force of my eye roll. "Though I find it hard to believe that you, an international award-winning actress, can be so easily charmed."

For the first time since we arrived, Amanda's smile slips. "It's because I've seen so much of that supposed 'Hollywood magic'"—she air quotes, though with her mittens it looks like puppet theater—"that I can appreciate something real when I see it." She attempts to cross her arms but fails thanks to the coat. With a huff, she gestures toward the stray dog. "Hideaway Harbor is charming. And you'd agree if you weren't being such a Scrooge."

Feeling a little guilty for raining on her small-town parade—but not guilty enough to get over myself—I drop my head against the siding and close my eyes. "You say *charming,*" I grumble. "I say *aggressively festive.*"

"Is that so?" The voice cuts in—cool, unimpressed, and in direct opposition to the warm wave of air that follows it.

I open my eyes just as the bakery door swings wide, and *she* steps out.

Dark hair pulled into a barely-contained bun. A smudge of cocoa on one cheek like war paint. A cranberry apron dusted in flour. Slip-resistant Crocs to match adorned with Christmas charms. And despite the holiday hue of her apron and the low-fi holiday music drifting out behind her, the woman herself looks anything but merry.

"Thank you for sharing your"—she gives me a slow, unimpressed once-over—"*unique* perspective on the town's holiday décor." Her voice is honeyed with just enough bite to qualify as legally passive-aggressive.

She steps fully onto the stoop, bakery box balanced on one palm, and offers what looks like a piece of cake to the stray dog—who perks up instantly, tail wagging like she just offered him a winning lottery ticket.

She tosses the treat. He catches it. Swallows. Trots away.

Then she turns to Amanda, and everything about her face softens.

"You must be Amanda Willis."

"I—yes." Amanda blinks, clearly caught off guard.

"Heard you'd be in town. The mayor wrote an article about it in *The Almanac*." She tips her head, giving me a better view of the beauty mark under her right eye. "Something about you lighting the Christmas tree tomorrow night in front of Town Hall?"

I've seen plenty of attractive women in LA. Dated more than a few. Celebrities, models, women with carefully tousled hair and strategically placed beauty marks.

So it makes *no damn sense* that my throat goes dry and my leather gloves creak from how tightly I'm clenching my fists from my sudden, irrational urge to act like that stray and beg this woman for a treat.

Amanda beams. "Yes. That's right."

"Welcome to Hideaway Harbor." She holds out the bakery box. "Two of each of my holiday whoopie pies."

I watch like a man observing a particularly tense chess match. Amanda's eyes flick to me occasionally, but the baker? She makes it clear I've been cut from the scene.

As someone who's spent his career carefully curated and

painfully aware of how every move plays in the court of public opinion, I'm *not* used to being ignored. Or called out.

Especially not by a wild-haired pastry assassin who smells like peppermint and poor impulse control.

Which explains the strange heat crawling up my neck when my gaze drops—unhelpfully—to the open collar of her chef's coat.

Right to the delicate slope of her collarbone.

"Wow." Amanda, lips forming an O at the box's contents, accepts it reverently. "Thank you."

I snap out of it, reaching for my wallet. "Let me pay you for—"

"No need." She lifts a hand, eyes still on Amanda. "I just thought it'd be wise to come out and meet you before you got swarmed." She thumbs toward the bakery window, where at least six faces are now smooshed against the glass.

"Your customers?" I blame the tone on jet lag. And possibly starvation. But it gets me what I want—her attention.

And *oof*. That look.

"Yes." Her brow arches like she's trying to illustrate how beneath her she finds me.

My frozen testicles begin to thaw.

"I'm Audrey Nouel, the owner and patissière of Making Whoopie"—she gestures to the holly-wrapped sign beside the door—"and a big fan of aggressively festive holiday décor." She turns back to Amanda. "Also a big fan of yours. *Loved* you in *Lift Off to Love.*"

Of course her name is Audrey. She's Audrey Hepburn incarnate.

And I've always had a thing for classics.

"Thanks." Amanda sounds sincere, but I can tell her focus has shifted entirely to the treasure trove in her hands. "Whoa."

The smile that lights up Audrey's face in response makes my chest feel like I've taken a sip of really good whiskey after closing a seven-figure deal.

She bats her lashes—fake-innocent. "My next suggestion for your visit would be to find someone who actually appreciates the town's charm."

I flinch, the barb landing.

"But if that fails..." She shrugs, chin tilting toward the shop next door. "Grabbing a coffee from Love at First Sip is the next best thing." And with that, she steps back inside.

Not a glance in my direction. Just the door shutting firmly behind her.

My next shiver starts below the belt.

"Ooh." Amanda, completely unfazed, lifts a glittering whoopie pie from the pale blue box. "This one has glitter."

Audrey

No man that smug, buttoned-up, and judgmental has any right being that good-looking. Especially not while standing in front of *my* shop, radiating disdain and disapproval like a space heater set to *condescend*.

I should've ignored him. Or snapped. Or handed him a whoopie pie and smiled while I told him to go to hell.

Instead, I got distracted. Lost my moment.

No picture with Amanda. No proof of my brush with fame.

And now I'm back inside Making Whoopie, facing down a bakery full of nosy locals who promised not to bombard the celebrity outside once I promised them gossip and a free pastry.

And while I may regret my too-strong reaction to the Burberry Grinch, I regret not staying outside a little longer to cool off even more. Because the second I step inside, I'm met by a press pool of whoopie pie enthusiasts turned amateur tabloid reporters.

—"Was she nice?"

—"Did she hug you?"

—"What was her favorite pie?"

—"Did she thank you?"

They lean in, a dozen heads bobbing in anticipation.

I spot Hudson at the back, rubbing his stomach like he just got elbowed.

Mia—phone now miraculously reclaimed from Hudson—is practically vibrating next to the window display. "Well?"

"We stayed put, just like you asked," Alice reminds me, arms crossed but eyes twinkling.

I inhale a deep, sugar-scented breath. *Fake it till you bake it.*

Making my way behind the counter, I rub my arms to shake off the lingering winter chill from standing outside sans coat. "Amanda Willis is absolutely lovely." I grab a tray of my experimental flavored pies.

"She *looks* lovely," Eileen murmurs, still gazing longingly out the window.

"She *is* lovely," I confirm, rounding the counter again and luring them toward the exit like one might a retriever with a biscuit. "Polite. Friendly. Effortlessly gracious." And genuinely enthusiastic about her free box of whoopie pies—which, frankly, is how I judge a person's character.

If Amanda Willis is even half as charming with the rest of the town as she was with me, Hideaway Harbor is going to stampede its way to that tree lighting tomorrow night.

My brain's already racing.

Can I bake enough extras to do a last-minute pop-up at the event?

Do I have enough boxes? Labels? Twine? Sprinkles?

Can I *make* the time?

I'm already running low on sleep thanks to last night's window display marathon and this morning's monster bake for the holiday flavor reveal.

But if I do pull it off—and if I *somehow* manage to get a picture of Amanda holding one of my whoopie pies? That's gold.

I know from my past job at the Ritz that a good post with the right hashtags could turn my respectable one thousand followers into something closer to... relevant.

Relevant enough to comfortably afford an assistant. *If* I could admit to myself that I need one.

"Did she say where she was going next?" Eileen asks, still holding her whoopie pie like it's a microphone.

I ignore the question and redirect.

"That's a new flavor combination I've been working on." I nod at the treat in her hand as the others swarm in and pluck theirs from the tray. "Spiced-vanilla cake with orange-cranberry buttercream and edible pine needle sprinkles."

Mia takes a huge bite and moans audibly.

Hudson turns a disturbing shade of red at the sound.

Alice moves her bite to the side of her cheek, chipmunk-style. "Divine as always, Audrey."

Feeling unreasonably pleased, I decide right then that the new flavor will be exclusive to tomorrow night's tree lighting. The tree lighting I will make time for.

My mind's already spinning with potential hashtags I don't have time to create.

"I directed Amanda to Love at First Sip," I announce loudly when no one shows any interest in heading for the door. "Said she wanted a coffee."

Eileen gasps—hands to heart, eyes wide. "Her *coffee order!*"

Alice groans. "Oh no."

"Yes!" Eileen spins toward her like a woman reborn. "Her coffee order will tell me *everything* I need to know about what kind of woman she likes."

Mia laughs. "I bet she orders an oat milk latte with fake sugar."

"Nah, something off-menu." Hudson strokes his stubbled jaw with one hand and waves his bag of pies with the other. "I bet my Jingle My Berries whoopie pie that she orders a green tea matcha chai with kombucha or something equally Californian and confusing."

Eileen pushes through the crowd like a woman on a caffeinated mission. "Only one way to find out!"

The bell over the door chimes like a starting pistol.

Bets forgotten, the herd mobilizes—coats zipping, boots stomping, a flurry of goodbyes flung in the air as the peanut gallery evacuates in pursuit of coffee-based matchmaking intel.

And when the last one exits, I'm left with the customers I haven't served and a line that's *finally* moving again.

In no time, the shop is full, the pies are selling, and the chaos feels... good.

Like possibility.

Like momentum.

Like *maybe,* just maybe, Making Whoopie is about to have its moment.

But as I fill new orders and replenish the display cases with trays of pies from the racks, my mind reels with all that I need to get together if I intend to make that moment happen. More pies. Social media posts. More pies. Signage. *More. Pies.*

I hand another customer their box and smile through the stress.

I'll figure it out. I always do.

Still, when a blond woman moves past the front window, reminding me of Amanda, a pang hits low and sharp.

I should've taken that photo when she was right there.

Not for clout. Not even for the algorithm. Not even for my mother.

Just for me.

But I didn't. Because I got flustered.

By a lawyer. A grinch. And a man my mother would absolutely adore with or without the law degree.

The very opposite of what I'm looking for. What I moved here for.

If I was ready to admit it.

Which I'm not. At all.

CROSS EXAMINE

Jack

I'm not as grumpy as I was yesterday.

A good thing, considering I'm currently standing on the outskirts of a large crowd gathered in the town square, waiting for Amanda to light the Christmas tree.

The enormous, *real* Christmas tree. Already partially lit by spotlights, like it's just waiting for its close-up.

I actually smile as children zigzag across the cobblestones in woolen hats with felt reindeer antlers stitched to the tops, while adults sip spiced cider and try to stop their toddlers from eating snow.

It might be the spiked hot chocolate Amanda left me with before heading toward the stage. But more than likely, my grinchlessness stems from a full night's sleep—and having recently consumed my weight in whoopie pies that could probably be FDA-approved to replace Xanax.

The moist cake sandwiches stuffed with icing, cream, and candy are the only explanation for how I survived both the townspeople's horrified expressions when they discovered what I did for a living and trailing Amanda through her Black Friday spending spree—which I'm pretty sure boosted Hideaway Harbor's economy by fifty percent.

Full and no longer sleep-deprived, I crashed at The Haven—a resort that feels like the love child of California hippies and Norwegian lumberjacks—and woke to find the town's Christmas décor decidedly less aggressively festive and more… tastefully magical.

There are twinkling white lights strung from every building. Red and green ribbons wrap the lampposts like peppermint sticks.

And in the center of it all stands the tree—an honest-to-God, thirty-foot Fraser fir crowned with a star that could rival the searchlights at a movie premiere.

There's nothing fake about the greenery or the cascade of snowflakes falling from the sky like a live-action Christmas card. No plastic cheer to roll my eyes at. No glitter bomb of commercialism to mock. Just actual trees, actual lights, and actual joy—all of it so sincere it short-circuits my ability to be a jackass about it.

Which, frankly, is unsettling.

Because if I can't pick it apart, I'm left with the other very real thing I've been avoiding since we landed in this sneakily charming snow globe: my feelings.

The over-the-top holiday spirit that silenced yesterday's inner Grinch has apparently made room for something worse—the dull, unspoken ache Amanda called out before I was eviscerated by the town's morally superior pastry goddess.

Only now it's not dull. And it has a voice.

It sounds like a feisty elf in a flour-dusted apron, slapping down trays of emotionally jarring whoopie pies and whispering, "You're lonely, Jack. And maybe it's time to expand your emotional vocabulary beyond 'annoyed' and 'contractually obligated.'"

And I can't seem to quiet this new and audacious inner voice.

Maybe because it sounds suspiciously like the woman who, just a few yards away, has set up a stall between one booth selling knit Santa hats and another hawking lobster claw ornaments that say *Merry Kiss-mas from Maine.*

Making Whoopie's town square pop-up booth looks like a wooden gingerbread cutout, accented in the bakery's signature cranberry red and sky blue.

The owner is wearing a logo-matching red puffer coat, her hair pulled into a low braided ponytail under a sky-blue knit hat topped with an oversized white pompom. Her cheeks are pink from the cold, and she's bracing one foot against a cooler as she tries to tape a sign to the front of her table for what appears to be the twelfth time.

Each time she leans forward, her braid slips over her shoulder. Each time, she huffs and tosses it back.

If possible, she looks even more stressed than she did at the shop.

I take a sip of hot chocolate and look away.

Immediately look back.

"What are you staring at?"

I turn toward the familiar deep voice and nearly drop my thermos. "Jesus."

Felix Jones, Hollywood A-list action star and my best

friend, is grinning at me, looking annoyingly down-to-earth in jeans and a buttoned-up navy peacoat.

Then again, his go-to celebrity look was always casual. I was the sidekick suit.

"Felix!" I pull him in for a quick one-armed hug, thump his back, and take note of what feels like a dad-bod situation under all that wool. "What the hell are you doing here, man?"

"I told you he'd be brooding on the edges of the crowd." Elizabeth Moore, his fiancée, bounces in her snow boots beside him, her wavy blond hair peeking out from under a white beret that matches her mittens. "You should've texted him."

Felix kisses her forehead, the gesture oddly more intimate than if he'd full-on made out with her. "I was afraid I'd let the surprise slip." He drops an arm around her shoulders, their feet shuffling closer in the snow.

The two of them together on one side, me on the other.

At least that's how it *feels*.

Stupid feelings.

"Surprise!" Felix jazz hands with his free arm, the move ridiculous enough to shake off my moment of selfish brooding.

Elizabeth tilts her head to one side, assessing me. "Good surprise?"

Moving past the physical and metaphorical separation between us, I wrap both arms around them, group hug style. "Great surprise."

And it is. Really.

When I step back, Felix's early smile is replaced with concern. "You okay, man?"

It's only then that I realize I held on a second longer than I probably should have, considering I'm not the most effusive guy to begin with.

"Uh, yeah. It's just, you know—" I gesture around us. "'Tis the season and all."

He chuckles, and the knot inside me loosens.

My eyes track back toward the whoopie pie booth.

Felix follows, turning back to me with a smirk that's graced more movie posters than I have fingers. "That the woman you pissed off?" He points.

"Don't." I grab his hand and lower it before anyone can notice. Before *she* can notice.

Elizabeth giggles.

I sigh. "Amanda told you, didn't she?"

"In great detail." Felix looks far too delighted for my supposed best friend. "Complete with hand gestures and character voices. It played like a one-woman Broadway show."

"Don't worry." Elizabeth relieves me of my thermos and takes a sip. "Amanda only made you sound *mildly* insufferable."

Before I can reply—or get my hot chocolate back—Felix's hands disappear into his coat. "Here. Hold this."

Something warm and horrifying is unlatched from the carrier strapped to his chest and deposited into my arms.

Mike Hunt, the hairless cat, blinks up at me from his fleece-lined vest and rubber-footed knit booties. He makes a sound that falls somewhere between a hiccup and a death threat.

"Oh no." I try to shove the feline back into Felix's arms. "Nope."

I would've rather the dad-bod situation I'd felt under his coat mean that I was now representing an action star with a beer gut than deal with the follically challenged demon now dangling from my outstretched arms.

Because where Mike Hunt goes, mayhem follows. A fact I learned far too well when Felix and Elizabeth got together.

"Why the *hell* would you bring this"—I shake my arms, his naked limbs flailing in the cold—"with you from New York?"

Elizabeth strokes Mike's chin but doesn't relieve me of him. "It's the busiest shopping week of the season, so I'm babysitting while my brothers and sisters-in-law are all hands on deck at the store."

The store being *Moore's*—a nearly one-million-square-foot luxury behemoth set in some of the priciest real estate in Manhattan. Think Harrods in London, only bigger.

While Elizabeth is one of the three heirs to the empire, she walked away, leaving her brothers to expand the brand—with the help of their brilliant wives—while she forged her own path.

Mike Hunt does a full-body shiver, and against my better judgment, I gather his dense, wrinkled little body against my chest.

He rewards me by stabbing one paw directly into my jugular.

Felix laughs as I cough.

The music from the speakers fades as the mayor takes the stage, Amanda beside him. She's glowing with that movie star wattage, waving at the crowd like she was born here, like she didn't just arrive yesterday in a rented SUV.

"Amanda looks good." Elizabeth gazes fondly at the stage

as the mayor launches into a rambling speech about holiday fundraisers and a cat sanctuary.

She and Felix were the other two people in Amanda's corner during her coming-out drama.

Mike Hunt—perhaps finally bored of attempting murder—retracts his claws, allowing me to tuck him deeper into my coat. "Yeah." I nod. "She's been pretty upbeat since deciding to produce her own films."

The mayor finally hands Amanda the mic.

She beams, pure star power wrapped in plaid. "This place is magic." Her breath curls into the cold air. "Thank you for such a warm welcome to your lovely town."

"Thank you for the purchases!" someone yells.

The crowd laughs.

"You're very welcome." Amanda winks. "Hideaway is such a special place. And while I came here because I heard about the amazing lineup of Christmas-themed events, all starting with this one right here"—she points to the tree—"after only twenty-four hours, I can tell it isn't the decorations that make this place special"—she finds me in the crowd and smirks—"no matter how aggressively festive—"

I snort.

"—but rather it's the people"—she gestures to the crowd, which seems to warm at her words despite the frigid temperatures—"all of you, who make this town truly one of a kind."

A collective *aww* rolls through the square, followed by mitten-muffled clapping.

She lifts her hand as if sharing a secret, but her voice carries clearly through the microphone. "The kind of special I very much hope to immortalize in film soon."

People gasp, clap, and nudge each other in excitement.

"But for now"—Amanda lifts her arms theatrically—"let's light this thing!"

A beat. Then—bam.

The star at the top of the tree flares to life, followed by a cascade of twinkling lights that ripple down the branches like a North Pole glitter bomb.

Felix lets out a low whistle. "It's like small-town Rockefeller Center."

"Seriously." Elizabeth, not meeting my eyes, murmurs, "Though some might not appreciate its charm."

I roll my eyes as Felix and Elizabeth share a laugh at my expense.

I'd double down on my earlier opinion of the town's décor, but even with a mostly naked cat lodged against my sternum, I can't find fault with Hideaway's coniferous spectacle. It's—well, kind of magical.

Elizabeth's eyes drift to the square. "I want one of those whoopie pies Amanda wouldn't shut up about."

"She said they were so good she briefly believed in soul mates again," Felix adds. "I feel like that's worth investigating."

I shift Mike's weight. "You two go. I'll stay here." I shove the cat forward. "Take this."

Elizabeth raises a brow, mittens to her chest. "Jack, sweetheart. How am I supposed to eat whoopie pies with a cat in my hands?"

Glaring, I pivot to Felix. "You have a carrier. I saw it."

Felix raises his hands but begins walking backward. "I need a break. You don't want me throwing my back out before filming starts next month, do you?"

"I—"

Mike emits a sound that can only be described as a death rattle, followed by a violent shiver.

"Fuck." I pull him back into my coat.

But not fast enough because by the time I look up, Felix and Elizabeth are out of arm's reach, blending into the crowd —leaving me alone with a velociraptor in cat form clinging to my chest and a rising sense of pastry-related dread.

"Bring me something!" I call after them.

Felix doesn't turn. Just lifts a hand. "We'll bring you your dignity if we find it!"

I sigh. The crowd is blissfully lost in the holiday spirit. Mike Hunt farts.

In seconds, the stench has smothered all sense of holiday magic.

Typical.

Stalking across the square, I lock eyes on the Making Whoopie booth near the stage, where my so-called friends are now chatting with its owner.

I'm going over there to return the cat.

That's it.

My impatience has absolutely nothing to do with the sarcastic baker who may or may not sell me a mistletoe-laced whoopie pie, and who is now laughing at something Felix just said.

Definitely not.

Just cat logistics.

Totally.

My new inner voice is annoyingly smug.

Audrey

In the past forty-eight hours, I've handed whoopie pies to two movie stars, and not once have I had time to process—let alone document—it.

Because when you own your own bakery and make the insane decision to also operate a booth outside of normal business hours—*during the holidays*—you forfeit things like sleep, sanity, and the ability to feel your toes after sunset.

I hand a Stuff My Stocking pie to Felix Jones and the tree-lighting-exclusive Oh, Tannenbaum to his gorgeous fiancée, both of whom smile at me like we're old friends.

Then the crowd hits.

Not drifts in. *Hits.*

The real-life celebrity endorsement slams into my booth like a peppermint-scented avalanche I was absolutely not prepared to ride.

Suddenly I'm boxed in by flannel and fleece and frantic voices.

"Two Santa's Cream-Filled Secrets!"

"One Hot Cocoa & Chill!"

"I'll have whatever Felix Jones ordered!"

My head's spinning, my cooler's cracked open, and I'm one order away from a full mental spiral when one of the three people wedged against the front of my booth waves a ten-dollar bill at me like I'm giving away more than just baked goods.

And then—because apparently tonight needed a final boss level of absurdity—I spot Amanda Willis' snobby lawyer shove a disturbingly festive hairless cat into Felix's arms like it's a cursed fruitcake before shouldering his way into the booth.

My booth.

He takes the ten-dollar bill from the customer's hand. "Coming right up."

But it's not coming right up. Because—*what the actual fuck?*

"Excuse me." Hands on my puffer-covered hips, I glare at the man invading both my personal and professional space. "Just who do you think you are to—"

"Jack Lourd." He pops open the cash box behind the counter and starts counting out change. "Nice to meet you."

I blink. "What—no—you can't just—"

"That's two Santa's Cream-Filled Secrets." He scans the labeled coolers like he owns the place. "I'd help with pie duty, but I'm guessing you know where everything is. This"—he gestures to the cash—"I can handle."

I open my mouth to argue, but he cuts me off again.

"And don't worry, I'm not going to steal your money."

"Well how do I—"

He nods toward Felix, now balancing the cat carrier against his chest and waving with his whoopie pie–holding hand. "He's my reference."

I make a strangled noise—equal parts fury and confusion.

How did this man—this human embodiment of condescension—wearing cologne that probably costs more than my beloved KitchenAid mixer—end up surrounded by *such nice people*?

Nice, celebrity, whoopie pie-endorsing people.

When a customer barks their order and hands me my booth sign, which has once again face-planted into the snow, I decide to both answer that question and verbally castrate *Jack Lourd* later.

Right now? Damage control.

Grabbing two SCFS pies, I bag them just as Felix calls out to the crowd, "Let's form a line, folks! I'll take a selfie with everyone while you wait!"

And just like that… order.

Sort of.

The lawyer—Jack—and I don't speak again, but we move like gears in the same machine.

And I hate that he's good at it.

Too good for someone who wore cashmere and judgment to my bakery like it was a courtroom.

He's calm. Efficient. And just charming enough to get away with it. Which, frankly, makes me want to slap a pie box over his perfect hair.

Ten minutes later, he hands off the last Oh, Tannenbaum to a teenager who squeal-screams "ICONIC!" and runs off to get her selfie with Felix. A selfie I'm hoping she tags both Felix and Making Whoopie in.

Elizabeth—now juggling the disgruntled cat and playing pseudo-photographer—catches my eye and smiles like this is all perfectly normal.

Between the two celebrities —Amanda has joined Felix in full selfie mode—the mob-like energy of the crowd, and the fact that we're about to sell out of whoopie pies, *none* of this is normal.

And yet, somehow, it's the lawyer that bothers me most.

Not because he's suddenly helpful and far too comfortable in a space he does not belong in... but because now I'm wondering just where the grinch from yesterday went.

Because *this* man—the one who just made a sixty-year-old, happily married woman *titter* while handing her a Hot Cocoa & Chill—smells like cedar and something luxurious and warm.

Which makes it hard to focus.

And I *hate* not being able to focus.

HALF-BAKED

Jack

I've negotiated multi-million-dollar contracts under tight deadlines. I've stood in the middle of milling extras, ignoring their barely contained hope that I'd pluck them from obscurity and turn them into the next big thing. I've stared down a wall of paparazzi screaming inappropriate questions at my friends, fishing for a reaction they could turn into a six-figure tabloid payday without so much as blinking.

But nothing—and I mean *nothing*—prepared me for a whoopie pie booth in a snowstorm.

And yet I stay.

Because somehow, despite the absolute insanity of it all—screaming fans, pie innuendo, and a frigid wind tunneling up the back of my very fashionable but very impractical coat—I can't seem to walk away.

Not from her.

Audrey Nouel, who glares like it's a competitive sport and moves behind that booth with the kind of speed that should violate at least three labor laws, is in the zone. Flushed. Flustered. Magnetic as hell.

And I'm the idiot with a law degree and a reputation for detached efficiency who just volunteered to work retail in a blizzard.

Why?

Because—like a jealous little brother watching the favorite son soak up all the praise—I couldn't stand seeing Felix charm his way into her good graces with nothing but a Hollywood smile and a naked cat while she kept looking at me like I'd started a petition to cancel Christmas.

And maybe—just maybe—my ego, which is apparently more inflated than I realized, didn't think it would be this hard.

I can practically hear the slow hiss of air as my overinflated hotshot balloon deflates in real time.

"Three Hot Cocoa & Chills and a Sleigh Me Softly!" a guy in a beanie yells like he's ordering from a ski-through drive-thru.

I turn to Audrey, who's already elbow-deep in a cooler. Without looking, she grabs a pastry bag with her other hand and slides the pies inside like she's been doing this since birth.

Assuming she's about to hand them to me, I reach in—and bump into her.

The cash in my hand flutters on the table like loose confetti.

She doesn't say anything, just *stares*, eyes narrowed and full of unspoken judgment, before grabbing the next order with military precision.

I scramble to regather the bills. Beanie Guy makes to walk off, then pauses and passes back a five. "You gave me too much."

I frown. "You're giving it back?"

"Of course." He looks at me like *I'm* the weirdo.

I watch him walk away, stunned, just as the next customer yells their order.

In LA, he'd be halfway down Melrose before I noticed—and probably halfway through leaving a two-star Yelp review claiming I shorted him.

Behind me, Audrey's already packing up the next pies with the ruthless grace of someone who's fought in frosting-stained trenches. Scoop. Stack. Seal.

Meanwhile, I'm over here fumbling through the primitive concept of exact change because according to the locals, no one in this town can run a card reader let alone get decent cell service without standing on a literal hill.

Still, when she wordlessly passes me another pie, I take it.

When she shoots me a look that could burn through snow, I meet it.

When she trips over a cooler lid and stumbles back into me, I catch her without thinking.

Her elbow brushes my chest.

My hand grazes the bare strip of wrist between her coat and glove.

We don't look at each other, but the air between us snaps.

A camera flash goes off behind us.

Felix, grinning like he's running for president, is now taking selfies with babies.

Audrey lets out a breath that's almost a laugh, and before I can stop myself, I swipe away a streak of frosting on her cheek with my thumb.

Her eyes meet mine.

A long beat passes.

"I didn't need your help." Audrey breaks the moment with a shot of pure-grade defensiveness.

I should back off. Let it drop.

Instead, I smile—because the glare she levels at me is fierce and, frankly, adorable. "I know."

That earns me a huff and an eyeroll.

But as she turns to get the next order ready, a fraction of a smile plays on her lips.

The magic feeling returns.

Audrey

"UNWRAP ME SLOWLY." Jack's voice is all velvet and wicked suggestion.

But it isn't the way he makes my already perversely named pies sound ten times as decadent or the past twenty minutes of our shared, non-stop action—bakery sales action—that causes my brain to stutter.

It's the lack of inventory.

The stark white bottom of the cooler burns into my eyes. "Damn."

Jack's charm falters. "What?"

I point to the empty box between us. "We're out."

The way he raises a single brow feels extremely judgmental. "Of Santa's Secret?"

"That and..." With jerky movements I open and close the lid of every cooler I stocked and dragged over to Town Square before the tree lighting ceremony. "... everything else, save for two Jingle My Berries and one Fireside Fling."

The Santa's Secret customer—a young mom with a baby on one hip and a toddler on his tip-toes peering over the counter—thrusts her twenty dollar bill at Jack. "I'll take all three!"

My unwanted booth partner, charm resurrected, takes the money and counts out her change while I hesitate to hand over the bag of whoopie pies.

"You sure?" I hate not giving the customer what they want.

But instead of disappointment, the woman beams. "Whatever Felix Jones ate, I'm eating." She pockets her change and adds, "Plus, these two"—she nods to the toddler beside her before adjusting the baby more securely on her hip and reaching out with her free hand—"don't care as long as it's sugar."

Once the pies have been handed over, Jack clears his throat and raises his arms. "Ladies and gentlemen of Hideaway Harbor," he booms like he's delivering a closing argument to the jury, "Making Whoopie is officially sold out."

The responding groan from the people still in line mirrors the one inside my head.

I should feel triumphant right now. Instead, I feel like

someone just handed me a participation trophy and whispered "Nice try" in my ear.

I'd vastly overestimated how much I could prep solo. And underestimated what a celebrity appearance—plus Jack and his very helpful friends—could do to a crowd.

As the crowd trickles off to find their sugar fix elsewhere, I grab a rag and start wiping down the counter as if the leftover crumbs are somehow responsible for my failure to anticipate being swarmed.

"Hey." Jack's shoulder nudges mine, the contact light but annoyingly effective. "You don't look thrilled for someone who just sold out."

Before I can answer, or re-clean my counter, Felix Jones and Elizabeth Moore approach the booth like returning conquerors, red-nosed and glowing.

"Whew." Felix shakes off the light dusting of snow from his shoulders. "Glad that's finished."

"Oh, get over yourself." Elizabeth, arms wrapped tightly around the hairless cat, leans against the booth's counter. "You know you loved it."

All smiles, they go back and forth teasing each other while Felix reaches out to relieve his fiancée of her feline burden.

Their camaraderie is light and easy, and I hate that it makes me feel heavy.

I gather the last of the crumbs, snap out of my funk, and plaster on a smile. "Thank you both so much." I meet their eyes. "Unlimited whoopie pies for life."

"Yay!" Elizabeth laughs, shaking out her arms. "Don't say that unless you mean it." She nods toward Felix. "He's got a mean sweet tooth."

Felix, now holding Mike like he's won an award, grins. "Big-time."

"Am I included in this lifetime supply deal?" Jack, who's been suspiciously quiet while I attempt to stop my self-recrimination, nudges me again. "Asking for a hungry friend."

I press a palm to the shoulder he keeps leaning into, suddenly very aware of how warm that spot feels. "I—"

"Woof."

As one, the four of us turn to find Skippy, Hideaway's unofficial mascot, staring at the hairless cat curled up in Felix's arms. But while Skippy's barks are usually 'got snacks?' barks, this bark sounds more like a 'there are enemies among us' alert.

Mike Hunt hisses, thoroughly unimpressed.

Sensing impending doom, Felix, still holding a whoopie pie, tries to tuck Mike inside his coat only to find one hand isn't enough to undo his buttons.

Skippy, shuffling forward, barks louder.

Mike, clearly over being threatened by the miniature yeti, decides to leap into action—literally.

Pushing off Felix's chest with his back legs, Mike launches himself into the air.

Not away from the dog.

At the dog.

Elizabeth gasps *Home Alone* style.

Felix lunges, but all he catches is one sad cat bootie.

Skippy takes one look at the rapidly approaching demon in a birthday suit and makes the only rational choice.

He runs—tail tucked, paws skidding, snow flying.

Mike Hunt gives chase, looking like a naked missile of vengeance.

People scatter. Squeals echo. Felix and Elizabeth take off after them.

"Holy shit." Jack's gaze follows the shrieking, flannel-clad trail of people parting like the Red Sea.

They're heading for the Christmas tree—Hideaway's enormous, thirty-foot symbol of peace, joy, and municipal liability.

Realizing Felix and Elizabeth are too far behind to catch up, I jump into action. Fisting my pile of crumbs, I exit the booth and cut around the crowd, slipping through a gap near the cider stand and sprinting to the stage. I reach it just in time to see Skippy gallop up and onto the platform, barreling around the tree in wide, frantic circles.

Mayor Locke dives to safety.

Meanwhile, Mike Hunt, possibly bored with the chase or finally realizing he's a cat and not a predator drone, leaves Skippy to run in useless circles and leaps into the tree.

Branches shake. Lights flicker. And then—*Fzzzt.*

Half the tree goes dark.

The glowing star at the top flickers like it's reconsidering its life choices.

Kind of like I am at the moment.

Mike's bald little head pops out between two branches about twelve feet up, eyes wide and ears flat like an evil ornament.

Skippy, now untethered from pursuit but still in full panic, keeps running.

I drop to my knees just ahead of him. "Treat!"

His massive paws skid on the snow-dusted stage as he slams to a stop in front of me. Forgetting about the naked predator stalking, he snuffles my jacket, drooling onto my puffer coat with familiar affection.

"Hey, buddy." I loop one arm under his chest and unfurl the other's fist of crumbs. "You want a treat?"

They're gone in one lick.

"I'll get you more later." I scratch under his chin with my newly slobbered hand. "A whole pie just for you, okay?"

Skippy gives me a full-body wiggle of agreement, his tail thumping against the snow like a drumroll. He's still panting, his tongue flopping sideways, when something shifts overhead.

A twitch. A branch shakes.

I look up just in time to see Mike Hunt hurtling toward us like a hairless grenade.

I pull Skippy closer and brace for impact.

However, it doesn't come in the form of a ten-pound cat, but rather a taller-than-average man in cashmere.

Jack, apparently having followed me, dives forward, arms outstretched like a wide receiver catching a Hail Mary pass made entirely of bad ideas.

The crowd gasps.

Jack's city-boy loafers hit a pile of pine needles.

I curse.

And then everything happens at once.

"WOOF!"

"Fuck!"

"Meow!"

"What the—"

We're a tangled mess of limbs, fur, puffer coat, and ornament carnage. Pine needles rain down like festive shrapnel.

There's a long, stunned beat.

When my brain reboots, I find myself flat on my back,

breath knocked out of me, and something heavy between my legs.

"Please tell me that was filmed," Felix says from somewhere above, half-horrified, half-delighted.

"Do you see what I mean?" Eileen asks someone.

"Oh, yes," a voice that oddly sounds like Amanda Willis answers. "You can count me in to help."

Somewhere behind a tree limb, Elizabeth whispers, "Mayor Locke, I'll cover the damage. All of it."

But it all fades—because the weight between my thighs just shifted.

Jack Lourd, city-boy lawyer and expert whoopie pie salesman, pine needles tangled in his hair and a very grumpy, very naked cat clutched securely in his arms like a football made of vengeance, looks up at me from his eyes-to-my-chest vantage point. "I caught him." He drops his forehead to my shoulder. "But I think your dog broke my spleen."

"He's not my dog."

"Well—" His laugh is low and winded. "For the record, this isn't my cat." He shifts, bracing himself, and it brings his hips snugly—*very* snugly—into contact with mine.

My brain stops functioning—*completely*.

Not because Jack Lourd is handsome. Well, not *just* because he's handsome. I already knew that.

But what I didn't know until this very second is that a man laughing while covered in tinsel and holding a pissed-off hairless cat as he's pressed between my thighs like a holiday fever dream is my new kink.

Yeah. I'm gonna need a new set of ovaries.

CASTING CALL

Jack

I'm walking the dog.

And as much as I wish that were a euphemism, it's not.

There's no leash. No ownership. No signed agreement. Just me, trailing behind a slobbering Saint Bernard with a bad sense of direction and apparently zero shame.

I have shame. So much that I spent the last three days post tree-lighting drama in my hotel room, only emerging when Amanda played to my overdeveloped sense of responsibility by mentioning she had seen Skippy limping.

Cut to me—once more freezing my man-bits off—Pied-Pipering Skippy to the local vet in the early hours of the morning via a trail of bacon bits left over from my bougie hotel omelet.

Thankfully, the vet declared Skippy the picture of tramp health.

Which is more than I can say for me as my neck, stiff from the cold, also aches from being hunched over my phone and laptop with poor Wi-Fi connection and no hope of expedited shipping on the one Ethernet cord that might've saved my sanity over the past seventy-two hours.

I tried to make the most of it by deciding to knock "learn to meditate" off my self-improvement checklist every time the spinning wheel of death hijacked my screen.

But while I may now qualify as a Buddhist monk by default, I don't feel the least bit enlightened. Or peaceful. Mostly, I feel cold. Unproductive.

And deeply ashamed of how many hours I've spent scrolling through the Instagram account of a local bakery named Making Whoopie for glimpses of the type-A baker whose thighs feel as if they left permanent scorch marks on my obliques ever since I landed between them under a rainfall of pine needles.

My cyberstalking started innocently enough. Felix and Amanda had tagged Making Whoopie in one of their many tree lighting selfies, and—seeing as I wouldn't be much of an agent if I didn't ensure my clients weren't accidentally endorsing something off-brand—I felt it was my professional duty to investigate.

Hours later, I was one of the many new followers of the Making Whoopie account and deep into the void of whoopie pie reels. I've seen every post. Twice.

I know which hairstyles the attractive patron favors—bun or braid—and how many seasonal Croc charms she owns—

infinite. Hell, I could probably recognize her piping technique in a frosting lineup.

My mind connects frosting and Audrey in multiple naughty ways, making me glad of the gust of wind that whips around the corner of Lobstah Lane and slices through my coat with enough power to one, cool me off and two, remind me why people wear hats.

Skippy trots on ahead, tail swinging, drool flinging, no limp in sight.

"Hey, are you the lawyer guy?"

I pause behind my Skippy pilgrimage just outside of a bookshop—the only shop that's apparently forgotten it's Christmas. Not a decoration in sight.

A bespeckled teenager steps outside looking warmer in her wool-knit sweater and jeans than I feel in my GQ-worthy cashmere crew neck and trench.

Before I can form a response to 'lawyer guy' that won't have me more hated than I already am, the teenager presses a tin of shortbread cookies into my hands. "That was super nice of you to take Skippy to the vet."

If I ever needed a weight to replace my kettle bells, this tin would be it. "How do you know about that?"

She scoffs, sounding very much like the teenager she is. "Welcome to small-town America."

"Ah." My mind tracks back to the vet's office, where the secretary behind the desk seemed unusually interested in my impromptu walk-in appointment with the town stray.

"Yep." She pushes her glasses up her nose. "I even know you paid for his visit—even though the town has a Skippy-fund."

Not wanting to dim her friendly attitude toward me, I

decide not to mention I had fully intended to bill Felix for Skippy's medical expense, plus my hourly rate.

"Hello!"

In unison, the teen and I turn toward the greeting to find a petite woman in a Nordic beanie and a puffer jacket two sizes too cheerful waving.

My cookie dealer waves back. "Hi."

"I'm Ida," the woman, now huffing and puffing in front of me announces. "Just wanted to say that it's such a pleasure for Hideaway to welcome such a lovely and caring man such as yourself, Mr. Lourd."

I glance behind me, sure she's addressing someone else. No one's there.

The teenager laughs.

"To check up on our poor Skippy like that." Another gust of wind whips around the corner, causing Ida to reach for her hat, securing it in place.

A hat I would pay serious money for right about now—despite how badly it would clash with my coat. Though it couldn't be any worse than the turbulent shade of red I'm sure my frozen ears are turning.

Ida leans in conspiratorially. "Never would've guessed a lawyer would do something like that."

Not wanting to speak on common decency for the entire population of people with law degrees, I make a noncommittal sound.

She pats my arm. "The town appreciates it."

Her sincerity hits in a strange, not-altogether-unpleasant way. "Well, if he was hurt"—I turn, directing the woman's attention down the road to where Skippy is making yellow snow a few shops down—"which he isn't, it would've been my fault. Only right I made sure he was okay."

Ida shimmies her shoulders and titters, looking pleased at my words.

The teen next to me excuses herself and heads back inside the bookstore. I have a feeling she was fighting a laugh.

"Yes, well..." The older woman clears her throat, once more leaning in. "Now that it's just the two of us, I was wondering..."

I brace, weirdly worried I'm about to be propositioned.

"Do you know anything about property lines?"

I blink, my mind obviously not quite as nimble in frigid temperatures to shift from canine health hero to land dispute consultant. "Uh, a bit."

Cut to me, ten minutes later, with a hand-knitted scarf wrapped around my neck given as legal tender for having listened to an epic tale of garden gnome warfare over a very disputed hedge.

And that's just the beginning.

By the time I catch up to Skippy—now dramatically flopped outside The Sweetest Thing candy shop—I've answered five legal questions, been greeted and thanked by a dozen people, given a sex shop gift certificate, an invitation to dinner from a peppy older couple on a late-morning walk, and am now the proud owner of a lobster Christmas ornament that was pressed into my hands by a woman who wanted to trademark her residential holiday décor "to keep looky-loos from copying my unique style."

Hideaway may lack cell signal or boundaries, but damn if it doesn't have heart.

Heart...

For some reason, my eyes trail down Main Street, stopping on a chalkboard sign stationed outside a sky-blue door.

Skippy whines.

"She wouldn't want to see me." Great, now I'm talking to a dog.

He huffs.

I look at my watch. "She's probably busy."

As if annoyed I'm making him move from his cozy snow drift bed, he gets up, nose pointed in Making Whoopie's direction like the hunting dog he isn't.

"Skippy." Now I'm *pleading* with a dog. "I fell into her crotch while holding a hairless pussy."

My crudeness falls on deaf ears as Skippy starts swaggering down Main Street.

And like the vet said I should—just to be safe—I follow.

Audrey

I'M HIGH. I can't tell if it's from my seemingly overnight success thanks to two celebrity social media endorsements, an above-average sugar intake, or the sleep deprivation caused by said overnight success and sugar intake.

Making Whoopie gained a few thousand new followers after the tree-lighting heard 'round Hideaway—and apparently, the country.

I've spent the last three days—including my one sacred day off, usually reserved for sleep—fulfilling an avalanche of large-order requests, dealing with pre-Christmas pie panic, and managing counter lines that could rival Disneyland on opening day.

A toddler in a puffy snowsuit screeches as he smashes his hands against the bakery display glass, leaving behind a constellation of sugar-frosted fingerprints. I slide a napkin across the counter with a tight smile at his mom, who's too focused on getting a TikTok of the cookie selection to notice that her child is trying to eat through the glass.

"Three Jingle My Berries and two Santa's Cream-Filled Secrets," I repeat back to the older man in the shearling-lined coat who ordered with the intensity of someone defusing a bomb. He gives me a thumbs-up and adds a sixth whoopie to the order for his wife, "the one with eggnog cream and the dirty name."

I box them up, slap a label on top, and pivot just in time to catch a gingerbread pie as it slides toward the edge of the cooling rack like it's attempting a baked goods escape.

I know how it feels.

Not that I'm not grateful to Felix and Amanda. I am. Exceedingly so.

Especially when I saw that my mother had liked that one post of Felix Jones biting into a whoopie pie.

I mean, does it also mean she probably saw the video of me being sacked like a quarterback by a man holding a naked cat and frosted redemption? Probably.

But I'm going to ignore that.

Just like I'm ignoring the customers waxing poetic about

Hideaway's newest golden boy—the lawyer with a heart of gold who rescued our precious town dog from paw-tricide.

A woman in a glittering "Eat, Sleigh, Love" sweatshirt leans across the counter and whispers, "Isn't it so sweet what that man did for Skippy this morning? Honestly, I didn't even think those lawyer types had hearts."

I hum noncommittally and use tongs to thrust a Sleigh Me Softly into her bag. Not passive-aggressive. Just... precision serving.

Never mind that I'm the one who got body-slammed into a thirty-foot pine tree. The one with a baseball-sized bruise on her ass cheek. The one squashed under a dog, a cat, and a lawyer in a pear tree.

But sure. Let's canonize Jack Lourd for being a decent human to a dog with a town trust fund.

I slide another gingerbread whoopie pie into a compostable box and hand it across the counter to a woman wearing a fur beret. It's gorgeous, and I want to ask where she got it, but I'm too tired to do more than—Smile. Nod. Repeat.

My eyes flick to the stack of mail Lumi, the postmistress, hand-delivered through the crowd earlier in exchange for a Maple Me Moan. The corner of one envelope is slightly greasy from its proximity to the spiced-rum buttercream.

I've hardly managed to do any administrative work in days. I only took time to double-check that the heat, electricity, and phone bills were paid before shoving everything else aside like emotional baggage in an overhead bin.

Emotional baggage I drum up the courage to unpack when the beret lady—my last customer—leaves.

Maybe, finally, a moment.

I wipe my hands on my apron and glance around the

empty front. No customers. No catastrophic messes. Just the soft purr of the convection ovens and the heady scent of allspice and cinnamon.

Taking advantage of the reprieve, I duck past the counter, weaving between cooling racks and prep table toward the mountainous pile of mail. On the way, I catch sight of the order sheet for tomorrow's café au lait order and try to work out the time I'd need to complete it, plus the ingredients I need to double-check, along with everything for my usual daily pies—which I've recently had to double, thanks to Making Whoopie's popularity.

Deep breath.

By the time I have the pile of mail in hand, my laptop open and have mentally reworked the math three times trying to figure it all out, I'm ready to make a deal with the devil himself for a reprieve and a cup of coffee.

Ding.

The bell over the door chimes. Soft yet forbidding.

Sighing, I drop the mail back on the prep table and head for the front, already preparing my face for round one thousand and ninety-seven of—Smile. Nod. Repeat.

Except this time, my smile falters and my Crocs come to a squeaky stop as I realize what I've somehow conjured in my exhaustion.

Jack Lourd—aka the devil—stands in the doorway, hellhound Skippy at his side, holding two to-go coffee cups and looking way too attractive for someone with wind-swept hair, red-tipped ears, and a scarf that would make one look as if they had strong opinions about early bird specials and perfectly steeped chamomile.

Figures. Joke about selling your soul for caffeine, and the

devil shows up holding a latte.

Jack raises one cup. "Dirty chai latte?"

My usual order—proof that if he's not the devil himself, he's at least in league with one.

I arch a brow, walk toward him, and enjoy the way his smile widens and then fades when I bend down toward Skippy.

"Hey there, buddy." Reaching in my apron pocket, I offer him one of the broken pieces of pie I keep around just for him. "How you doing?"

In answer, Skippy swallows that palm-sized piece in one go and then circles to face the door, silently asking me to let him back out to complete his daily rounds.

Which I do.

Leaving the door open, I pluck the offered cup from a now-frowning Jack and salute him in thanks before pivoting on my heel, muttering, "Don't let me stop you from your heroic dog-watching duties" before heading back to my pile of mail, having too many other things to do than trade passive-aggressive banter with a man who never asked how I was after taking me out with a diving tackle.

In the kitchen, I drop back into my desk chair, take a long drink of latte, and start sorting mail.

The door chimes closed.

A beat.

Then footsteps.

Huh.

Out of the corner of my eye, I watch him round the corner as I toss envelopes into piles—junk, Christmas card, Christmas card, junk, junk.

"So." Jack comes to a stop beside one of the cooling racks. "How are you?"

Christmas card. "Busy." Bill.

"That's good."

Is it, though? I pause, letter in hand, at the thought.

Of course, busy is good. It's what I wanted. What I said I needed so that I could feel justified on focusing on the *other* reason I wanted to move to Hideaway.

Shaking my head, I tap awake my laptop and double-check that my November expenses are logged before setting up December's log.

"Wait." Jack rounds the prep table between us and leans over my shoulder. "You have Internet here?"

Damn it. "Yes. I have Internet." I lean back, away from whatever delicious cologne he's wearing. "We're not that out in the sticks, Hollywood."

He lets out a low chuckle. "Tell that to The Haven's Internet service provider." Pushing off the table, he takes a few steps back.

I breathe in air untainted by Jack and let it out in a shaky laugh. "Yeah, well, they're more remote—and I'm pretty sure against anything that would keep their guests from relaxing." I grab the stack of remaining mail and begin sorting again.

"Yeah, I guess that makes sense." He leans against the wall next to one of my cooling trolleys, looking far more delicious than the whoopie pies next to him.

First my nose, now my eyes. I can't trust my senses around this guy. Shifting in my chair so he isn't in my direct line of sight, I focus on my piles—Christmas card, kitchen equipment catalogue, utilities bill.

"Hey, what flavor are these?"

"Experimental dozen." I toss the growing pile of junk in the recycling bin before it topples over. "Twelve varieties I'm testing."

Junk, *The Almanac*, Christmas card.

The growing pile of Christmas cards from people in town makes me feel generous. "Help yourself." Plus, maybe if he's got a pie in his mouth, he'll stop talking. Or better, *leave*.

I hear the rustle of parchment paper, then silence, followed by a muffled hum of appreciation that I try not to find satisfying—or naughty.

An envelope catches my eye at the bottom of the unsorted stack.

Heavy bond paper. Too narrow to be a Christmas card. No return address. And it's thick and official-looking in the I-mean-business kind of way.

Curious, I tear it open—and stop breathing.

CEASE AND DESIST

The edges of the paper blur slightly the longer I stare at the letter, my mind screaming the heading too loudly to comprehend anything written after.

Jack says something, his voice soft and tentative, but I can't make it out.

I blink, hoping the rapid movement will allow me to focus, to read and comprehend.

It doesn't.

"Audrey?" Jack's voice is louder now, followed by his palm, heavy and warm, dropping on my shoulder. "What's wrong?" His touch and gentle shake finally jar me out of my mental spiral.

This time when I blink, I'm able to focus—on him. And whatever he sees in my expression darkens his own.

"I, uh..." Clearing my throat but still not trusting myself to speak, I hand him the letter.

His eyes scan the document before lifting his gaze to mine. "Cease and desist over the use of the name Making Whoopie."

Hearing the words out loud makes me want to upchuck my chai.

"Did you register your business name with the state?"

I think back to those early weeks—permits, equipment quotes, tax ID forms. Did I register the name? I kind of thought I did... but now I can't remember.

Before Maine, any legal advice or needs I had, I used my mother's lawyer in the city. But when I came here, I was so focused on proving myself, proving that this was a good move, that I did everything myself. And I have done since.

And there was a lot. Much more business know-how than an expert baker realized.

Business loans, equipment, overhead, taxes, marketing, ad spend... so much so that I just can't remember anything about registering Making Whoopie's name.

The name that someone, somewhere else in Maine, is claiming they own and insisting I stop using—*or else*.

Jack's hand gently squeezes my shoulder.

Warm. Steady. Real.

"Listen, I'm not licensed to practice law in Maine, but I know enough to say this is meant to scare you. It doesn't mean you have to stop working—not until any real legal action is taken by the other party."

He pauses, as if expecting a response.

I manage to nod.

"And I have a list of lawyers who *can* practice in Maine thanks to Amanda wanting to shoot a film here. I can call them." He shrugs. "I mean, they're entertainment lawyers, but they'll know enough to get us pointed in the right direction to take care of this."

Us? The word overrides the 'Cease and Desist' refrain looping in my mind.

Whatever he sees in my expression has his lips tilting upward. "I mean, I already spent the better part of the morning offering free legal advice to half the town on matters of lawn-gnome custody and reindeer-induced property damage. Why not add a commercial dispute to the list?"

My gut twists. This time it doesn't have to do with the very real and worrying legal problem but with him lumping me together with every other small-town legal problem he's been solving on the street corners.

Which is dumb. Because of course this is no big deal for a hotshot city lawyer like himself to deal with. It's fine if I'm just another ridiculous Hideaway resident with a legal issue he can resolve to alleviate his boredom while he bides his time in aggressively decorated small-town America.

His condescending nonchalance is much better than the emotional jabs I'd take if I asked my mother for help.

Better the devil you *kind of* know.

Decision made, I shrug off his hand and offer my own. "You're hired."

OVER-BEATEN

Audrey

I have a squatter problem.

From my spot near the cooling racks, I watch Jack Lourd—my bakery's newest, most irritating cohabitant—rifle through my business files while I pipe cream into pies in the lull after the Sunday morning rush.

Three days after I hired Jack, and I'm already second-guessing myself. I'd been prepared to shell out my hard-earned money for legal services. I hadn't been prepared to pay by surrendering my sanctuary to a stranger in the name of "reliable Wi-Fi."

Jack, probably sensing me staring for the umpteenth time in the last ninety-six hours, glances up from his laptop. I promptly drop my gaze to the piping bag in my hands.

"Need something?" His voice is far too amused for my liking.

Feigning nonchalance, I shrug. "Just wondering if you happen to know about Maine's squatter laws."

I don't need to turn my head to know he's smiling. For someone who complained about small-town holiday charm before blindsiding its Christmas tree, he's been awfully jovial lately.

It's annoying.

"I'm not that well-versed in your state's adverse possession laws, no."

"I see." Twisting the top of the bag, I push cream toward the fluted tip when movement in my peripheral makes me glance his way.

Elbows on the table, chin propped on his fists, he looks entirely too pleased with himself—like my bakery is his own personal corner office.

"Is that your way of implying I'm overstaying my welcome?"

I hum noncommittally and, piping bag ready, lean over my pastries.

"So you finally hired yourself an assistant?"

I jump, not having heard the bell over the door chime, sending a jaunty loop of cream across a row of pies.

Awesome.

"Oh—good morning, Mrs. Bradford." I set down the piping bag and grab a towel. "Ah, no. He's just, uh, using my Wi-Fi." I wave toward Jack, who's typing away like he's negotiating a movie deal. "You know." I wipe up my mess. "Important Hollywood stuff."

The phone rings. Before I can move toward it, Jack rises from his seat and lifts the landline from its cradle. "Making Whoopie, where every craving has a happy ending."

I shiver, suddenly reconsidering my playful marketing slogan.

Jack's eyes meet mine, a lazy smile playing over his lips. "Jack speaking. How can I help you?"

I swallow.

"Hollywood stuff, hmm?" The gleam in Mrs. Bradford's eyes is more "the knitting circle is going to love this" than I'd like.

My customer-service expression tightens. Tossing the towel in the laundry bag, I step to the counter. "Your usual Sunday order?"

She nods, eyes merry as the holiday.

At least the townspeople seem to be enjoying my squatter problem. At this point, I can't tell whether the increased traffic is thanks to Making Whoopie's recent celebrity endorsement or its new cashmere-loving, six-foot-something mascot with eyes the color of dark chocolate ganache.

Not that I was staring at his eyes. I just happened to be making dark chocolate ganache when he looked up. That's all.

I hand Mrs. Bradford the dozen assorted pastries for her grandkids. "Hope the kids enjoy the new holiday flavors."

"Oh, you know they will." Her expression softens. "You've made me the coolest meemaw in town."

A pang of jealousy knots my hands into fists. "I'm sure that has more to do with how much you love them." I would've loved a grandmother like Mrs. Bradford.

A few more customers filter in, and I wonder if I'll have to save the pastry piping for later.

"Can I help you?" Jack slides in beside me, the heat of him lingering along my arm like static electricity.

I tell myself the goosebumps are from the front door

constantly opening and the subsequent winter air gusting through. I do not believe me.

As a proud, card-carrying Type-A control freak who color-codes her grocery list, letting someone else take over my bakery—even for five minutes—should make me break out in hives.

Instead, I get back to piping while my lawyer/cashier/squatter charms Mrs. Perrault into the last Stuff My Stockings whoopie pies and a half-dozen mini fruitcakes, leaning on my counter like it's a velvet-roped Hollywood club instead of an innuendo-laden bakery.

A slip of paper from the order he just took is waiting on my prep counter—visible but neatly out of my way. An order I might not have had time to make if Jack hadn't been manning the counter.

"What do you recommend, Mr. Lourd?" The elementary school principal arches her brows like she's asking for more than a pastry suggestion.

I over-pipe a pie.

Readjusting the now half-empty bag, I try to tune out the counter flirting and finish the Morning After Mint whoopie pies—yet another order Jack took.

And while my mind might wander into unhelpful territory when it comes to my lawyer, I must admit that I've never been less stressed about work.

And with a possible lawsuit looming, that's saying something.

The murmur of Jack's voice, too low to make out, sends the woman into a fit of giggles.

Who would've thought that the man who grinched his way into Hideaway would start acting like one of Santa's elves?

If Santa's elves were six feet of broad shoulders, smug charm, and the kind of hands that make you wonder what else they're good at besides kneading bread—which he did yesterday, helping me make dough.

It seems I've just replaced one problem with another.

Because while I usually fall asleep to the soundtrack of my never-ending to-do list, last night I was replaying the way Jack's large, strong hands worked my dough.

And that made for a very *different* kind of restless night.

Jack

"SAW SKIPPY THIS MORNING." The vet, Dr. Eli Bennett, grins as I ring him up. "Healthy as ever."

"Yes." I hand him his change. "If anything, he seems rather pleased with the extra attention and treats everyone is giving him since Saturday."

"Don't let that stop you from bringing him in." Eli, as he asked me to call him, laughs good-naturedly. "My practice could always use more helicopter pet dads with black Amex cards."

Shaking my head, I give in to laughing at myself. "Yeah, I might've gone a little overboard on asking for the full work-up of tests for Skippy." Grabbing a couple of broken cake pieces, I toss them into a small bag before adding it to his order. "For your patients. Tell them they're Skippy-approved."

His grin spreads. "They'll be thrilled."

The bell over the door jingles as he leaves, marking the end of customers for the day—and there have been *a lot* of customers. Every day since I started working out of Audrey's kitchen has been busy, but the weekends are something else entirely. The Winter Market opened yesterday, and a lot of out-of-towners drove in, all saying they had to stop by 'the bakery Felix Jones and Amanda Willis raved about.'

They came, in addition to the locals who greeted me without surprise, having already been informed through the local grapevine that I'm working Making Whoopie's counter. Greeted with large smiles, no less.

Apparently, in just a few days, I went from persona non grata to Hideaway's non-celebrity guest star.

Between establishing Making Whoopie's start of business date and calling in a few favors to some trademark lawyers, I've bagged orders, greeted customers, and even made change from the register without Audrey eyeing me every time my hand dipped into the cash drawer. Progress.

Through the doorway, I watch the reluctantly trusting baker scoop batter into cake molds, her motions quiet yet precise.

Baking Audrey is different from Order-Taking Audrey. The perpetual tension between her brows is gone, her expression soft. Her love of baking is visible in her almost-smile and the subtle flare in her wrists when she pipes a line of frosting or uses chopsticks to individually place sprinkles on top of a pastry.

Not that frazzled, snappish Audrey didn't have her own appeal. But happy Audrey? She's dangerous.

She licks a smear of frosting off the back of her hand without thinking, and my brain instantly queues an entire highlight reel of thoughts that definitely violate the attorney-client handbook.

She's my client now. And seeing as I'm leaving after the holidays, it would be beyond dumb to mix business with pleasure. I don't start things I have no intention of finishing.

I retreat to the table I've commandeered as an office—the one in the back corner and the most out of the way. Sitting down, I glance over my latest research on the screen. Whereas I should be answering the pile of unread messages from California—producers, clients, a studio head who doesn't understand time zones—I'm instead combing through statutes on business names and registration requirements in Maine.

I'd forgotten how much I liked business law. The puzzle pieces of legislation and precedent. The satisfaction of things lining up neatly. I gave it up to help Felix launch his career, thinking it would be a temporary detour. Ten years later, the detour has become the road, and I've forgotten there was another route entirely.

Now here I am, in a snow-covered fishing town, enjoying the hell out of practicing the kind of law I walked away from.

I snap the laptop shut and lean against the doorway to the kitchen. "I think I left my scarf here the other day."

Audrey doesn't look up, still piping. "I brought it upstairs with me yesterday to get it out of the way." She might as well have said 'You're in the way.'

I probably should wonder if something's wrong with me, finding her faux grump attitude a turn-on.

She sighs heavily at my silence and puts down the piping bag. "I'll go—" An oven timer goes off, Audrey's eyes cutting to it then to me.

Holding up my hands, I take a step back. "You just bake." I thumb over my shoulder at the door leading upstairs. "I'll run up and get it."

Grabbing her oven mitt with one hand, she shuts off the timer with the other. "I don't know." Hand on the oven handle, she pauses, biting her lip. "I don't usually have people up there."

I laugh, misreading her hesitation. "Promise I won't judge any dirty dishes in the sink."

That gets me an eye roll before she opens the oven door. "I never leave dirty dishes in the sink." She wafts the hot air escaping the oven in front of her, her cheeks pinking in the heat, the fine tendrils around her face blowing from the convection fan. "Fine, go ahead."

I blame the mix of cloves and nutmeg for the hard swallow I have to take.

Pulling out the tray, Audrey further dismisses me by turning to place what looks like gingerbread house pieces on a cooling rack. "Your scarf's on a coat rack, to the right of the door when you enter."

Nodding even though she can't see me, I make my escape from the provoking smells.

On the stairs, as the scent of Audrey's baked goods fade, a thrum of curiosity and anticipation hits me. While I may have scoffed at Making Whoopie's holiday decor when I arrived in Hideaway, I've since come to enjoy it. Tasteful and homey, just like the goods Audrey bakes.

So I'm curious to what her own personal space looks like. I half expect garlands, twinkle lights, a tree covered in tiny whoopie pie ornaments— something even *more* festive than the bakery below since Audrey wouldn't have had to worry about the décor getting in the way of her baking.

But when I open the door and find the scarf right where she said it would be—hanging neatly from a coat rack by the door—nothing else is as expected.

No tree. No garland. No lights. And definitely no mess.

I take two steps into a small living area on the left: denim loveseat, coffee table, TV. Behind that, a small kitchen as immaculate as the bakery's at closing time—but without the cinnamon sugar scent.

The tiny island that doubles as a dining table is spotless, except for a stack of cookbooks with a legal pad tucked between them like a makeshift bookmark.

It's the opposite of downstairs, where—in the front of the shop—every surface glows with holiday cheer and the air is sugar-scented. Audrey's apartment is basic. Functional. Like she's poured every ounce of herself into the bakery and left nothing for her own space.

Something about that… lands. I know exactly what it's like to live entirely at work and leave the rest empty because you're never really there.

Feeling as if I've seen something private, I start toward the door to grab my scarf when a framed photo catches my eye. Audrey, hair short, in a chef's coat, and a woman who looks like a slightly older, blond version of the younger Audrey next to her standing in front of the Ritz in New York. I know the building. I've stayed there more than once. And whereas the woman—probably her mother—is smiling widely into the camera, Audrey is smiling at the woman.

I pull the scarf from the hook, but the image sticks with me.

CLOSE-UP

Audrey

The Chowder House Rules smells like butter, corn, and impending regret.

I fidget with the bottom of my pale blue sweater while Jack sits back after ordering a bowl of said chowder, scanning the mixture of blue and cherry wood paneling like he's filing away the details. His gaze lingers on a porthole mirror and the carved wooden buoys strung above the kitchen pass-through. "I like this place. If the food's good, I wouldn't mind eating here again."

"This is a work lunch." The votive lit inside a Mason jar flickers violently from the bounce of my restless leg beneath it.

When I asked Jack yesterday if we could review where I stood with the cease-and-desist order, I pictured us spending my day off at the bakery.

I could get ahead on tomorrow's orders and this weekend's gingerbread competition designs, and he could speak fluent legalese without me nodding off. Win-win.

But no.

After last night's snowfall prevented him from getting to the bakery this morning for coffee and pastries—something I always have in supply—Jack insisted on a lunch that wasn't delivered or microwaved. Unlike the frozen entrée army currently staging a coup in my walk-in freezer.

One brow lifts. "I'm aware." He breaks off a corner of cornbread, the warm squares bleeding butter into their napkin nest. "But if I'm going to tell you what I've been doing on your behalf"—he leans in, forearms braced on the table, voice pitched low enough to curl heat up the back of my neck—"I won't have you distracted by batter or an oven timer."

A burst of laughter rises from a table near the bar, blending with the muted clink of silverware against ceramic. Somewhere behind us, the kitchen door swings open and releases a puff of briny steam that smells faintly of buttered lobster.

I grab a piece of cornbread, more to keep my hands busy than to eat. "And what exactly have you been doing?"

His fingers drum once on the tabletop, like he's choosing where to start. "First, I established the date Making Whoopie—the one under your ownership—began operating. In business terms, that's your first use in commerce." Jack pauses, as if making sure I'm following. "Second, I found invoices, supply orders, and even the article in *The Almanac* from your opening week. All of it proves you've been using the name longer than the other guys."

I frown, thinking back to two years ago and my foray into small-town life and entrepreneurship. "Did I actually keep that article?"

A faint shake of his head. "No. But that's what your reliable Internet connection was used for." The curve of his mouth lands somewhere between smug and infuriating.

The warmth in my ears spikes.

"You didn't really think I was just squatting in your bakery for Wi-Fi so I could scroll social media, did you?"

I answer by not answering.

Jack's smile shifts into a smirk at my silent admission. "Though I have to admit, a lot of my time was spent learning how to be a baker's assistant."

My expression flattens. "Do you really think that after four days of answering the phone and ringing up customers you have the skills to call yourself a baker's assistant?"

He chuckles. "No, not really." His eyebrows raise. "How about cashier boy?"

I bite my tongue, stopping whatever comment I was about to make that would insinuate there was nothing *boy* about him. And all pervy thoughts aside, it's true that even when customers had to wait longer than normal for service, they always left smiling—thanks in large part to Jack's people skills.

Avoiding his eyes, I manage, "Yes, you can definitely add that to your list of skills." Feeling grateful for all his hard work, I add, "I'd even tack on people pleaser."

Something shifts behind his eyes that makes him seem pleased, but it's gone in a second. "Now *that's* generous praise."

I shrug, playing it off. "It's the holidays."

"Well, for someone ready to go twelve rounds over the sanctity of Hideaway's Christmas lights, I was surprised to discover you don't attend many of the town's holiday festivities—and that you're living in an apartment without so much as a strand of tinsel."

Having forgotten he was in my apartment yesterday, I suddenly find the condensation trailing down my glass extremely interesting.

He leans forward, brows pinched. "Now how does that end up happening?"

I grab my water, the cold glass feeling arctic in my hot hand. "I'm focusing all my attention on the shop."

"Uh-huh." His tone makes it clear he's not buying it.

But thankfully, as he watches me chug down my tall glass in an attempt to cool down, he must decide to pivot instead of press the matter. "Well, you'll be pleased to know what I learned when I looked into the company that sent the cease-and-desist. They are set up in Bangor, which may have a larger client base being in the city, but it turns out they only filed their state registration three months ago." He wipes his thumb along his lip, erasing the distracting smear of butter.

Annoyed at the diversion, I blink a few times to refocus. "Which means…?"

Jack's grin widens. "Which means that *you* have senior common law rights in Maine for the business name Making Whoopie." He shrugs as if he didn't just pop the balloon of anxiety swelling in my gut since I received that letter. "They probably just hoped you didn't know that. Or that you didn't have an awesome lawyer to tell you."

The look he gives me feels equal parts smug and intimate,

the kind of heat that almost pulls my focus from what's important.

"Wait." I replay what he said and not what he looked like saying it. "So my business is *not* doomed?"

Our waitress chooses that moment to set down two steaming bowls, and the scent of sweet corn and cream is almost as soothing as what I *think* Jack just told me.

"Not if we move fast." He scoops a spoonful of chowder, blowing across the surface, his pursed lips pulling my thoughts into dangerous territory. "I've already sent a response asserting your prior use. Then I compiled and background checked a list of nearby Maine lawyers who can step in if they try and take things further, as well as looked into the steps to apply for a federal trademark if needed."

I pause in picking up my spoon. "You did all that since Wednesday?"

He hums happily over his first taste of Hideaway's finest comfort food before answering. "I was also fielding calls to Los Angeles, negotiating an endorsement contract for Felix, and looking into this state's filmmaking laws for Amanda."

"Wow." I stare into my chowder because apparently the hard-working, case-juggling lawyer side of Jack is...kind of impressive.

It's not like I thought he didn't know what he was doing. I wouldn't have hired him if I didn't think he could do it, no matter how convenient his timing was in my moment of legal need. But the fact that he could juggle all of that without looking flustered, swamped, or even remotely out of his depth?

Must be nice.

Taking my stunned silence for gratitude, Jack's gaze shifts

past me to a passing dessert tray, then slides back with a glint I don't trust. "You can thank me with dessert."

The warmth from the chowder fades under the weight of his look. I focus on my bowl, chasing a kernel of corn with my spoon. "What, my lifetime supply of whoopie pies isn't enough to appease you?"

One brow lifts. "I didn't know I was included in that offer." A beat passes before his smile curves up nice and slow. "Dangerous thing to offer up your whoopie to a man with a sweet tooth."

Jack

SHE BOUGHT ME DESSERT.

It's chocolate and dark and decadent but in no way comparable to Audrey's whoopie pies.

I don't know if I should take the slice of chocolate cake as her drawing a line between us after I made the joke about offering up her whoopie or if it's simply her thanking me for the work I did for her.

Why I made the joke in the first place is beyond me. I already told myself not to mix business with... whatever this thing is between Audrey and me.

I thought helping settle her worries over her business name would make things less awkward.

I thought wrong.

Because there is something about seeing her in something other than her chef's coat, or the way the table rattles from her leg bouncing beneath it like she's bracing to bolt, or the way her brown hair flashes auburn in the candlelight that has me wanting to make bad decisions.

A family of four laughs at the table beside us, and across the room, the bartender is busy slinging drinks to the guests on barstools.

Clearing my throat, I refocus. "How's the cake?"

She cuts off the tip of the cake wedge, bringing it to her lips without meeting my eyes. "Good."

"Good, huh?" I cut myself a bite. "Coming from a James Beard winner, that's high praise."

Her fork stops halfway to her mouth. "You googled me?"

"I *researched* you," I correct. "Big difference. My investigation uncovered that you were the pastry chef at the Ritz-Carlton in New York and, yes, a James Beard Award winner."

Her lips purse to one side. "That was a long time ago."

"Long time?" I force my eyes to hers and *not* her lips. "I'd argue that. Four years isn't so long."

After a beat, she wraps her lips around her bite of cake.

Clearing my throat, I sit back. "And unless I'm mistaken, they don't just give out James Beard awards like Santa does candy canes."

I'm rewarded—tortured?—when her lips twitch around her fork, as if fighting a smile.

I grab my knife and butter a piece of cornbread I have no intention of eating. "So what was it like working at one of the world's most prestigious and well-known establishments?"

She exhales a soft laugh, more weary than nostalgic.

"Intense. Glamorous on the outside, relentless on the inside. You're surrounded by marble floors, crystal chandeliers, gold-trimmed menus… and a kitchen that runs like a battlefield. Ten burners going at once, pastry bags lined up like ammunition, and everyone moving so fast you learn to pivot without spilling a drop of sauce."

Her fork trails through the cake like she's stirring up old memories. "And I had a small army of *real* assistants"—she does smile then, a sly one that speaks of our inside joke—"people whose entire job was to prep, fetch, clean, restock... basically anticipate what I needed before I knew I needed it." She glances up at me with a self-deprecating shrug. "At the Ritz, if I wanted a bag of powdered sugar, someone sprinted for it. In Hideaway, I sprint—and usually trip over a mixing bowl on the way."

I try to picture her in that gleaming, high-stakes kitchen—chef's coat pressed to perfection, a brigade of people orbiting her every move—and it's almost impossible to match with the Audrey I know now, hair tied up, cranberry Crocs squeaking across the bakery floor. And yet… the version of her in Hideaway feels more *her*.

"I don't regret leaving, but… I do regret not being more grateful for them." A soft, almost reluctant smile tugs at her mouth before she sighs with longing.

I keep my voice soft, not wanting to disturb her comfortable reminiscing. "Why did you leave?"

She sets her fork down, eyes cutting to the family of four near us. "I always knew I wanted something different, even when I first started working at the Ritz. Something… slower. More real." She grimaces. "But when the Ritz makes you an offer, you'd be an idiot to pass it up."

The way she says the last makes me think she's quoting someone else.

"So what was your breaking point?" I press, curious now in a way that has nothing to do with research. "The moment you decided you were done with the Ritz?"

Her mouth tilts like she's debating whether to admit it. "A wedding. For a groom I'd already baked a wedding cake for five years earlier."

I blink. "Same guy, different bride?"

"Yep. First wedding—six tiers, sugar roses, fondant lace. Picture-perfect. Second wedding—eight tiers, more sugar work, imported edible pearls. Bigger, flashier... emptier." She shakes her head. "I remember standing in that kitchen, piping the same man's initials onto a different cake topper and thinking, *This isn't romantic. This is a business transaction with matching napkins.*"

I lean back, imagining her in that gleaming hotel kitchen, surrounded by perfection that suddenly seemed hollow. "That was it?"

"That was it." She presses her fork into the side of the cake, shaving off a sliver.

It's quiet for a beat as I let it sink in—Audrey, a pastry chef at the top of her game, leaving it all for Hideaway so she can bake for people who come not for a bigger spectacle but because they can't stop thinking about the last bite.

And now I get why my jet-lagged, bah-humbug slam on Hideaway kept me parked at the bottom of her esteem for so long.

"So..." I pick up my fork once more. "Who's the woman in the framed photo on your bookshelf?"

She chokes on a bite of cake. "The photo?"

"Ah, yeah." I draw out the word, my fork halfway through the cake, pretty sure I've just jinxed myself and taken the conversation in a direction Audrey did not want to go. "The one by the coat rack?" I slide her water glass toward her with my free hand in case she needs it. "I saw it when I collected my scarf."

"Oh." She takes a sip. Then another, buying a few more seconds. "That's my mother." She speaks like it's nothing, but there's a subtle shift in her posture. "That picture was taken on my first day at the Ritz." Something flickers in her eyes before she focuses on the cake crumbs on her plate.

"I bet she's proud of you." Hell, *I'm* proud of her and we just met.

Audrey's fork hesitates just long enough for me to notice before she answers. "She was very proud of my job at the Ritz."

I could leave it there. I don't. "But not Making Whoopie?"

She exhales through her nose, not quite a sigh. "My mother's an accountant. Numbers are her love language. To her, it made no sense to trade in a well-paying, high-prestige job for a small-town business when..." She stirs her fork through the crumbs. "When twenty percent of all small businesses go bankrupt in the first year."

"Yeah, but Making Whoopie just passed its second year, and if the crowds streaming in from open to close that I've witnessed firsthand are any indication—you're nowhere near going bankrupt."

"Fifty percent of new businesses fail in the first five years." Her reply is rote, like she's repeated it a hundred times. Or heard it from her mother even more. I watch her tuck a loose strand of hair behind her ear. She's talking facts, but I can hear the subtext—the way her mother saw the risk without seeing the dream.

Not wanting to talk badly about anyone's mother, I settle for, "She, uh, sounds practical."

"She is." This time the sigh is longer, quieter. "And she's not wrong, statistically speaking. Or a bad mom." Her gaze stays on the plate, voice even. "She just had to raise me on her own when my dad left, and then fought her way through a male-dominated career. She didn't want me to struggle." She shrugs her shoulders. "Still doesn't."

I study her, the way her shoulders square up even as her voice softens, and something in me shifts, like a wall I had braced inside me giving way.

"I'm pretty sure my mom was proud of me, too." The words scrape out before I can stop them. "She passed when I was younger. But she—" I clear my throat, forcing a crooked smile. "I remember she had this way of making everything feel... easy. Even when things weren't."

Audrey's eyes flick to mine.

"Guess that's why Hideaway threw me more than I expected when I first got here. All the holiday cheer, the traditions, families everywhere—it reminded me of everything I'd had and lost." I let out a slow breath, the words coming easier than expected. "My parents and I lived in a small town in Oregon before moving to Los Angeles, and most of my good memories of them are from then. So walking into Hideaway..." I shrug, not sure how to finish that sentence.

"I'm so sorry." Her voice is soft, guilt edging her words. "I didn't realize, and I wasn't very nice when—"

"Hey." I wave my hand across the table as if trying to thin the air that's become heavy with things I didn't mean to confess. "You couldn't have known." I lean back in my chair, trying to portray the picture-perfect image of an emotionally stable and successful man. "And now that I'm not jet-lagged and I've retired from Skippy patrol, I actually like Hideaway for the same reason I first didn't—it reminds me of my parents."

Audrey's expression turns hopeful.

"And I've especially liked working out of your bakery and" —I gesture around me and the nautical décor overlayed with Christmas trimmings—"going to places like this." I meet her eyes and smile, hoping to restore some of our previous ease. "I mean, now that I've gotten decent sleep, I can really appreciate the town."

Not taking the bait, Audrey asks, "You said your parents died when you were young. How young?"

"I was ten."

She winces, and I rush to follow with a softer note. "But Felix's mom, Sofia—she lived down the street. She stepped in when no one else could and basically adopted me. She's been like family ever since."

Something gentle crosses Audrey's face—sympathy but also curiosity, like she's cataloguing the people who matter most to me.

"Bottom line," I add, keeping my tone light, "Sofia and Felix have been my family for years, and I'm *fine*."

The furrow in her brow eases a little.

And then the waitress slides the bill onto the table.

I snatch it up before Audrey can even reach for her wallet. "You can get the next business meeting." I pull out my wallet and tuck my card inside the small black folder.

Her mouth opens like she wants to argue—but instead,

Audrey closes it, a reluctant smile tugging at her lips. "Fine. Next business meeting."

The heaviness eases, replaced by something lighter. Not quite safe, but not uncomfortable either.

Good thing this is just business.

OBJECTION!

Audrey

The problem with good intentions is that they look suspiciously like dates when you're carrying a picnic basket.

"When I said you could get the tab for the next business meeting, I didn't know it was going to come with a side of tree." Jack stands at the entrance to Pine & Dandy, one brow cocked, his breath fogging in the cold air like punctuation to his amusement.

I shift the basket to my other hand, the containers inside clattering like sleigh bells. "Well, uh… I wanted to thank you for all your help." The words sound lame even to my ears. Who thanks someone with flannel-clad tree cutters, sleigh rides, and hot chocolate stands that smell like sugar and woodsmoke?

Me, that's who.

This excursion seemed like a good idea this morning. After three straight days of tourist buses slamming into Making Whoopie—customers either asking for whatever Felix Jones posted about on social media or trying to catch a glimpse of Amanda Willis mid-whoopie pie bite—plus prepping for the upcoming gingerbread competition, I'd also been replaying what Jack said at the Chowder House. How Hideaway reminded him of his parents. About how the town's holiday magic may have initially stung, but it also sparked something unexpectedly good.

And I thought… maybe he'd like Pine & Dandy. The whole cut-your-own-tree experience complete with horses jingling past, tamed reindeer roaming the forest, and hot chocolate that tastes better because your mittens are damp. A small-town classic that might feel less like loss and more like home.

But now, standing at the entrance with Jack at my side, his amused expression melting into something softer, something dangerously more intimate, I'm second-guessing everything.

"Besides." I tug my scarf tighter with my free hand. "You were the one who complained about my apartment being holiday deprived."

He looks ahead to the clapboard barn decorated with swaths of pine garland, the corner of his mouth twitching. Not quite a smile but suspiciously close. "That I did."

Stifling a humph, I shuffle forward across the snow dusted ground. Jack follows, catching up to take hold of the basket for me.

It's nice. Not just his gentlemanly act but Pine & Dandy's atmosphere. I remember it from when I visited Hideaway before I moved here. Before I opened my bakery and suddenly didn't have time for the very things I moved here for.

The farm smells like every candle Yankee ever tried to bottle—pine needles crushed underfoot, woodsmoke from chimneys, sugar drifting out from the barn's bakery counter. Kids squeal as a pair of horses jingle past, pulling a sleigh heavy with bundled families. Off to the side, a pen holds two of the farm's reindeer, lounging like disinterested celebrities behind their wooden fence while children press mittened hands through the slats, begging them to "do the nose thing."

Jack's gaze lingers on the reindeer. "Tell me you don't actually make people pay to see Rudolph's understudies."

"Only three dollars," I say, straight-faced. "Five if you want a selfie."

That earns me a low chuckle, warm enough to chase away the chill.

"So what's the business angle here?" Jack shoves his hands in his coat pockets as we stroll past the rows of pre-cut trees, eyeing them like he's ready to negotiate. "You're going to write off a Douglas fir as a deductible?"

"No business." The words almost stick in my throat for how unusual they are. "Just a well-earned, small-town thank you experience."

Jack was right— I don't partake in the local festivities that drew me to the town. After Making Whoopie opened its doors, I kept saying I'd make time once that first crucial year of a new business's first year was behind me. Then it was once I'd paid off the equipment. Then once I hit a certain follower count on social media. All benchmarks I thought my mom needed before she'd finally admit I'd done a good thing by moving here—that she could be as proud of my little shop as she'd been when I worked at the Ritz.

Only then could I launch my main objective. Which, ironically enough, began with a Christmas tree farm. Just not this one.

Jack nudges my shoulder with his, guiding me back to the present. "Does that mean I've become baking assistant material?"

Between answering the phone, ringing up customers, and juggling his telework, he's started sticking around after hours to 'help' me prep for the gingerbread house competition this weekend.

I smile remembering Jack's expression when he *finally* got all four sides standing somewhat straight. "Getting there."

He puffs out his chest as best he can in his new thick winter coat. "Nice."

Having given up his city-slicker cashmere trench, Jack, in between lawyering and baking assistanting, managed to find a legitimately warm winter coat from a local shop.

It's unnerving how good he looks in his small-town-guy uniform.

We shuffle forward in line at the hot chocolate hut, where a college kid in a knit hat and Dansby's "Tree Crew" sweatshirt mans the pump-top thermoses. He perks up the second he sees Jack.

"Wait. You're Jack Lourd, right?" He fumbles his phone out of his pocket, thumb already hovering over the camera app. "So, uh—does that mean Amanda Willis or Felix Jones are coming, too?"

Jack's mouth flattens in a way I've started to recognize as his polite Hollywood no. "Not today."

The kid's shoulders slump. "Dang." He slides his phone back into his pocket with a dejected sigh, like Jack just told him Santa wasn't real. "Hot chocolate then?"

"Yes," I answer for both of us, stepping in before Jack can reach for his wallet.

The kid fills the thermoses I brought from home, still craning his neck one way and then the other as if Jack was lying and a celebrity might suddenly appear out of the snow-dusted evergreens. I hand Jack one, my gloved fingers brushing his.

"Thanks." He takes a sip, eyes on me, the whipped cream hitting his upper lip.

I stare a beat too long before jolting forward, waving toward the row of picnic tables set up between the hot chocolate stand and the barn glowing with white Christmas lights. "Come on. First, lunch. Then, spruce."

Jack

THE PICNIC BASKET has been raided down to crumbs and empty Tupperware.

Audrey fusses with the lids and napkins like she's running quality control for NASA, while I lean back against the splintered picnic bench—full and content and watching the farm move around us.

A sleigh rattles past, pulled by two heavy horses draped in bells, the sound carrying across the field like someone pressed play on a Christmas soundtrack. The white clapboard barn nearly blends in with the snowscape if not for the Christmas light trim blinking against the winter gray sky.

It's a scene straight out of a Bing Crosby movie, and I like it. And yet—sarcasm comes easier than sincerity.

"I should tell Amanda about this place." I sip the last of my cocoa. "Pine & Dandy would make a killer set for her holiday film. Though honestly..." I gesture toward the barn, the sleigh, the kid now crying because the reindeer ignored him. "It's not like the world needs one more Christmas tree farmer romance. Women flocking to the guy in flannel like he invented chopping wood? Bit overdone at this point, right?"

Instead of a shared laugh, I'm met with flashing eyes. "I forgot—your idea of romance is a prenup and a nondisclosure agreement." Her eye roll looks aspirin-worthy. "God forbid anyone wants something simple, or"—she jabs a mittened finger toward the rows of evergreens, their branches glittering with snow—"something real."

The jab lands square in my chest, sharper than I expected. I open my mouth, then close it again. For once, I've got nothing.

She notices. And instantly her shoulders drop, a guilty sigh slipping out. "Sorry. That was... uncalled for."

The wind whistles through the rows of trees, carrying the faint scent of pine and woodsmoke. She reaches into the basket for the last cookie, fiddling with the wrapper.

"I might be a *tad bit* sensitive to the whole Christmas tree farmer trope." She grimaces before dropping her eyes to her hands. "And I may not have been *one hundred* percent honest about why I moved to Hideaway."

Fully invested, I lean forward, elbows braced on the picnic table. "Go on."

She huffs a laugh at the exaggerated attention. "There might have been a week after Christmas when I was recovering from a busy holiday season at the Ritz, and I binge-watched a bunch of holiday romance re-runs."

"And were there Christmas tree farmers involved?" I can't help but tease.

Another eye roll, this one far less aggressive. "In about half of them." She shrugs. "What can I say, it turns out I'm a sucker for a man in plaid wielding a saw and driving a vintage pick-up truck."

Oddly, that bit of information stings. Because even in the new shapeless-yet-warm shearling lined coat I bought to replace my cashmere trench, I'm nothing like she's describing.

Her cheeks flush pink, the kind of color I know isn't from the cold. She sneaks a glance at me, embarrassed. "And I guess somewhere between the snowball fights and the inevitable barn dances, it hit me that a Christmas tree farmer was exactly what I wanted."

I nod. "But why the big secret? As you've said, you're not the only person intrigued by Christmas tree farmers—if the sheer number of movies featuring them is any indication."

"Well…" She hands me the cookie. "I didn't think my mom would understand." Her lips twist to the side. "She's kind of like you."

Frowning, I tip my head. "Why do I feel like that's not a compliment?"

Audrey shakes her head, laughing. "I respect my mom

enormously for raising me on her own, but I think because of that—and my father leaving—she doesn't put a lot of stock in the whole husband-two kids-dog-PTA-meetings lifestyle."

I take a bite of cookie, my suddenly dry mouth making it hard to swallow.

"What?" Her voice is light, but there's a defensive edge in her eyes. "Sound lame, Mr. Hollywood?"

After a hard swallow, I clear my throat. "Not at all." My voice is steadier than I expect, softer too. But inside, the words slam into me. Because Audrey Nouel is sitting across from me, confessing her Hallmark-movie dream, and I know damn well that's not me.

I'm not flannel and PTA meetings. I'm Hollywood contracts and cross-country flights. I'm the very life she left behind.

It doesn't matter, I tell myself, focusing on finishing the cookie I'm too preoccupied to taste. But when the cookie is gone and the silence between us grows, I have a sneaking suspicion I'm lying.

I GRIT MY TEETH, the saw biting into the trunk with slow, steady strokes. "You sure this is the one?" My voice is muffled under layers of tree branches.

"It's straight. It's full. It'll fit in my apartment without bringing down the ceiling. Checks all the boxes." She sounds smug as hell, while I'm crouched under a fat Douglas fir with snow seeping into my gloves, sawing away like a man auditioning for Lumberjack of the Year.

So much for all those action-hero workouts with Felix and his six-figure personal trainer. Wilderness survival training would've been more useful than the six-pack I developed.

"You sure you still want to do it all yourself?" She sounds more amused than impressed.

Not that I'm trying to impress her.

The saw slips forward, and I have to reseat it into the pathetic excuse for a cut I've managed in ten minutes. "I got it."

I don't, but I'd never disclose that to someone with a Christmas-Tree-Farmer-Hero complex.

Besides, Audrey brought me here for the whole "cut your own" experience. It would be ungrateful not to follow through.

Snow shakes off the branch above me, melting on the exposed skin at my neck. I shiver, the saw slipping again.

Cursing under my breath, I admit that maybe part of the reason I've insisted on doing this alone is to prove I can. As if a clean cut through a ten-inch trunk might magically qualify me for the Norman Rockwell painting Audrey wants—one I have no intention of delivering.

"Fine." Audrey's tone sounds suspiciously amused. "But if that tree falls on you, you can't hold me legally liable."

I swallow back a sarcastic retort and get to sawing.

Another ten minutes later, with Audrey having wandered off to refill our hot chocolate, I've got a pain in my back that I'm pretty sure only Lars, the masseuse at The Haven, can fix —but at least the tree is finally about to give way.

That's when something sharp jabs me in the ass.

"Um, Audrey?"

No answer—unless you count a deep huffing and the sound of snow being pawed.

The jab comes again, harder this time, knocking me sideways out from under the tree. I sprawl into the snow, and when I look up, I come face to face with antlers. Two sets of them, one reindeer snuffling aggressively at my coat, the other circling like backup muscle.

"Uh—Audrey?" I repeat, my voice cracking.

"Oh my god."

I tip my head to the right, just enough to see Audrey halfway up the hill, thermos in each hand, eyes wide.

"Um, stay still, Jack."

Duh. But I don't say it. Because I'm pretty sure I once saw a documentary about reindeer that emphasized how aggressive they could be.

A giant snout nuzzles the side of my neck.

Or was that a moose documentary?

Well, whatever it was, these two didn't get the memo because my playing-possum strategy is met with two of Santa's wingmen deciding I'm their new human lollipop.

Blitzen, by the name tag jangling from his harness, begins snuffling lower.

"What the hell is happening?" I whisper to Audrey, who's now wide-eyed, her gloved hand covering her mouth.

"I think—" She lowers her hand, only to snort when Donner muscles in—"I think they think you're a *girl reindeer.*"

If you've ever wondered what a reindeer tongue feels like in your ear—don't.

"Why the hell do they think that?"

"Um... maybe your coat?"

"What?" Giving up on playing dead, I try sliding myself out of range.

Audrey waves at something—or someone—in the direction of the barn before turning back to me. "Its color does look an awful lot like their hides."

I squint my eyes shut, protecting my vision from both a tongue lashing and the sight of Blitzen's undercarriage getting dangerously close to my face. "Is that your way of telling me my new coat is reindeer porn?"

Audrey snickers. "And you *were* on all fours under the tree for an abnormally long time."

"Way to kick a guy when he's dow—*oomph*."

Donner's snout just got a little too friendly with *my* undercarriage.

Audrey loses control and wheezes a laugh before regaining her composure.

Thankful it was a nose and not an antler or hoof, I flail backward, boots slipping, while my alleged tormentors grunt happily and continue their assault.

And then it clicks. Audrey's not panicked. She's entertained. Which means...

"They're tame, aren't they?" I hiss, arm up to protect my face as Blitzen and Donner argue with body bumps over who's going to grope me next.

Her reply is a fresh round of giggles.

The handler, who Audrey was probably signaling earlier, jogs over, shaking a bucket of feed, and just like that, Donner and Blitzen forget all about me.

They trot back to the pen, leaving me used and abused as well as damp, pine-scented, and fairly certain my future obituary will read: *Fondled by festive livestock.*

Audrey's still laughing when I stand, brushing snow and reindeer hair off my coat.

"This is why I should've purchased the new Moncler parka and just paid for expedited shipping."

Then, as if on cue, the tree behind me topples over, whacking me in the back and sending me head first, ass-up into the snow.

CRUMB COAT

Audrey

The bakery is quiet.

Ovens sigh themselves to sleep. The last trays of gingerbread house pieces cool on the racks. Outside, Hideaway Harbor has emptied, the clatter of boots and chatter of townspeople drifting toward the docks where the lobster-trap Christmas tree waits to be lit.

Normally, I'd feel a pang of wistfulness at missing out—the whole town gathered under twinkling lights, Santa arriving by boat, a crustacean deity glowing from the top of a pyramid of traps.

But considering that the last tree lighting ended with me getting pancaked in the town square by a Saint Bernard, a Hollywood agent, and a satanic cat, wistful isn't exactly what I'm feeling.

So while everyone else is bundled in scarves and mittens

to ooh and ahh over the town's mascot—Larry the Lobstah—twinkling from on high, I'm content to be surrounded by my cooling racks and my gingerbread-domination blueprints. Here in my sugar-scented sanctuary, I am safe from vengeful animals and the unnecessary distraction of broad male shoulders.

I glance at Jack's corner—that's how I've come to think of the desk I once used for stacking business papers until it was commandeered in the name of trademark law and questionable Wi-Fi. My Croc'ed feet tap with restless energy as I spread another blueprint on the prep counter, rattling through my box of pencils like a woman searching for a lifeline.

Knock. Knock.

Straightening, I groan, tossing my colored pencil back in the box. "We're closed!" I call, even as my feet betray me and head toward the door.

Another knock. Louder this time.

Thinking it's some poor caffeine addict who overshot the coffee shop, I flick on the front light. And freeze.

It's not a lost tourist or a hangry peppermint-mocha hopeful.

It's Jack.

He stands in the glow of the streetlight, collar turned up against the cold, juggling two enormous shopping bags that look ready to burst. His grin is so wide it tugs one out of me too.

Which, of course, sets off alarms ricocheting in my chest.

It isn't until his smile slightly dims that I realize I've been staring and letting him freeze on the doorstep.

Rushing over the last few steps, I open the door. "If those

bags contain your human cruelty lawsuit against Pine & Dandy's reindeer that you want me to witness, I'll sic Skippy on you."

Still smiling, Jack turns sideways to fit through the door. "Ha ha." He hefts the bags higher, proud as a kid showing off their Christmas morning haul. "I come bearing your much-needed holiday cheer."

The twisted paper handles look ready to tear from the weight of whatever's inside. "What are you talking about? I got a tree, remember? Or are you purposely blocking out any memory related to the reindeer incident?"

"You're awfully jokey for someone who has a dead tree in a literal mop bucket of water leaning against their apartment wall."

"All Christmas trees are dead, Jack. That's what happens when you cut them down. They die."

"Yes, but when you decorate them, like a normal person, they feel alive."

I peek into the top of one of his bags and jerk back, nearly blinded by the glare off a jumbo package of tinsel crammed on top.

"You got my tree decorations?"

Jack nods, moving past me into the kitchen. "Decorations. Lights. The whole nine yards."

"Jack..." I warn, "tomorrow is the gingerbread competition." I point to the blueprints.

He levels a flat stare, one brow barely twitching like even his face can't be bothered.

"Besides, where's Amanda?" I cross my arms, bracing myself even as doubt prickles underneath. "You haven't exactly been spending much time with the client who brought you here to figure out how to film a movie."

"One, Amanda is happier than an actress at the Vanity Fair Oscars afterparty. Apparently there was a taffy pulling spectacle at the candy shop that Amanda has become infatuated with which morphed into something mildly pornographic that she decided to follow with witnessing a tree made of lobster cages get lit by a Santa arriving by boat at the harbor."

I snort at the image.

"And two, I think it's pretty clear that if Amanda Willis wants to do something, she does it—whether or not her lawyer-slash-agent approves."

I smile, despite knowing I'm continuing a losing battle. "Must make tough work for the lawyer-slash-agent."

He sighs dramatically. "You have no idea."

We share a moment of levity before I shake it off and point to my prep table. "Well, I still need to—"

"No, you don't." His tone is light as he sets the bags directly on top of my gingerbread blueprints, but his eyes leave no room for argument. "You've done more than enough already." He taps an uncovered section of my design. "You added a boathouse, for Santa's sake."

I fold my arms, frowning. "What's wrong with a boathouse?"

"Nothing, if you're the architect for the Gingerbread Vanderbilts wanting to build their extravagant Maine getaway with room enough for their yacht."

A reluctant laugh sputters out, undermining my position and making Jack grin.

"But seeing as there is no such thing as Gingerbread Vanderbilts"—he eyes the multiple sheets of gingerbread house pieces I made in triplicate cooling on my racks—"you've done enough."

I don't have much of an argument. Because he isn't wrong. I *have* gotten more done this year than last. Both for the gingerbread competition and normal day-to-day orders for the bakery. Since Jack began working out of my bakery, I've even been able to sleep more than six hours a night. And for any baker during the holiday season—small shop or Ritz—that says a lot.

"So what?" I pretend to be put out. "You want to play Martha Stewart now?"

"No." He straightens, his cheerful expression back in place. "Martha has taste. I have… enthusiasm." He picks up the bags again—this time from the bottom. "We're decorating our tree."

Our tree.

Grateful he can't see what I am sure is a very goofy and lopsided grin on my face—the massive bags conveniently blocking his view—I guide him toward my apartment entrance in the back. "Fine. But only because it may actually be criminal in Hideaway to abandon a tree in such a sad, naked state."

"Exactly." His voice is softer, muffled behind his mountain of holiday spirit. "We wouldn't want the town gossips judging you, now would we?"

I scoff, thinking of how little Eileen would care about my undecorated tree but how much she'd salivate over the idea of Jack dusting it in tinsel.

Minutes—and a few stumbles—later, we're in my apartment, straightening our cut-your-own Pine & Dandy special in the new tree stand Jack bought.

Satisfied with how it looks, Jack tears into his bags, pulling out boxes. "Lights first."

I squint at the labels. One hundred LED lights. Ten different settings. User friendly.

I'm starting to sweat.

"Then decorations." He attacks the second bag by simply overturning it—spilling tinsel, ornaments, and a tree topper onto the sliver of rug not already swallowed by the circumference of the six-foot tree.

I sift through the pile. "Is this a Larry the Lobstah ornament?"

Jack nods, prying open the first box of lights. "Yeah. I got everything in town." The neatly coiled strand immediately knots itself when he yanks on the wrong end. "Between the Christmas market and this insane holiday store next to the bookshop, I may have blacked out and panic-bought trying to get us everything we need."

I eye the ceramic flamingo in a Santa hat cozying up to the delicate blown-glass angel in its little coffin of bubble wrap and think 'need' is a very generous word.

Jack, not done exploding Christmas in my apartment, hooks up his phone to my speaker.

"All right." He claps his hands together. "Let's do this."

And do this we do.

We untangle lights, burst packages of tinsel, and use enough electrical connections to worry a fire department—all to the soundtrack of Jack's curated holiday playlist that consists of Dean Martin, Mariah Carey, and the Beastie Boys.

It's eclectic to say the least.

Just like the tree.

"So." I eye his placement of a giant glitter pickle. "Did you have a theme or something in mind when you picked out the ornaments?"

Jack grins, a ribbon clamped between his teeth. "You mean besides Christmas?"

I roll my eyes and hang a red velvet bow next to the Santa Astronaut ornament that's chrome painted. "Yeah, besides that."

He rolls his eyes back at me. "I didn't realize trees needed a theme."

Stepping back, I assess the ornament composition. "Well, what does your tree usually look like?"

He hangs a strand of tinsel over an ornament of a teddy bear dressed as an elf. "I don't have one."

When he bends down to grab another decoration, I remove the tinsel and drape it over the end of a branch. "Really?"

"Don't look so surprised." His eyes narrow on the teddy bear ornament before placing the bow—this one leopard print —next to a turquoise ball. "You didn't have one either."

"Yeah, but I just thought since you seemed so shocked over my lack of tree that trees must be a big deal to you."

He shrugs, tossing up tinsel. "Since I usually spend Christmas at Sofia's house, I didn't think it mattered if I had one or not at mine." He leans closer to the tree and inhales deeply. "But in Los Angeles, real trees are hard to come by. At least ones that last through the actual holiday with most of their needles." He digs through the decorations, unearthing a plastic snowflake on a red hook. "But this..."—his hand stills, the grin sliding off his face like melting ice—"tree reminds me of the ones my parents had when I was little." He blinks, clearing his throat and hanging the snowflake. "I don't remember much, but I do remember the smell." He steps back, admiring his handiwork, seemingly satisfied with the cluster of ornaments and tinsel he adorned just one section of tree with.

I spend the rest of Jack's playlist following him around, reshuffling and re-spacing his—*our*—decorations.

Jack

"LET ME JUST SWITCH THESE TWO..." Audrey moves around our tree, muttering under her breath as she fixes my questionable bow placement.

Our.

The word slips through my head uninvited, lodging deep like a splinter I don't want to pull out.

"Ready?" I squat in my new fleece-lined khakis—another local purchase I made and one that I hope does *not* attract local wildlife—and hold the plug dramatically by the outlet.

Audrey rolls her lips, trying not to laugh.

God, that half-hidden smile is enough to wreck me.

She nods, eyes dancing. "Ready."

I shove the plug in. The tree detonates.

White, red, multicolor—every strand on a different setting. A disco supernova. One blinks like an ambulance flatlining, another twinkles like a Vegas marquee, and a third glows steadily, smug as hell.

Audrey throws her hands up, laughing, and I can't look away. Not at the chaos. Not at the glitter now dotting her cheekbone. Just her, radiant in the gaudiest light show ever conceived.

"That"—her voice shakes with laughter—"is by far the ugliest tree I've ever seen."

"Uh." I stand, hand on chest, mock-offended. "How dare you?"

But when she points at the angel tree topper wobbling like it's had too much sacrificial wine, it's hard to keep a straight face.

I shrug, a chuckle catching in my throat. "You may have a point."

We laugh together. And in our shared amusement over the catastrophe we've built, something shifts. An emotion catches in my chest—like a lock clicking open. I don't want the moment to end.

I get my wish, as it doesn't end so much as transforms—the laughter fading while the air thickens between us.

She steps closer. Too close. Close enough that I catch the scent of pine on her sweater, sugar on her skin.

Her hand lifts, tugging a tinsel strand from my hair, and I forget how to breathe.

"Jack?" Her eyes hold mine, unguarded.

"Yeah?" The word comes rough because she's so close, her lips parted like she might say something that'll undo me completely.

"I love our tree," she whispers.

I was right—*Our*.

Nat King Cole croons "O Holy Night" from my playlist as something inside me reorients.

Her lips curve, and I feel like I've been walking off-kilter for years and just found solid ground.

My hand lifts before I can stop it, brushing glitter from her cheek. "Me too."

And then we kiss.

Soft. Sweet. Tender.

Until it isn't.

Our mouths part, and heat punches straight to my ribs. My tongue grazes hers, tentative at first—a question I've been dying to ask but never thought I could. She answers without hesitation, pulling me closer.

I grab hold of her waist to steady myself, but soon my touch turns greedy. I need to memorize the feel of her through the soft knit of her sweater. I need to absorb her heat and leave a trail of mine in return.

Her fingers fist the fabric at my chest, pulling me closer. Each brush of her lips sharpens my senses, the taste of sugar giving way to spice until I'm half-drunk on the very flavor of her.

The kiss builds like the tree—every reckless ornament, every mismatched piece stacked higher and higher until the whole thing glows. By the time the chorus swells, I'm ready to do what Nat King Cole sings—fall on my knees.

Client status, her family-life goals, me nearing my Hideaway expiration—none of it matters. Only this kiss matters. Only her.

Then—my pants vibrate.

And not in the good way.

Audrey

THE SUDDEN COLD where Jack's mouth had been on mine feels sharper than the draft sneaking through my apartment's single-paned windows.

I just kissed Jack Lourd. Or did he kiss me?

Does it matter?

Oh my god, oh my god, oh my god.

"Sorry." Looking more flustered than I've ever seen him—and I've seen him dive-bombing a Christmas tree with a naked cat in hand—Jack pulls his phone from his pocket. He frowns at the screen like he'd love nothing more than to pitch it into the harbor. "I'll turn it off."

"No." My voice is louder and harsher than I intended. "Ah, I mean, you should take it." My lips are still tingling, and my pulse hasn't slowed since he kissed me—I need a minute. Or fifty.

His gaze flicks to mine, brow furrowing, like he can't quite decide if I'm brushing him off or being polite. For a heartbeat, I think he'll ignore it despite my permission. Then he exhales, swipes, and suddenly his voice is polished, professional, clipped. So very different from when we fought over where to place the two turtle doves on our tree.

"Jack Lourd." Whoever talks back on the other end has Jack's frown deepening. "Yes. I know who you are." There's more chatter on the other end, and I'm suddenly conscious of my silent apartment— the music having shut off when Jack's phone rang. "When is the movie supposed to start filming?" He runs a hand through his hair, no longer dusted in tinsel. "And the contract?"

Dropping to my knees, I busy myself with cleaning. The shiny wrappers from his ornament spree, scraps of ribbon, cellophane from the lights—my hands gather them up, crinkling and snapping, not wanting to hear my internal thought process highlighting just how bad of an idea that kiss was. But how *good* it felt.

While Jack continues speaking fluent Hollywood, I can hear the harbor festivities happening outside a short distance away. Getting up from the floor with my pile of festive trash, I make my way toward the front window. Through the frosted panes I catch a blur of motion—scarves and hats bobbing under the lampposts, all heading to or from the harbor, where fireworks are soon to go off.

Behind me, Jack paces the length of the room, his voice sharp. "Residuals are capped against international box office —hello? Can you hear me?" He pulls the phone away, frowning, then tries again. "You'd need to—hello?" He stops midstride, listening to nothing, and finally lowers the phone with a muttered curse.

"Who was that?" I ask, aiming for casual.

Jack pockets his phone, his gaze never leaving mine, eyes stormy with something that makes my breath catch. "Potential client."

Client. As in movie star. As in Hollywood. As in where he lives, all the way across the country. "Do you need to call them back?"

He shrugs, taking a step toward me. "I can call later." His tone is easy, his eyes intense.

Oh my god, oh my god, oh my god.

I back up a step, not sure if I'm ready for whatever his expression means. "Maybe you should call them now?" I try for nonchalance. "It's never a good idea to turn down business."

For a moment he studies me, eyes searching, as though he suspects that my unaffected countenance is forced. That I don't mean what I'm saying.

He'd be right, but I double down on my poor acting skills by checking my nails.

Pausing, he frowns harder before giving me a cautious nod. "I guess that's true." His words come slowly.

Ignoring the hypocritical stab of disappointment at his agreement, I keep a smile on my face and tilt my head toward the door. "Go. I'll finish up here."

He hesitates like there's something he wants to say before grabbing his coat off the back of the couch. Still frowning, he shrugs it on, the shapeless bulk looking decidedly un-Jack-like. "I'll see you soon." He says it like a question.

"Sure." The word comes out flatter than I meant, like it already regrets itself. "Yeah."

Yet as soon as the latch of my apartment door clicks shut, leaving me alone with twinkle lights and the pounding of my libido that sounds an awful lot like my heart, I'm absolutely sure of two things.

One, I'm the biggest idiot in Maine for sending him home instead of to my bedroom.

And two, that I'll be wide awake regretting it until sunrise.

HALF-BAKED

Audrey

Oh my god, oh my god, oh my god.

The words—on endless replay since last night's kiss with Jack ended far too soon—are still beating against my skull harder than the Christmas carols blasting from the community center's loudspeakers. Only now they're accompanied by the fact that I'm flustered, frazzled, and *at least* two gumdrops short of looking put-together.

Which is not how I wanted to show up for the gingerbread competition.

But this morning? I overslept. After spending half the night tossing and turning in bed, replaying a kiss I should've filed under *one-and-done* but instead kept analyzing from every conceivable angle. And much to my dismay, fantasizing about how I wish the kiss would've ended— as in not until we were both naked and his Christmas playlist went on repeat—didn't do anything to cool my downtown ovens, so to speak.

The result of my overactive imagination and unhelpful lusting? Puffy eyes, bedhead barely wrestled into a braid, and a heart and mind about to emotionally and physically collapse—especially after what one of the competition judges, Eileen Burrows, just told me.

"I'm sorry, what?" I blink at her as she smiles at me from behind the sign-in table, pen poised like she's orchestrating a wedding rather than a bake-off.

"I could've sworn I told you, dear." She frowns, but I *swear* there's mischief in her eyes.

Taking a deep breath, I glance down the row of tables set up for the showdown, each one loaded with gingerbread slabs, piping bags, and more gumdrops than a dentist's worst nightmare. Every team is neatly paired off—husbands and wives, siblings, parent-and-kid duos. All bright-eyed, sugar-hyped, and grinning like this is the most fun they'll have all season.

Everyone except… me.

Because no. Eileen most definitely did not tell me about the partner requirement. But arguing with Eileen Burrows is like arguing with Santa Claus—even if you win, you lose. So instead of protesting, I paste on a polite smile, hoping it hides the flush creeping up my neck. "Must've slipped my mind."

Eileen, cheeks rosy and Christmas tree brooch winking under the fluorescent lights, taps her pen on the clipboard. "I thought that might be the case when I was double-checking the sign-ups this morning." She beams and makes a dramatic flourish next to my name. "So I arranged a partner for you."

My stomach sinks. "A... partner?" I squint hard, trying to read her looping scrawl upside down.

"Mm-hm." Eileen extends her arm, covering the clipboard, and pats my hand as though she's bestowing a blessing from the love gods themselves. "Such a perfect fit, you'll see."

And right on cue, a familiar voice rumbles behind me.

"Sorry I'm late."

Oh my god, oh my god, oh my god.

I freeze. My spine locks up, my braid feels too tight, and I'm ninety-nine percent sure the heat flooding my cheeks could melt my entire gumdrop stash.

Slowly, I turn.

And there he is. Jack Lourd in a Henley that clings to his chest in ways no fabric has a right to, dark stubble shadowing the jaw I'd spent half the night imagining beneath my lips. He looks maddeningly awake, maddeningly put together, and not at all like a man who should have the power to unravel me in front of half the town.

My oh-my-gods multiply.

Eileen clasps her hands together like a fairy godmother who's just orchestrated the ball. "Perfect," she announces to no one in particular—except the hundred or so Hideaway residents already sneaking glances our way.

Perfect?

I want to argue. To insist this is the opposite of perfect. That I don't need a partner—especially not *this* partner—to get through the competition.

But Jack's gaze catches mine, a flicker of amusement in his eyes that tells me he knows exactly what I'm thinking. And worse, he looks like he's enjoying it.

"The competition will be in two forty-five-minute parts with a ten-minute break in-between."

Eileen hands us our name badges—*Team Whoopie*—written above them. "Good luck!"

Jack

I ALMOST DIDN'T COME.

After the way Audrey shooed me out the door last night, showing up at a gingerbread free-for-all seemed like a surefire way to dig myself deeper into whatever hole I'm already in. But then Eileen Burrows—the same woman who runs a matchmaking empire out of a coffee shop and thinks she can strong-arm anyone with a latte—called my room at The Haven while I was briefs-deep in legal research over my potential client's movie deal, whose deadline suddenly got pushed up.

Eileen's message was clear: Show up at the community center now or Audrey would have to forfeit the competition.

And apparently not all lawyers are complete bastards because I came.

Not that I should've been surprised to learn Audrey wasn't the one who signed me up as her partner. I overheard Eileen at the sign-in desk, cheerfully announcing she had "solved Audrey's problem."

But instead of irritated, I find myself… relieved.

Because Audrey Nouel—James Beard winner, Michelin darling, bakery owner with frosting in her veins—looks flustered. Not polished. Not untouchable. But cheeks pink, hair askew, eyes wide as she realizes she's been cornered.

And if the look on her face is anything to go by, she wasn't as unaffected by our kiss last night as she wanted me to believe when I took that phone call.

The call that took longer than I'd expected. The one that made the opportunity in LA so sweet it should've had me salivating.

And yet all I felt was annoyed—at it costing me an opportunity with Audrey.

Now standing here with a 'Jack' name tag to slap on my cashmere Henley, I can't help thinking maybe this competition is my shot at getting a do-over.

"You two better hurry," Eileen chirps, practically glowing with matchmaking glee. "The competition is about to begin."

Audrey mutters something that sounds suspiciously like *fuck it* under her breath and grips the handle of her supply wagon like she's about to march into battle.

I fall into step behind her because apparently that's my role now—back-up gingerbread grunt. She yanks the wagon forward, but the thing wobbles and squeaks like it's carrying bricks instead of flour and candy.

I plant a hand on the back of the cart and give it a shove. The load jerks forward, suddenly lighter, and she shoots me a startled look over her shoulder—braid swinging, cheeks pinker, looking equal parts flustered and furious.

"Relax," I murmur, thinking that I've somehow been elbowed into a domestic fantasy I didn't know I wanted. "I'm only here to keep the wagon from collapsing before the house does."

The corner of her mouth twitches—half annoyance, half amusement—but she says nothing and lets me push the wagon. I count that as a win.

On our journey down the hall, people wave and call hellos to Audrey, who acknowledges with a nod but not much else. It's like she's already in battle mode.

I'm more than a little surprised when a few townspeople call out to *me* by name. I guess selling most of these people pies for the past week has made me more than Amanda Willis' agent or Skippy's dogwalker. I make sure to wave back with the hand not pushing the cart.

When we finally reach our assigned table, Audrey begins lining up supplies with the precision of a military general. Piping bags, candy bowls, sheets of gingerbread—all squared up, symmetrical, and waiting for her command.

"Do not touch anything until I tell you." Still squaring bowls and piping bags, she doesn't so much as spare me a glance.

I raise both hands in surrender. "Scout's honor."

She finally glances up, one brow arched. "I highly doubt you were ever a scout."

She's not wrong. But if she thinks I'm above sneaking a Red Hot the moment her back's turned to get her to lighten up, she doesn't know me at all.

I slide one from the bowl, pop it into my mouth, and bite down with exaggerated satisfaction.

Her head jerks at the sound, hair lashing around like a whip. "Are you serious right now?"

I grin, sugar and spice sticking to my tongue. "Just a little quality control."

Her brows are still pinched, but I swear the corner of her lips soften. But before she can reprimand me or smile, a voice booms through the microphone at the front of the room. "Ladies and gentlemen, boys and girls—welcome to the Annual Hideaway Gingerbread Showdown!"

The crowd cheers, a mix of holiday sweaters and Santa hats bouncing as people clap. The energy is almost electric, festive chaos pressing in on all sides.

The announcer continues, "You'll have two hours to create the most spectacular gingerbread structure you can dream up. Houses, castles, cathedrals—we've seen it all. Remember: teamwork makes the dream work!"

Audrey exhales like she's about to enter the Hunger Games, then smooths a hand down the front of her pastry chef coat.

For a second, with her black slacks hugging her legs in a way that doesn't feel regulation uniform and her eyes gleaming with deadly pastry intent, I forget that this is supposed to be a gingerbread competition and not a seductive gladiatorial combat demonstration.

The countdown begins. Ten, nine, eight…

She grips a piping bag and thrusts it at me like a weapon. "Don't squeeze until I tell you to."

I take it, resisting the urge to say *'Yes, chef,'* and bump her with my shoulder. "You got this, Audrey."

My sincerity catches her off-guard, and her eyes hold mine. For a split second, I swear she's remembering what happened the last time we were this close—that kiss, the one that's been replaying in my head ever since. Her mouth opens, then snaps shut. She turns back to the gingerbread slabs like they're the only things that matter.

Three, two, one—

The whistle blows, and Audrey immediately gets to work, hands flying. Meanwhile, I'm still holding the piping bag like it's a loaded gun and wondering if frosting someone's apron counts as contempt of cake.

Audrey

THE WHISTLE SHRIEKS, and the whole room surges with energy—bowls rattling, kids shrieking, couples elbowing each other over gumdrops.

I brace myself for having to waste time incorporating Jack into my carefully planned strategy.

But instead, he rolls his shoulders back, squeezes the piping bag once to test the flow, and gives me a sharp nod like he's reporting for duty. "Walls first?"

"Yes." Relief loosens my spine, and I'm suddenly extremely thankful for Jack inserting himself into my gingerbread competition prep this past week, even if it was just in between mooching off my Wi-Fi and juggling Hollywood emails.

He crouches to eye level with the slab, his hands rock-solid as he pipes a line of icing, while mine tremble slightly as I join the edges. The wall seals tightly, cleaner than if I'd done it alone.

"Next?" he prompts, calm and focused, and damn if my chest doesn't squeeze.

I grab the next rectangle of perfectly baked gingerbread from my prep line-up. "Other wall."

Piece by piece, we fall into a rhythm. I direct, he executes. His piping is deliberate, his hands surprisingly deft for someone who spends most of his life with contracts instead of confections. Every so often he throws me a glance, like he's checking to see if I approve, and each time I have to swallow the ridiculous urge to tell him he could proudly add baker's assistant to his résumé—and that he's the best I've ever had.

Even at the Ritz, with properly trained assistants, I never felt as relaxed as I do with Jack by my side. He doesn't try to outshine me or sneak in his own flair—he just... supports.

And for the first forty-five minutes of the competition, I give orders like a drill sergeant at the gingerbread Olympics, and Jack steadily complies.

By the time the halfway whistle blows, our house structure is standing tall. Undecorated, but with the hardest part behind us. For the first time since I overslept this morning, my shoulders unclench, my breath sliding out in something close to relief.

Letting out a sigh, Jack sits back in one of the chairs we've been given and scratches his neck while I circle our table like a building inspector with a clipboard.

"When they blow the whistle to start again, we'll install the candy cane porch columns, followed by the gumdrop pathway." Moving to the cart, I double-check that I have all the required candy lined up in the correct order to mirror my instructions. "We'll leave the roof shingles for last to make sure the icing has time to fully cure so the roof can bear the weight."

"That sounds like a well-thought-out plan." Portia, owner of the Sweetest Thing Candy Shop, stops by our table, Amanda Willis behind her.

"Oh, hey." I straighten to attention, my old days of competing in international showcases coming back to me. "Thank you, judge."

Portia rolls her eyes. "Thank you, judge? Really, Audrey?"

"Sorry." I shrug, feeling sillier than I'd like. "I guess old habits are hard to break."

"Yes, well, break this one. It feels weird for a friend to be so formal."

Friend. Yes, I guess Portia and I are friends. I feel guilty even having to second-guess that. Portia has always been someone I can talk to since I moved to Hideaway. It started with me using her candy in my creations, and now sometimes when we talk, work doesn't even come up.

Have I really been so busy that I haven't noticed?

"Jack, what's with the stiff shoulders?" Amanda whacks her agent on the back. "You getting old on me?"

"Nah." Jack laughs, but it doesn't quite meet his eyes or smooth out the pinch between his brows. "Just making sure I don't screw things up for Audrey."

Heat hits my cheeks hard and fast, the truth sinking in—I've been less festive teammate and more sprinkle drill sergeant.

"Well, aren't you the considerate one." Amanda laughs, hers more natural. "Though I don't think you have anything to worry about." She gestures to our gingerbread compound. "No one else has gone this big or looks this perfect."

I follow her hand, for the first time taking in the other tables.

And while Amanda is right—ours is the biggest and most professional looking—there's something everyone else has that mine lacks: fun.

Across from us, a teenage girl fist-bumps her dad over their slightly cockeyed gingerbread lighthouse. Next to them, a young married couple smear frosting on each other's noses like it's cake at their wedding. And to our left, two women from the local garden club play rock-paper-scissors to decide the color of Pop Rocks for their gingerbread mulch.

All of them are smiling. None of them are worried about perfection.

"Get ready to restart in five minutes!" Eileen shouts from the loudspeaker at the front of the community center.

"I need to look at the other tables." Portia hurries off, but Amanda stays.

Jack gets up. "I'm going to run to the restroom." He glances at the clock. "Or should I not chance it?"

If everyone around me smiling and laughing wasn't enough to knock some sense into me about how over-the-top I was being, the fact that Jack would worry about inconveniencing me enough to not use the bathroom does.

"Go." I point him in the right direction. "No need to rush. It's fine."

He looks startled at that last word. "Okay." He takes two steps and stops. "I'll be right back, promise." Then he jogs off.

"Talk about not wanting to leave your side." Amanda snorts. "Sheesh. He's got it bad."

I blink once, trying to decode her meaning. "Got what bad?"

"His thing." Amanda looks at me quizzically. "For you."

"I'm sorry?" My fingers worry the hem of my chef's coat.

"Girl." Amanda tilts her head and gives me the look only best friends and exasperated older sisters perfect. "It's pretty obvious."

"What are you talking about?" Unless she knows about the kiss—and even then, I don't think anything is obvious.

Amanda gives me the universal *duh* look. "Uh... he hasn't left your side since we got to Hideaway."

Not meeting her eyes, I rearrange my perfectly straight lines of edible glitter by color. "I hired him to take care of a legal issue for me."

Her brows climb. "You did?"

"Yeah." I flick a crumb off the table, as if that settles it. "And in return for payment, I let him use my Wi-Fi."

Amanda snorts sharp and disbelieving, making a couple kids at the next table glance over. "He doesn't need your Wi-Fi."

My pulse hiccups. "He doesn't?"

"Ah, no." She taps her chin, thinking it over. "Well, maybe in the first few days, before the Ethernet cable he ordered arrived. But he's had that for ages. He's always working when he gets home from the bakery—in his room, what with Los Angeles being a few hours behind us."

"Oh." The sound around me thins, like all the oxygen's been pulled out of the community center.

The time difference. I'd completely forgotten about that.

"Then why did he always show up right when the bakery opened if people were still sleeping in LA?"

Amanda cocks a hip, looking at me as if I asked why water is wet. "Seriously?"

Portia laughs at something Eileen says at the front of the room, drawing Amanda's attention—and softening her gaze.

I'd be interested in that detail if I wasn't still trying to work out what she just told me.

"Got to go be an epic judge sidekick." Amanda winks at me. "Wish me luck."

And I know she's asking for more than just luck with judging. "Good luck."

"You too." And I know we both mean more than just luck with the gingerbread competition.

She saunters away, passing Jack as he jogs down the aisle toward our table.

He pulls up short at my look and checks his watch. "I made it, right?"

"Yes." The word catches, and I clear my throat. "Plenty of time."

"One minute!" Eileen bellows, causing teams to resettle around their tables.

"Hey." Jack drops a hand on my shoulder. "You okay?" He glances behind him at my perfectly proportioned and executed gingerbread mansion with unattached boathouse. "I didn't mess anything up, did I?"

"No." I shake my head hard, for some reason finding it difficult to get the words out. "You did great."

His chest puffs out, looking surprised but pleased. "Yeah."

"Yeah." I laugh, the escaping air loosening something else inside me. "Totally."

OFF-SCRIPT

Jack

The second whistle blows, and suddenly it feels like I've stepped into an entirely different competition.

Same table. Same gingerbread mansion. Same sugar-fueled crowd buzzing all around us. But Audrey? She's not the same woman who barked orders at me for the first hour like Gordon Ramsay on a peppermint bender.

Something's shifted.

"What do you think?" She holds a jar of candy canes in one hand and gumdrops in the other.

I blink, sure I misheard her. "You're asking me?"

"Yes, you." A laugh slips out of her, quick and real, like it escaped before she could stop it. "Don't look so surprised." She rattles the candies. "Candy canes or gumdrops?"

"Candy canes." I draw out my answer, trying to figure out who flipped Audrey Nouel's switch and how.

She nods like I've passed a test and presses one into place, the peppermint gleaming against the white icing. Then, without fanfare, she nudges the piping bag into my hands. "Your turn."

I look at her, waiting for the punch line. "My turn for what?"

"For the boathouse dock." She motions to the bare gingerbread slab jutting out like a pier. "You're in charge of the boat."

I almost laugh, convinced she's messing with me. But when she continues to stare at me expectantly, the amusement fades to confusion. "You trust me with that?"

The same Audrey who nearly came unglued when I piped an uneven line of icing that would be hidden inside the house, lifts her shoulders with a shrug. "Why not? You've got good hands." She says it lightly, like she's talking about my penmanship, but something in her voice takes me back to her apartment, our Christmas tree and last night's kiss.

I clear my throat and dirty mind, worried I might inadvertently start competing with the candy canes for the stiffest line at the table. "Okay then."

I start slapping gingerbread slabs together with icing mortar, fashioning something vaguely resembling a skiff. My "boat" looks about as seaworthy as a shoebox, but Audrey's not correcting, not critiquing, just steadies the bowl of icing when I reach for it or slides a gumdrop across the table without a word.

And when one of my licorice railings sags sideways, she snorts. *Snorts.*

"Don't laugh," I protest, trying to right it, but she's already shaking with laughter, her hair falling over her shoulder.

"It's charming," she insists, eyes bright. "Authentic." She dabs a fingertip in a blob of icing stuck to the back of my hand before it can slide onto our masterpiece. "Hideaway boats are supposed to look a little weathered."

Her touch lingers for a beat too long on the edge of my knuckle before pulling back, eyes on the gingerbread like nothing happened.

Every time I fumble—licorice railings sagging, candy oars tilting—she covers the mistake with a sprinkle of sugar or a swirl of frosting, smoothing over my flaws like she's been doing it forever. And each time, her mouth curves in that restrained little smile, the one that tells me she's enjoying this more than she'll admit out loud.

Together we add a sheet of blue sugar glass for the "water," the boat perched at the dock with a gummy fish leaping beside it. She anchors it with icing ropes while I pipe snowdrifts along the dock.

It doesn't look as professional as Audrey's painstakingly designed blueprint. But it looks… alive. Joyful.

I glance at her, hair slipping loose from her braid, face glowing in the warm overhead lights. She catches me staring, but instead of looking away, she stares back, smiling.

Someone across the room laughs, drawing her attention for a moment. When she looks back, her eyes are wide, her brows lifted. Hopeful. "Are you having fun?"

She has no idea.

"Big time." My smile feels unnaturally large.

Somewhere between straight candy-cane railings and my sad gingerbread dinghy, it became less about supporting her and more about us spending time together.

And damn if I don't want more.

Audrey

"We've got this." Jack nudges his shoulder against mine, his cadet-straight posture comically at odds with the powdered sugar streaking his Henley.

Our mansion stands tall behind us as Jack and I—and all the teams—line up at the front of the community center with their builds displayed.

I may not agree with Jack's certainty about winning the showcase, but even so, I nudge him back. "Yeah." We share a smile that lasts a beat longer than friendly.

His eyes drop to my lips, and I—

"Testing."

A nervous energy zings through me as Eileen taps the microphone. But it isn't about the competition. It's about what I've been secretly planning to do with Jack after the competition. To show him just how much I appreciate him. For today, the past weeks at Making Whoopie, and last night in my apartment.

"Ladies and gentlemen, bakers and builders," she begins, her voice carrying easily over the crowd, "what a Showcase this has been. I've seen gumdrop gardens, peppermint porches, chocolate chimneys, and one questionable jellybean outhouse." The crowd chuckles, and Eileen grins. "And I can honestly say this year's creativity and teamwork has outdone them all."

She sweeps her arm toward the lineup of houses. "Now some of you will be leaving with ribbons today, and some with nothing more than a sugar hangover and sticky fingers. But every single one of you is taking home something sweeter —memories made right here in Hideaway Harbor."

Eileen's gaze lands on me, holding for a second before moving along.

"As for the prizes: first, second and third place winners will each receive gift certificates to the community center, good toward registration fees for spring sports and classes." She pauses. "And exclusive to our *first* place champions is their picture in Hideaway's very own *Almanac,* and"—she draws it out, eyes sparkling—"in the Bangor regional paper, the *Bangor Daily Chronicle.*"

Murmurs ripple through the crowd at the mention of the regional coverage. My pulse kicks up a notch.

I glance back at our mansion, standing tall with candy-cane columns, a winding gumdrop path, and Jack's gingerbread boat bobbing off its licorice dock. It looks impressive.

But not perfect. Not the polished replica I envisioned in my carefully drafted blueprints. The kind of thing I never would've submitted when perfection was the only acceptable outcome.

Even so, I've never loved anything I made more.

Eileen hands over the microphone to Portia, whose vibrantly colored hair and tinsel extensions catch the overhead lights. Amanda, usually glued to her side, has slipped away so as not to upstage the competitors.

Portia smiles at the crowd, the hand holding the microphone stacked in a multitude of candy bracelets. "I'll start with the honorable mention for most creative concept…"

I take Jack's hand in mine.

Startled, he looks down at our hands before frowning at me. "You okay?" he whispers out the side of his mouth, trying not to draw attention.

Portia drones through the early awards.

Trying not to let the sudden rush of emotion show, I wink at him. "Win or lose, I had a great time with you today."

That shocks him more than me holding his hand. "Yeah." His posture loosens, shoulders relaxing as he twists toward me. "Me too."

"And not just today." I hesitate, then push through. "Every day since you arrived has been great. Fun, even."

Jack arches a brow, disbelief tugging at his mouth. "Even the first day?"

I chuckle quietly. "Well, maybe not that first day."

"Even last night?" His grin tilts, more sin than humor, his eyes locking on mine.

The room gets warmer.

"Yeah." I squeeze his hand. "Even last—"

"Team Whoopie!" Portia's shout reverberates across the community center, slicing through the moment.

For a second, it doesn't even register. But then cheers erupt, claps echo off the rafters, and Eileen bustles toward us with the blue ribbon.

I won.

I actually won.

Jack engulfs me in a hug, his warmth crashing into the high already flooding my veins.

No—I squeeze him tighter—*we* won.

Joy bursts through me, impossible to contain, and I bounce in his arms like a cork popping free.

Not just because the *Almanac* photographer is on his way, or because the *Bangor Daily Chronicle* will run my bakery's name for all of southern Maine to see—including the bakery that tried to steal it. And not just because it's another notch of prestige to wave in my mother's face.

It's about more than that. About letting go. About joy without ROI.

I step back to accept the ribbon Eileen hands me. Jack bows extravagantly like he's just accepted a Tony Award, making me roll my eyes so hard I lose my balance. Grinning, I shift toward him—straight into his chest.

"Careful." Jack steadies me, his hand firm on my elbow. But it's too late.

My Crocs betray me.

One sole catches on the custom charms I ordered on Etsy. Rubber catches on rubber, and I stutter-step backward, apron strings tangling around my legs.

I stumble—*hard.*

Jack grabs for me, but the skid-resistant Croc shall not be moved, and together we topple.

Backwards.

Right into our award-winning gingerbread mansion.

The destruction is spectacular. Glorious. Cinematic, even.

And while normally no one falling into rubble could note the details, I'm blessed—*cursed?*—with an out-of-body experience enabling me to home in on every second of destruction: the foam board platform giving way under my elbow, an earthquake-like crack in the zigzagging beneath the mansion, the front wall collapsing, the gumdrops sinking into the fissure.

Jack hits the table next, the jolt collapsing the roof, frosting shattering like snow in slow motion. His lovingly constructed gingerbread boat catapults into the air, arching beneath the fluorescent lights like Icarus' doomed wings flying too close to the sun.

Powdered sugar, blue Pop Rocks, and candy cane shards explode upward like fireworks, coating us—and everyone within five feet—in sweet broken debris.

Jack and I land with a thud, the platform cleaving in two, remnants of our masterpiece sliding in on us like a candy avalanche.

The entire room goes silent.

Blinking past the sugar mist, my eyes land on the Bangor photographer, camera frozen midair, mouth wide open.

A kid in the audience pauses mid-bite, cheeks bulging with contraband gumdrops.

Portia and Eileen stand frozen, clipboards dangling uselessly at their sides.

Jack's arms are still around me, cushioning my fall. He stares down at me, eyes wide, sugar dusting his stubble—horror etched deeper than the day he accidentally became Blitzen's side-piece.

No one moves. No one breathes. As if they're all waiting for my cue.

Waiting for the pressure bubbling up inside me to erupt onto the stunned silence.

And yet even with the full impact of what happened sinking in, what overflows isn't tears or anger.

It's laughter.

It breaks free, sharp and loud, until my head is tipped back against the boathouse rubble, my braid tangled in licorice ropes.

Jack's horrified expression cracks into a grin, and his laugh joins mine—low at first, then rich and unrestrained.

That's all it takes.

The crowd erupts. Giggles from kids, chuckles from parents, a full belly laugh from Portia that rings over the loudspeaker.

Our masterpiece is rubble, but the joy is intact. Maybe more than intact—it's doubled.

And for the first time in my life, losing doesn't feel like losing at all.

INDECENT EXPOSURE

Jack

She should've been devastated.

Her perfect gingerbread house and my amateur boat house collapsed like a New England roof in an ice storm, gumdrops rolling across the floor, icing sliding down like sticky snow.

Instead, Audrey laughed.

Really laughed—head tipped back, cheeks flushed, shoulders loose. Like it didn't matter that she'd closed the store on a busy holiday weekend all for a chance at the free advertising and prestige that winning the Gingerbread Showcase would bring her—only to have the whole town watch her bakery pride nosedive into rubble before the newspaper photographer could snap their picture.

I felt that laugh in my chest. Suspiciously close to my heart.

Even now, after we packed up the gingerbread crumbs and loaded it and the rest of the paraphernalia onto her cart and rolled through the back entrance of Making Whoopie, that same happiness still radiates off her, illuminating the dimly lit bakery.

Just this morning she was cool, dodging eye contact, pretending our kiss by the Christmas tree never happened, focused entirely on work and winning. Now she tosses her scarf aside, hair tumbling out of its icing-covered braid, looking at me like she just won another James Beard award.

"Thank you for today." Her voice is low but laced with something more sensual than gratitude.

I blink, caught off guard for the umpteenth time today. "For… what?" I add a touch of flirt to my voice, very much liking the mood she's creating. "Adding gingerbread demolition to my ever-growing résumé?"

Her mouth tilts, sly and soft at once. "For making it fun."

Her words shouldn't undo me the way they do. But the way it sounds like she couldn't have had fun without me and the way she's looking at me—like I'm a lot more than a consolation prize—hits harder than Felix's personal trainer in the boxing ring.

I want to ask, cross-examine her like a witness—*What changed, Miss Nouel? What made you go from ignoring Exhibit A (our kiss) to Exhibit B (launching yourself at me)?*

But then she moves. Her arms wind around my neck, her body presses flush against mine, and for once, the lawyer in me shuts up. Helps when her mouth covers mine.

We stumble farther into the kitchen, her lips fierce, her laugh breaking between kisses. My back slams into a rack of cooling trays, sending a metallic crash echoing through the empty room.

"Sorry," she gasps, already tugging at my scarf like it's personally offended her.

"Don't apologize." My hands tangle in her hair, sending a drift of powdered sugar into the air. The stuff glitters down like we've triggered some kind of bakery snow globe.

We turn, bumping into the counter, a mixing bowl clattering to the floor. My curse is muffled against her mouth.

She grins, her fingers fisted tightly in my shirt.

I reach out to brace myself, but instead of the table, my palm meets a leftover piping bag on the cart from the competition. A sharp squeeze and *pfffft*—icing squirts across the stainless steel surface in a perfect arc.

Audrey freezes, eyes wide. "You—" Her voice cracks into laughter. "You just frosted my table."

"Not the worst euphemism I've ever heard." I lick a streak off my finger, slow and deliberate.

Her cheeks flush pink, then she yanks me to her. Her mouth is cinnamon and sugar and something uniquely hers, and I'm a lost man.

We careen sideways, my elbow knocking a whisk off the counter. It spins across the tile, a metallic *wheeeeee* that might as well be cheering us on.

Her sweater rides up under my hands, warmth meeting my palms. I pull it the rest of the way off, pale skin more luminous than any string of Christmas lights I've ever seen. Her cranberry-colored bra, a perfect match for her Crocs, hits me hard in both the chest and the groin.

"Merry Christmas, Jack," I mumble like a prayer as I stroke the curve of her waist with my thumb.

Her laugh turns into a moan as she arches into me.

God, she's gorgeous—hair wild, lips kiss-swollen, laughter and heat blending until I'm not sure which is making me harder.

The prep table gleams behind her, spotless save for the long, curing ribbon of icing I inadvertently piped.

I hoist her onto it, then drag a finger through the rogue frosting before smearing it across the tops of her breasts, sticky and sweet.

She looks down at the white line, then back at me, incredulous. "You decorating me?"

"What can I say?" I suck the cream off her skin as I reach behind her to unclasp her bra. "You taught me well." Her breasts, freed, weigh heavy in my hands, her toes curling against my hips.

Before I can lick every bit of frosting, she reaches for my shirt. Seams stretch and rip, and one of my Henley's buttons pings across the floor. And then her hands skim my chest, but instead of frosting, her nails leave trails of heat.

I bury my mouth against her neck, biting just enough to make her gasp. She clutches at me like she can't get close enough, and hell, I feel the same—like I've been starving and suddenly stumbled into a feast.

Her jeans are a battle. Tight denim, my impatient fingers, her wriggling hips—it's chaos that sends a container of cookie cutters from the shelf beneath the table tumbling to the floor in a chorus of metallic jingles. And when her pants are finally off, inside out in my hand, I feel like I've just won an Oscar—and Audrey's the trophy in cranberry lace and fuzzy holiday socks.

"Sexy," I rasp, dragging the lace away, my frosting-coated

fingers making a mess of her. "Festive." Leaving the sock on, I kiss its arch.

She rolls her eyes, then gasps when my fingers stroke her open. Wet, hot, already ready for me.

I bend, tasting her, proving myself right—that she's sweeter than frosting.

Lost to sensation, Audrey braces her heels on the table, lowering her knees, allowing me better access to feast.

In seconds, her earlier amusement is replaced with whimpers of need, then moans of urgency as I press my tongue deeper, savoring longer.

"Jack." The word breaks from her, wrecked and pleading.

I kiss my way back up her trembling body, leaving a trail of lust and sugar smeared across her belly. Her hands drag at me, pulling me closer until I'm braced between her thighs.

She's wild, radiant, spread out like temptation itself. The woman who has no time for nonsense but relishes holiday décor. Whose work ethic could rival a Fortune 500 CEO's but who laughed through today's failure. A woman who—most thankful of all—has stopped pretending she isn't affected by this thing between us. This need.

My forehead drops to hers. "Audrey—"

"*Now.*" The whisper is soft and urgent.

And God help me, making quick, yet sticky work of my belt and zipper, I'm right there, poised at her entrance, the world collapsing to sugar, steel, and the woman spread out beneath me like the sweetest sin.

Audrey

"PLEASE, JACK—JUST… INSIDE ME."

The words tear out of me, raw and desperate, like I've been holding them back since that first kiss under the tree. No—longer than that. Probably since he put his hand in my till box at the Christmas tree lighting and saved Skippy and me from feline annihilation.

"Protection?"

"I'm good." I turn my head, licking frosting off his wrist where it braces beside my head. "And I'm on birth control." I catch his eyes. "You?"

"Yes." He drops his head. "Totally good. Promise."

I reach down, wrap my hand around him—thick and hard and throbbing. "Now." I touch the tip to my entrance and shiver.

"Fuck." With one hard thrust, he's inside me, stretching, filling, claiming, until my head tips back against the stainless steel and a broken sound escapes my throat.

"*Yes*," I breathe, clutching his shoulders. "Yes, yes—"

He groans, forehead pressed to mine, pushing deeper until the world blurs to sugar and heat, and everything else falls away.

I'm not thinking about margins. Or how closing the bakery this afternoon might cost me six dozen whoopie pies' worth of sales or whether losing the Gingerbread Showcase was a PR misfire. For once, I'm not running a cost-benefit analysis on my own heart.

I couldn't if I wanted to. Because he starts to move.

Each thrust rocks the table beneath us, steel squeaking against tile. My legs lock tighter around his hips, dragging him closer, urging him harder. A forgotten pan crashes to the floor, a bowl falls to the ground, making lazy circles on the floor, and my ass slides over a slick of icing.

We laugh, then moan—breathless, gasping, greedy. His mouth finds mine again, hungry, claiming, tasting like cinnamon and trouble. I arch into him, sticky and undone, choosing this—choosing him—over the safe, tidy spreadsheet of what my life is "supposed" to look like.

He grabs the edge of the table above me. Metal bites his knuckles as he braces, as if he's anchoring both of us to this exact second. The angle shifts—deeper, sharper. My nails rake down his back. "God, Jack—don't stop—"

His other hand slides between us, fingers circling my clit. Teasing. Tapping. Circling. Pinching.

White-hot pleasure explodes low in my belly, building fast, sharp, unstoppable—my hips bucking as the orgasm tears through me, electric and inevitable, leaving me shaking and smeared in sugar like I've been blessed by the patron saint of bad but good decisions.

Jack thrusts once more, stilling on a groan that echoes around us, his breath hot against my neck, his body heavy and perfect.

The refrigerator humming and the tiniest jingle from a renegade cookie cutter settling under the table are the only things tethering me to reality as the heat of him pulses inside me.

Then a lazy drip of frosting slides off the cart's edge onto the table beside me with a plop.

I giggle, both of us moaning with how my muscle contracts around him as I do.

Jack hums against my neck. "You're pretty happy for someone who had her baking sanctuary violated." He lifts his head, eyes skimming our crime/sex scene. "Not to mention every health code in Maine."

He's right. The me before Jack would've measured the risk, counted the cost, wrung the joy out of it until it looked like safety and success. The me before Jack would've needed a return on investment.

I swipe a finger across my frosting-smeared hip and hold it up. "Seven, at least." I touch it to his lips. "Exhibit A."

He then licks it clean with a wicked grin.

My heart does a somersault.

I think about this morning, about how I dodged his eyes like I could avoid gravity, like pretending not to want him would make it true. I think about Eileen's knowing look, the town's gossip, and my mother always urging me to be safe and precise.

The plan has always been "do it right." The path has always been "don't mess it up." But right now the only thing that feels right is messy and sweet and a little ridiculous.

He kisses me again—slow this time, a tasting-me kiss, a *you're-not-alone* kiss. My chest pinches with an ache as it expands. Giving me more room to breathe. To enjoy.

Skimming my sides, his hands ease me upright, shifting me higher onto the table while he pulls out of me. Then, kissing my knee, he bends to make sure my fuzzy socks are in place like they're—*I'm*—precious cargo.

And I realize, with a tiny shock, that I'm... happy. Not

everything's great, thanks for asking while I tally shortfalls in my head. But in-this-moment-enjoying-life happy.

"Should we be worried about customers?" Jack steps back, grabbing his shirt off the ground.

"Making Whoopie is closed for the day." I move to get down, but Jack stops me by putting his shirt over my head. Once my arms are in, he lifts me off the table, setting me down gently.

I move in a circle, careful to avoid cookie cutter shrapnel. "Which is probably a good thing."

"Hideaway Harbor is resilient." He nods solemnly, finding my Crocs by the door and slipping them on my socked feet. "And well-frosted."

"Over-frosted." I glance at the carnage of piping bags. "I'm going to have to disinfect every square inch."

"I'll help." His promise lands warm, making me smile.

I plant a hand on the counter and lean into it, for once at ease with sharing my space with someone. "Oh, you'll help, Hollywood."

His gaze drags over my mouth, slow and heated, before he hooks an arm around my waist and pulls me in, kissing me.

We don't get around to cleaning up until much, much later.

SUSTAINED

Audrey

It's hot.

Not the usual I-slept-under-too-many-blankets kind, but the solid, steady warmth of a man stretched out beside me, his arm heavy around my waist like he's holding me in place. Which—let's be real—he kind of is.

Normally on a Monday morning I'd already be in my kitchen, elbows deep in batter, juggling invoices with one hand and a whisk with the other, wondering when I'll have time to get groceries. Even on my "day off," there's dough to test, emails to answer, a spreadsheet whispering my name.

But not today.

Today, I'm tucked against Jack Lourd, Hollywood shark turned unexpected bed-warmer, and I'm staying put. I don't spring out of bed. I don't even check the time. I just breathe in the faint scent of my rosemary mint shampoo clinging to his hair from yesterday's much-needed shower after our rampant kitchen sex and let myself have the novelty of lying still.

Jack's hand shifts against my stomach, fingers curling with sleepy instinct. The move sends a slow ripple of awareness through me. My heart stutters, my body already remembering every place his mouth lingered last night.

"Morning." His breath tickles my ear, his voice rough with sleep.

"Morning." My whisper comes out more like a sigh than a greeting. I'm exhausted—happily so—and content to let go of my plans for laundry, bookkeeping, maybe finally facing the disaster that is my spice cupboard.

For a long, perfect stretch of minutes, neither of us moves. And when we finally do, it's not to get out of bed. It's to tangle closer, to kiss slowly and lazily, to remind ourselves that frosting isn't the only thing worth licking off skin.

The soft pads of his fingertips circle my breasts before gliding down my stomach, goosebumps chasing after them. And when they dip between my thighs, I arch into them.

His laugh rumbles against my mouth, low and wicked. "That's a yes, then?"

"Yes." My nails scrape lightly down his back, and he shudders. "But quiet." I don't want anything to break this moment, not even our voices. I just want to feel.

Jack must agree with my plan because without another word, he rolls me beneath him with an ease that makes me immediately forget how to breathe. His weight pins me in the best way, heat seeping through every place our bodies touch.

I expect urgency, another round of last night's desperate hunger. But this is slower, indulgent. Jack kisses me like he's memorizing the taste, like he can't quite believe I'm here, letting him in again.

My hands trail lower, deliberate now that I'm not as ravenous or rushed, mapping the strong lines of his back, squeezing the firm curve of his ass.

Jack groans at my shameless exploration, hips flexing toward me, his cock pressing hard against my stomach.

Set on testing every reaction, I slide my hand between us, finding him thick and already straining. Wrapping my fingers around him, I stroke once, then again, teasing.

"Audrey…" It's a plea and a warning.

One I take no heed of as I circle the tip with my index finger, smearing precum around the ridge, savoring the way his eyes darken.

The blanket slips as he rises up, bracing on his knees. I don't have time to be embarrassed by my vulnerable sprawl or to worry about what I look like in the morning light streaming through my bedroom window. Because I see him. And Jack Lourd has never looked better than when the only thing grazing his body is sunlight.

His shoulders are broad, his chest lightly dusted with hair that matches his dark-chocolate eyes. His biceps flex as he grabs my legs, pulling them toward him until my ass slides up his thighs. My stomach, soft as it curls in this new position, feels exposed—until I notice the ridges of his impossibly defined abs and think how unfair it is that a man who eats at least one whoopie pie a day looks carved from stone.

And then thought vanishes, because he's pushing into me.

The pressure. The stretch. The heat. All of it burns away any lingering thought.

Jack's head falls back, exposing the sinewed tendons of his throat. "Fuck."

My legs tighten around him automatically, pulling him deeper.

"Audrey." Large hands grip my hips, and he thrusts once—twice, his breath ragged. "You feel…" He groans, moving again, first shallow, then deep, then shallow, dragging me to the edge with each deliberate rhythm.

"So good." The words spill out before I can stop them, half plea, half dare.

His eyes burn, his pace quickens as his mouth crashes back to mine, and the world narrows to heat and rhythm and the dizzying ache of wanting.

Wanting him.

Maybe wanting too much.

But the thought is gone as his cock finds that perfect spot inside me, setting me free of every second-guess as I ride the wave of release. My cry echoes in the room, my hands grasping at his wrists, nails biting into his skin as pleasure rips through me.

Jack curses, low and rough, as my body clenches around him. His rhythm stutters, then drives harder, faster, until with one final thrust he spills into me with a guttural groan that vibrates through my bones.

My bed frame creaks in protest as Jack lowers himself over me, his weight delicious and grounding, his chest heaving against mine.

I smooth a hand down his back, feeling the tremors still shivering through him. He nips at my jaw, then presses his forehead to mine, laughter ghosting over my lips.

"I'm pretty sure that counts as my cardio for the day." He

places my hand on his chest, the feel of his heartbeat pounding wild against my palm.

I smile, breathless, and don't move my hand. I just keep it there, memorizing the rhythm that proves I'm not the only one who's undone.

Jack

"LET'S just head to the market." Audrey yawns the words as she steps out onto Main Street and turns to lock the door behind her.

The woman's running on sugar, orgasms, and sheer stubbornness, and I know burnout when I see it.

"Coffee first," I declare, steering her toward the café before she can argue. "Non-negotiable."

She shoots me a look, like I just suggested she frost a cake before it cooled.

I loop my fingers through hers and keep walking. "You're half-asleep and look like you're about to face-plant into a snowbank."

Her lips twitch, but she doesn't push. Which is how I know she's really exhausted.

The bell over the door jingles as we step inside Love at First Sip, the smell of nutmeg and espresso wrapping around us as every person inside turns to look.

Audrey tugs me toward the counter, rattling off her order at the young barista like muscle memory. "Dirty chai latte. Extra shot."

"Black coffee," I add, ignoring the way Eileen Burrows pauses mid-step with the espresso beans when she spots us.

It's an awkward few minutes as we wait for our drinks, her hawk eyes never leaving us. Then, in a voice meant to carry, she says, "Well, don't you look merry and bright."

Her gaze doesn't stop at my face. It drops lower—to the icing smears still ghosting across my Henley from yesterday's gingerbread fiasco.

Audrey groans into her latte.

Oops.

But before I can brush it off with a joke, Eileen vanishes into the back, reemerging seconds later wielding a long-sleeve tee with a glittery café logo like she's about to knight me into her secret order.

"Off with that mess." She holds up the shirt like a mother dressing a toddler. "On with this."

Audrey mutters something about divine intervention and closes her eyes as if in prayer before grabbing our drinks from the counter.

Her unusual reluctance for caffeine makes sense as I remember Hideaway's small-town status—where nothing goes unnoticed.

Eileen arches one imperious brow. "Arms up." She shakes the shirt impatiently while Audrey burrows her face deeper into her scarf, mortified.

Which is all the encouragement I need.

Grinning, I peel off my jacket, grab the hem of my Henley, and tug it over my head in one motion. The corner table of silver-haired ladies audibly gasps. If my career ever tanks, it seems I've got a fallback as a coffee shop calendar pin-up boy.

Eileen assesses me rather like a cowboy judging a horse at auction. "And you'll need cream for those claw marks on your back."

Audrey chokes on her latte.

I grin, slide the tee over my head, and spread my arms like I'm auditioning for a holiday latte ad. "How do I look?"

Eileen winks. "Like caffeine and gossip."

Which, judging by how Audrey nibbles her lower lip, is apparently not a bad look on me.

"There now." Eileen dismisses me like she's just stamped my passport into the land of small-town gossip. "You two go enjoy yourselves."

Honestly? I've closed tougher rooms.

But none of them made me feel this accomplished.

Or this proud.

Audrey

"Larry the Lobstah loves you."

That's the message painted on the six-inch plastic lobster ornament Jack just purchased from a stall in Hideaway Harbor's Winter Market and is now holding up like a proud papa.

"Wow." I nod, wide-eyed over the steam curling off my hard-earned latte. "I never knew plastic to glow such a vibrant orangey-red."

Jack drops it into my hand with a grin, like he's daring me not to love it.

I tuck my newly gifted ornament into a rapidly filling shopping bag as Jack and I wander down Lobster Avenue with insulated cups warming our palms, the market alive with smells that make my stomach growl.

Sugared almonds, fried dough, and hot cider steeped with cinnamon sticks. If joy had a flavor, it would taste like this street. And while it's unusual to find me out and about like this even on my day off, the real part I didn't see coming by taking a chance on slowing down?—Jack by my side.

Of course, leave it to Eileen Burrows to make sure my slowing-down epiphany came with a side of humiliation.

And now? Now my morning humiliation has gone mobile. Because as Jack and I stroll hand in hand through the market, I catch more than one sidelong glance. A whisper behind mittened hands. A raised brow from a crochet clubber nudging her friend.

It doesn't take a degree in small-town anthropology to know exactly what's happening: The rumor parade has officially left the café and marched straight into the Christmas market.

Catching me staring at the sparkly logo across his chest, Jack flexes like he's auditioning for a holiday latte ad. "I feel like your town has sponsored me."

I take an extra-long sip of cinnamon foam to hide my groan.

He grins like he won the lottery.

Another sip hides my matching smile.

The whole street hums with pedestrian traffic—parents with strollers crowd the stalls, the older kids not yet out of school, while a brass trio attempts "Deck the Halls" just off-key enough to be charming.

"Let's head this way." Jack gestures toward a booth where a woman stirs almonds in a copper kettle. "Always wanted to try those."

Nodding, I toss my empty cup into a trash bin. Before I can tuck my hand into my coat pocket, Jack takes it in his own.

This time, there's nothing to hide my smile.

Hand in hand, we pass the rows of wooden huts—one stacked high with mittens, another gleaming with carved ornaments, another fragrant with pine wreaths and beeswax candles. The glowing windows of Town Hall and the white stucco church frame the scene, wrapping the whole street in twinkle lights.

Jack buys us a paper cone of roasted almonds, still hot enough that he needs to juggle it between his hands before offering it like he's presenting a winning case.

"Careful." One side of his mouth kicks up. "This won't be easy to lick off like your icing."

Heat flickers low in my stomach, completely unrelated to the almond I pluck from the cone. It's warm and sweet, but the taste is nothing compared to the look Jack gives me.

We keep walking, weaving past couples swinging shopping bags, kids sticky with candy canes, teenagers daring each other into wasabi popcorn. The brass trio stumbles into "Jingle Bells," one note sliding sharp enough to make me wince.

At the end of the avenue, fudge is displayed in neat squares between nutcrackers, and my mind wanders to fudge whoopie pie fillings. Double chocolate. Call it Fudge Me Twice. Maybe even—

Jack nudges me with his elbow, his expression soft. "Day off, remember?"

Right. A day off.

Smiling at his reminder, I take a deep breath of holiday-heavy air. Linking my arm through his, we drift toward a wooden bench beneath a lamppost wrapped in garland and twinkle lights.

Jack dusts it off with his coat sleeve before tugging me down beside him.

Our bags at our feet, the scent of sugared almonds rising between us, we sit in comfortable silence and people-watch. Across the way, a little boy argues with his mom over why a giant stuffed lobster should count as a "necessary purchase." A couple in matching plaid coats take turns holding up ornaments for each other's approval. A dog in a red sweater tries to steal kettle corn from a distracted toddler.

Jack leans back, stretching his arm across the back of the bench until his fingers graze my shoulder. Not possessive—just... there. Warm, steady.

I let my head tip until it brushes his sleeve, the sequined logo peeking through his open coat winking at me. For once, I shelve my to-do lists, table my business plans, and silence the voice that says I always need to be doing more.

I'm just... here. In the town I came to because I wanted this exact feeling. The bustle, the cheer, the slow rhythm of a December day where everything tastes sweeter because you're not rushing through it.

And maybe my picture-perfect future—the flannel-wearing Christmas tree farmer and two point five kids I drafted as carefully as a gingerbread blueprint—was never the pièce de résistance I needed.

Maybe what matters is how life feels. And right now, with Jack beside me, it feels like more than enough.

Jack

I'M HALFWAY through pretending to admire a display of hand-carved reindeer when a familiar voice calls out behind me.

"Lourd! Got a second?"

Dr. Eli Bennett strides over, tall and steady, munching roasted almonds from a paper sack. "I've been looking for you. Wasn't sure where to find you with the bakery closed today." His wry smile pulls one from me in return.

"Enjoying the day off." I look pointedly at the green scrubs under his parka. "I take it you're not?"

He scoffs. "Yeah, no. But don't worry, I'm not here about Skippy's overdue shots." He pulls a packet of papers from his coat. "Could use a lawyer's eye. And with Hideaway's view on lawyers…"

We both laugh, knowing full well how Hidies feel about my line of work.

Taking the papers Eli hands me, I pause, thinking how

different my reception has been lately. Less wary. More welcoming. "What have we got here?"

Eli taps the top of the stapled documents. "I've been renting my clinic space for ten years. Landlord finally offered to sell me the building, but the terms..." He shakes his head. "Let's just say I don't trust them."

I skim the first page, and the noise of the market fades. Inflated purchase price. Maintenance clauses that put all the liability on Eli. A line about 'restricted renovations' that might as well chain him to the status quo.

"You're right," I tell him, pointing at the clause. "This is stacked against you. You'd be paying like an owner but living like a tenant."

Eli exhales, half relieved, half frustrated. "That's what I thought. So what would you do?"

I hesitate, the desire to help fighting against the state's restrictions on my legal reach. "I can tell you what's wrong. I can even outline what a fairer deal would look like. But I can't actually fix it. I'm not licensed in Maine."

"So you know how to help, but you're not allowed to?" Eli frowns. "That's gotta be frustrating."

I nod, recognizing the same weight in him. A fellow high-responsibility guy. "Exactly."

"That's a shame." The vet studies me, his expression thoughtful. "Because a guy like you could do a lot of good here. Even as an outsider—and a dreaded lawyer—people here already trust you."

The words catch me off guard, landing heavier than they should.

When I glance across the square, I spot Audrey at a booth with Portia, laughing over a stocking the length of her leg, her cheeks pink from the cold, her dark hair curling around the shoulders of her red coat. She looks like she's exactly where she belongs.

And suddenly, I can picture it.

Not me on a red-eye back to LA. Not me tied to A-list clients and residuals and box office percentages.

Me here. Next to her. Practicing law that actually helps people. Solving problems that matter.

And damn if I don't want it.

COOLING RACK

Audrey

"Merry Christmas!"

The last customer leaves with a wave, and I flip Making Whoopie's lock and turn the sign to *Closed* before humming my way back to the counter. It's three o'clock, which in Hideaway Harbor means scrubbing cocoa powder off marble and sweeping up sprinkles, the day's chaos distilled into sugar confetti.

"That's not going to work for my client." Across the room, Jack is camped out at his corner table, dress shirt fastened with cufflinks, hair perfectly coiffed. "As per the contract, it states we have first right to..."

While my ovens cool, his world is just heating up—noon in Los Angeles is prime time for lunch meetings. He's on Zoom, earbuds in, nodding at a wall of Hollywood faces on his computer screen while I hum "Deck the Halls" and feel a delicious burn between my legs that has nothing to do with today's baking.

Jack might call sex his new cardio, but this morning's session had me flying through orders like I'd mainlined espresso.

I pause, cloth still in hand, as the thought sharpens. Is it just sex—or sex with Jack? Because somehow, instead of dragging through the day, I'm buzzing. Since he spent the night after the gingerbread competition, we've been together, save for him grabbing a bag from his hotel to save me from the embarrassment of having to ask Eileen for more coffee shop merch.

It's only been one full workday since things changed between Jack and me, yet every task feels lighter, every batch quicker, even the paperwork less soul-sucking. Like when he pops behind the counter between Zoom calls to steal a kiss or when he's ringing up a long line of customers as I ice cakes. Sharing the day with him makes the bakery feel less like a grind and more like a life.

Almost like the life I imagined when I decided to pull up stakes at the Ritz and come to Hideaway.

The phone rings.

Jack starts to rise, as if from habit, and I wave him down. "Finish your meeting. I've got it."

His answering wink sends another slow burn through me.

With what I'm sure is a grin that screams *sexually satisfied baker,* I lift the receiver off the wall. "Making Whoopie, where every craving deserves a happy ending. Audrey speaking."

"Hi, sweetheart." My mother's voice clicks sharp through the receiver.

"Oh, uh, hi, Mom." From the corner of my eye, I see Jack's head pop up from his laptop. "What's going on?"

"I just wanted to say your cupcake tower looked great." Her voice is surprisingly free of the anxious edge it usually carries when she's talking about my business.

But I don't have time to relish that because—"I'm sorry, Mom. My what tower?"

"Your Winter Wonderland cupcake tower," she says. "The photo in the *Bangor Daily*. Very ambitious."

I laugh, baffled, thinking back to the gingerbread contest and wondering if the paper used an old photo since my house was demolished before they could get one for the article. "I've never made a Winter Wonderland cupcake tower." The thought slips out before I remember who I'm talking to.

"Well, that's odd." Paper rustles in the background. "Because it says *Making Whoopie* right here under the picture. White chocolate trees, sugared cranberries—lovely presentation." A beat. "Oh." There's the anxious tone I know so well. "It says below to contact Margery for your baking inquiries."

As the judgment in her silence stretches, I wind the phone cord around my hand and cross to the pile of unopened mail, flipping through bills until I find the newspaper, scattering pages until I land on the food section.

Making Whoopie Wins Blue Ribbon at Bangor Winter Sweets Showcase.

Only it isn't *my* Making Whoopie. It's the other bakery. Two bakers I don't know—but one who I'm guessing is Margery—beaming behind a glittering tower of cupcakes crowned in spun-sugar snowflakes.

The floor tilts under me.

"That's the other bakery." My voice comes out strained. "The one using my name."

Silence stretches, then Mom clears her throat. "Audrey, what does that mean for your bakery if someone else is winning awards in Maine under the same name?"

I have no good answer. "It means..." Spinning on my heel, I clutch the receiver. "It means I have to get back to closing up." The words tumble fast. "Love you, Mom."

I hang up before she can say more, palms sweaty against the receiver.

When I turn, leaning my back against the wall, I find Jack watching me, his laptop closed. He must've ended his call early.

"What happened?" His eyes flick to the paper spread across the counter. Picking it up, he skims the headline and swears under his breath.

"Unbelievable." He shoves a hand through his hair. "Not only are they still using your name after I proved prior use, but now they're plastering it across the state paper?" He looks at me, hard but not unkind. "Don't worry, Audrey. I'll take care of it. They want to push? Fine." He slaps the paper back on the table. "I'll push harder." He cradles my face in his hand, eyes drilling into mine. "You don't need to carry this." He kisses my forehead like it's settled, case closed.

"Okay." I force a smile. "If you say so."

On the outside, I'm sure I look calm, full of confidence in him and his ability to handle this.

On the inside? I'm unraveling. And whereas just five minutes ago, before my mother's call and before the article in the paper, that unraveling felt freeing—like the tightly wound ball of anxiety and nerves that's kept my business and me going these past two years finally wasn't needed—

Now? Now the loose threads feel like nooses wrapping around my neck, choking back the happiness Jack seems to think I've earned.

"Sam." Jack's on his cell, his voice, sharper now than on his Hollywood call, echoing in the tiled kitchen. "I need your help with something."

Leaving him to it, I pick up my towel once more, rewiping already clean counters and absentmindedly polishing circles into nothing.

Maybe Jack was wrong. Maybe I haven't earned it. Maybe while I've been busy with him sneaking kisses behind the counter, I've been letting the one thing I built for myself slip away.

Jack

MY BALLS WILL NEVER BE the same.

Not after—*hopefully*—surviving their first cold winter since dropping at the ripe age of twelve, late bloomer that I was.

That's the errant thought that hits me just as the sharp salt-and-pine tang drifts up from the harbor as I turn off

Hideaway's Main Street toward the square, the cold air clouding in front of me.

Another day in Hideaway where shop windows glow with strands of lights, the whole street already dressed for December like it's auditioning for a postcard. Another day spent in Making Whoopie—only this one not as easygoing as yesterday's. Before Audrey's phone call from her mother. Before the article in the paper.

Having volunteered to bring the Sweet as Honey Corny as Sin whoopie pies—cornbread cakes filled with honey cream cheese icing—that Audrey made for the Chowder House Rules restaurant for Clam Chowder and Cornbread Appreciation Day, I took a detour on the walk back to the bakery to clear my head.

Skippy found me two steps in, as if waiting for me like our walk was preplanned.

He trots a few paces ahead of me, nose buried in every snowbank like he's on an FBI sweep. Calling it a walk is generous—I'm mostly following him around while he zigzags from lamppost to mailbox.

My mind's not on him anyway. It's not even really on my testicles, cold under the dress slacks I wore because my locally bought flannel-lined jeans are in the wash. Audrey's wash. And while my mind should be on the new client and their contract negotiations, along with the potential wave of income it would bring to my agency, it's not.

Instead, my mind is back in the bakery. Back to yesterday afternoon, to Audrey's expression when she was on the phone. Her voice, brittle, uncertain. *"That's the other bakery. The one using my name."*

I hate it. Hate that she thinks she's slipping, hate that

someone else is muddying what she built. Hate that it feels like my fault.

Maybe it is.

Since then I've already redrafted the cease and desist in my head multiple times before having a colleague in Maine send one out this morning. The guy laughed when I mentioned *Making Whoopie,* but he agreed to put it on his letterhead, make it official. Then I stopped by the Post Office to give Audrey an extra sense of security.

All of it should've felt like a win. Instead it feels like bailing water from a sinking boat with a thimble. Not when Audrey's confidence is unraveling. Not when she's looking at me like maybe I'm part of the problem.

"Afternoon, Lourd!"

I glance up as Mayor Locke barrels out of Town Hall, scarf trailing, cheeks red from the cold. He claps me on the back like we've been neighbors for years. His laugh echoes across the street, loud enough to make Skippy jump, tail dropping.

"Didn't expect to see you still here." The mayor's grin widens. "Hideaway Harbor must be working its magic." He eyes me up and down, from the top of my windblown business cut to the tips of my Cole Haans. "We locals—we need to be less judgmental. Because I'll admit, not a single one of us would've bet a Hollywood man could settle in here. We all thought you were too polished, too temporary." He steps back, gesturing at everything he just assessed. "But look at you now—working cases for Bennett, helping out at the bakery"—he points to Skippy retaliating from his scare by marking Town Hall's shrubbery as his own—"dog in tow. Guess that'll teach us to keep our mouths shut, huh?"

I force a laugh, keeping it light. "I've just answered a few legal questions and wiped down a counter or two."

Skippy trots back to me, and without thinking, I dig into my pocket for the bakery scraps I've started keeping there.

The mayor chuckles like I've just proven his point. "Mm-hm. You keep telling yourself that."

Feeling an odd need to clarify something even I'm not sure of, I add, "Besides, I'm not even licensed to work in Maine."

"That's easily taken care of." He tips his head knowingly. "I know a lawyer in Portland. If you partnered with him, Maine allows you to practice here without taking the bar exam again."

"Maine also allows you to apply for reciprocity if you've been practicing out of state long enough," I state, more to myself than to him.

The mayor grins like I've just confessed something. "See? I knew you were already thinking about it." With a wink and another clap on my back, he stomps off toward the diner.

Leaving me standing there, snow soaking into my shoes, the word echoing like a hammer blow.

Yes, I've looked into becoming legal in Maine. But in my head it was for Amanda. For business. Hollywood business.

But was it?

Pictures flash too easily in my mind—Audrey dusted in flour, me sitting at the tiny wood table in the corner. Daily chats with the locals. Seasons changing along with the flavors of her whoopie pies. Quintessential small-town life. Audrey's dream come true.

Suddenly, my reminders of my own happy childhood feel less like warmth and more like fractures. Shortcomings.

I don't know how to be that man.

My memories consist of my mom singing off-key carols while burning butter cookies. Of my dad pretending not to mind when the tree leaned sideways in the stand. It was chaotic, imperfect, real. But then it was gone. A car accident and a funeral and nothing steady ever again.

Now all I know is clients, contracts, the next deal. Not homes and holidays and permanence.

Skippy barks at a snowplow rumbling past, then lopes ahead again. I shove my hands into my crumb-filled pockets and follow. The cold stings my face, but it doesn't clear my head the way I hoped. Yet by the time we circle back toward the bakery, I've plastered my easy smile back in place. The one I haven't used since handing Audrey her dirty chai latte after making sure Skippy wasn't limping.

The one I reserve for business. For noncommittal responses and vague offerings.

The door jingles as I open, Audrey looking up from sweeping the floor. "Have a good walk?"

Smile in place, I nod.

She nods back before getting to work, letting me know that on the outside I must look steady. Unchanged.

But on the inside, I'm anything but.

PROOFING

Audrey

The scent of fried clams and chowder fogs up my little apartment like a New England perfume. Cartons from Chowder House Rules litter my tiny kitchen table, steam curling in the air until the windows haze.

"Pretty nice of the restaurant to send this over for free." Jack spears a clam fritter with his fork before I've even opened the napkins.

I roll my eyes, unstacking the cartons. "If it was free, I wouldn't have taken it." I put the plasticware they packed with the food in a drawer and pull out my silverware, feeling the need to be a bit fancier with Jack here. "Small businesses need to support small businesses." I grab two bowls from a cabinet for the chowder. "This was a barter." I gesture to the brown paper bags covering my small island. "I made cornbread whoopie pies for Clam Chowder and Cornbread Appreciation Day, and they made me chowder."

"Small-town economics. Carbs for carbs." Jack helps pour the chowder from the carton into the bowls. "I like this system." His grin is crooked, easy, the kind of grin that feels dangerous because it makes my insides go gooey. "Kind of like the scarf I got for settling the garden gnome dispute."

I glance at the scarf hanging on my coat rack. The same scarf that's been there every night this past week and stayed there until morning. While Jack hasn't given up his hotel room, he also hasn't been there in some time.

"Yeah, I figured you'd be a fan of the barter system." I point my spoon at him. "Seeing as I'm paying your lawyer fees in whoopie."

Jack grin makes the heat off my chowder seem frigid. "Both the treat *and* the activity."

Avoiding his eyes for fear of combusting, I dig into my food like someone who worked a twelve-hour day—because I am. I've been waking up earlier than usual, leaving Jack behind in bed as I creep downstairs, trying to make up for the moments during the day when he distracts me.

Oddly, even with the extra hour, I don't seem to be getting any more done.

Finishing his chowder, Jack wipes his mouth with a napkin and leans back. Casual. Too casual. "Got word from my Maine contact today."

My stomach tightens.

His expression is as nonchalant as his tone. "The cease and desist went out by certified mail."

The words hang between us, meant to be good news. He watches me, almost too invested in my reaction.

I nod, forcing a smile. "That's great." Last week when we discussed this over the very same meal, it was. Then I'd felt lighter, like someone had finally pulled a sack of flour off my chest. Tonight? Not so much.

His answering frown tells me I'm not as cunning as I'd like. "I'm handling this, Audrey. I promise." He reaches over, squeezing my hand. "In fact, I also—"

I lean across the table and kiss him. Quick, decisive, chowder-flavored. "I know. And thank you." My smile this time, lips still tingling from his, comes easier.

Frown gone, Jack kisses back, warm and sure, until he stops to lick my chin.

"Jack!" I push at his shoulder, laughing even as I wipe the salvia from his tongue off my face with the back of my hand.

"What? I was just cleaning up your chowder drool." His grin is wicked, his eyes lit with that infuriating Hollywood sparkle that makes him look like he could sell sin in a snowstorm. "Waste not want not."

"You've been spending too much time with Skippy." I wad up a napkin and throw it at him. "And I don't have chowder drool."

He dodges, catches me around the waist, and suddenly I'm in his lap, a bowl balanced precariously on the edge of the table as he recaptures my lips.

I laugh into his mouth, the sound softening as his hands slide under my sweater. The heat between us is always there, always a little shocking in how fast it flares.

And then, out of the corner of my eye, I see it—the tree.

The one we decorated together. Our lopsided Pine & Dandy special, standing proudly in my living room with Larry the Lobster dangling crookedly from a branch. Multi-colored lights blink, white lights glimmer warm and steady, the whole tree casting a bipolar festive glow in my apartment.

The sight squeezes something in me. I remember how he tangled the lights instantly, how I teased him for his terrible ornament placement, how we laughed until my sides hurt. And then… our first kiss under its glow.

I still feel wary. The bakery name fight isn't over, my mother's voice still rattles in my head, and Jack is still Jack—Hollywood, contracts, big shiny world.

But the tree is here. And so is he. That's enough.

For now.

Jack's mouth trails along my jaw, his breath hot against my skin. I wrap my arms around his neck, pulling him closer.

"You taste like chowder," he murmurs against my throat. "But I should probably work off all that cream and cornbread."

I grin up at the ceiling. "A late-night cardio session?"

He chuckles, low and dangerous, before lifting me in his arms.

I murmur a word of thanks to Jack's celebrity trainer as he takes a step toward the bedroom. I grab his wrist—not to stop him but to redirect him. "Couch."

His grin is pure male satisfaction. I roll my eyes, but my pulse is racing as we half-collapse onto the tiny sofa, laughter muffled under the weight of kissing. His hands are everywhere—gentle, greedy, grounding.

I moan into his mouth, the sound shocking me with how much I want him, how much I need this reminder that not everything is fragile.

We continue working out with the tree lights glowing and

pulsing next to us, holding my doubts at bay for one more night.

Jack

"HAND CHECK." Amanda, her head poking in the door with a red and green hat looks like a festive meerkat, eyes me standing behind Making Whoopie's counter next to Audrey.

The two of us roll our eyes in tandem, raising our hands like we're under arrest.

"Oh." She pouts. "That's disappointing."

"What is it that you want, Amanda?" I drop the arm closest to Audrey around her shoulders. "You're letting out all of Audrey's heat."

She steps inside, the door ringing shut beside her. "Be at Love at First Sip in five. It's Peppermint Mocha Appreciation Day." She points at Audrey before swinging her finger at me. "Put on your merry faces."

Audrey, face red from either the ovens or embarrassment, goes back to finishing off a tray of mini whoopie pies by sandwiching dark brown cakes around pale-pink swirls of icing. Flour dusts her cheekbone like highlighter. "You go. Represent Making Whoopie." She claps her hands clean. "And don't come back without my dirty chai. Extra dirty."

"Define extra." I lift my hand she just escaped, my index finger brushing the white powder off her face.

Her eyelashes flutter. "If it's not morally questionable, it's not dirty enough."

Amanda snorts, breaking the moment. "I like her."

"I'm aware." I pull back, disappointed in the interruption. Since the phone call with her mother, Audrey's been…distant. Here. But not.

I haven't brought up the other bakery since telling her that I had her cease and desist letter sent out, but I can tell the situation is like a bruise she keeps bumping, so I've let it rest.

Audrey points to the tray of thirty-six perfectly identical mini whoopie pies, glossy tops catching the light. The filling smells like peppermint and something darker, richer—chocolate? Espresso?

"Pairing special." She tucks parchment under the edges. "Tell Lucy and Eileen it's for sampling with the mochas."

I think back to the phone orders I took since officially helping out this past week in the shop. "When did they order this?"

"They didn't." Audrey shrugs, her eyes cutting to the side. "But it's a party. And parties need snacks."

Amanda, having come around the counter, reaches for one. I smack her hand away, feeling oddly protective of Audrey's generosity. "Those are for customers."

"But I *am* a customer." Amanda pouts, dramatically shaking out her hand. "By the way, what are they called?"

Audrey's lips twitch. "Kiss My Mocha."

Amanda holds up her hand. "Nice."

Looking embarrassed but still smiling, Audrey high-fives her.

Amanda turns her raised palm to me. "Eh?"

Leaving her hanging, I turn to Audrey. "Why don't you bring the pies over?" The owners of Chowder House Rules also asked after Audrey when I delivered their surprise whoopie pies yesterday. "I'm sure Lucy and Eileen would want to thank you."

"That's okay. They won't even notice if I'm not there. Besides"—she points to the timer set on the counter—"the new batch for Little Italy is about to come out."

Knowing Audrey is never going to see how much she's appreciated in this town if she doesn't make time for it, I pick up a potholder. "I could take those out for you while you go next door."

The look Audrey gives me tells me that while the faith she has in my customer service has grown in leaps and bounds, that hard-fought trust has not translated to baking tasks.

She grabs a spatula and points at the door. "Go, Hollywood. Mingle. Be festive."

I drop the potholder.

"*I'm* festive." Amanda, still pretend pouting, can't hide the glee in her eyes from seeing me get my marching orders.

Audrey smoothers a smile before kissing me. Quick. Warm. Mint on her tongue, sugar on mine.

It's the first time she's ever initiated affection in public, and it makes me forget how sentences work.

Turning back to the oven, but not before I see her cheeks darken, she adds, "Whoever brings me back a chai gets to be the first to taste test my new whoopie pie flavor."

Amanda grabs the tray of mini pies out from under me, hitching the tray on her forearms before sliding around the counter and quick-walking to the door. "Come on, Jack!"

Shaking my head, I follow, taking the tray from her and casting a last look at Audrey, who's already sliding the next sheet into the oven before stepping out into the crisp afternoon.

Once again, Hideaway Harbor is a snow globe come to life —flurries sifting down lazily while the harbor bells ping somewhere out in the gray. The Winter Market stalls across the square wear their garlands like beauty queens. People bustle with paper cups and knit hats and the kind of cheer that makes my Los Angeles reflexes brace for a punchline.

"Are you staying past Christmas?" Amanda asks as we pass the crowd still gathered on the sidewalk walking toward the coffee shop chanting "Pep-per-mint! Pep-per-mint!"

Amanda's tone is casual, the way a rattlesnake might casually admire your shoes before striking. "Because you should really let the Haven know in case they need your room for other guests." She bumps me, making me stutter step to keep the whoopie pie tray level. "Or are you staying somewhere else? Like the favored local bakery?"

"And you?" I angle the tray away from her interference. "Have you officially checked out due to spending most of your time with a certain candymaker with rainbow hair?"

Color climbs her neck, perfectly matching her hat. "Don't jinx it."

I nod and so does she, a silent truce forming as we pass by the large chalkboard sign that reads PEPPERMINT MOCHA APPRECIATION DAY in hand-lettered loops so enthusiastic they look like they might hug you.

Inside Love at First Sip is cacophony. Steam hisses. Milk frothers scream. A toddler in a reindeer sweater tries to eat a candy cane like a drumstick. The whole place smells like a milk chocolate chip ice cream cone that's been melted over a campfire. Eileen is airborne—figuratively, but still—floating from table to table with a garland headband, and a barista I've never seen before is behind the counter doing five things with two hands while also managing the playlist and probably orchestrating the tides.

"Kiss My Mocha whoopie pies from Making Whoopie." I set the tray on the bar beside the espresso machine. "For pairing with the peppermint mochas." There's a collective sigh from those within sniffing radius. "On the house."

The barista's eyes go wide. "Audrey," she breathes, like it's an answer to prayer.

Eileen claps, then mashes my arms to my side with a hug. "Of course. That girl thinks of everything."

"She does." Something in me straightens—that possessive ribbon I pretend I don't carry around tightening under my ribs. Because this is what Audrey never sees: the way people's voices soften when they say her name. The gratitude that slides into the conversation when they mention the box she sent to the school fundraiser, the late-night batch she whipped up for a wake, the way she remembered that Mrs. Callahan's husband prefers marshmallow fluff in his peppermint whoopie because he lost his dentures last summer and icing is a war zone—all things locals have stopped to tell me about during my stay in Hideaway.

The line moves. Cup after cup topped with a swirl of whipped cream and crushed candy cane. Amanda peels off to chat with the barista—apparently having already met them—angling for information from the frazzled barista about Lucy, the regular barista's relationship with a man named Enzo.

I give Eileen Audrey's dirty chai order to mark on a cup,

then lean against the end of the bar and watch the town do what the town does—bump shoulders, trade gossip, shove cookies into mittened hands, and exclaim happiness over Audrey's thoughtful mini pies.

Yesterday was the cornbread pies for Chowder House Rules, before that, she rolled out Take the Gun, Leave the Cannoli for Little Italy—a pistachio-cannoli whoopie that made grown men whimper—and priced it at cost so the deli could make the margin. They worked so well, Audrey's currently making them more.

And the week before that, she dropped off a tray at The Perfect Package—this town's least subtle adult store—because they were running a couples' workshop, and she thought a red velvet whoopie with edible glitter might be "on theme."

And then it hits me. *Of course.*

They have a day for chowder. A day for cornbread. A day for wool socks. If Hideaway can sanctify footwear, it can sanctify its state treat—its unofficial love language, courtesy of the woman who's been quietly stitching this town together with sugar and butter for two years.

Audrey calls herself an outsider. And she means it. Believes it. Meanwhile, the town has already tattooed her on its heart.

My phone buzzes. Hollywood rings at a different frequency; I swear I can hear it in my bones before the screen lights up. I glance down at the name. The agent who's been circling me for a week, foaming at the mouth for me to sign her client. Big. Bankable. Press release kind of big.

Amanda's back at my shoulder before I can decide if I'm going to answer. Her eyes flick to the screen, a magpie for shiny names. One brow climbs.

I let it buzz out. Silence hums in the space it leaves, surprising as snow in August. Not relief, exactly. More... alignment. As if all the pieces that have been wiggling loose finally click.

"Who was that?" she asks, but she already knows.

"Agent." I take a swallow of a sample peppermint mocha, my sinuses burning in candy cane protest. "The one who wants me to take on her client, Scott Evans."

Amanda's mouth actually falls open a fraction. She repeats the name low and quick, like she doesn't want to spook the possibility. "You just—didn't pick up?"

I scan the room until Eileen's headband appears again, bobbing like a buoy. "Eileen," I call, and she beelines as if I've offered her state secrets and a pony.

Amanda pinches my sleeve. "Jack."

"I need your help with something," I tell Eileen, ignoring Amanda's blatant curiosity.

Eileen leans in. "What kind of help? Planning? Baking? Discreet meddling? Overt meddling disguised as charity?"

"Something along those lines." I nod at the peppermint-chanting crowd who just entered seeking warmth and drinks. "I'll come by after close." My voice drops, uncharacteristically earnest. "And I want it to be a surprise."

She makes the kind of expression people make at kittens and baby showers. "A surprise." Her voice is reverent as if invoking the Holy Ghost. "We do adore surprises here in Hideaway."

Amanda bumps my shoulder, reminding me of her presence. "You're going to tell me what the surprise is?"

I take another sip of peppermint, the whipped cream on

top tickling my nose. "Not unless you want to tell me how you came to admire the local candymaker's lollipops."

She tries to glare through a smile. Fails. "I would if you told me how sweet Audrey's pies are."

I snort into the leftover whipped cream in my cup. "Good one."

Lucy slides a to-go cup across the bar with Audrey's name scribbled on the side decorated with hearts. "Dirty chai." She winks. "Extra filthy."

Eileen fans herself. "I don't know what that means, but I'm both scandalized and delighted."

I cradle the cup, warmth seeping into my fingers, sugar noise still buzzing in my ears. Outside, flakes thicken. Inside, a chorus of "Deck the Halls" tries to decide on a key and fails with gusto. The tray of pairing whoopie pies is half gone already, crumbs like confetti across the bar.

This is not my world, not the way LA was—contracts and cameras and conversations that always tilt toward leverage. But it's not *not* my world either. It's a place where someone can march into a coffee shop with a tray of free dessert because it'll make their neighbors happy, where an entire town will line up to celebrate a flavored latte like it's a coronation, where a man who has been very good at being alone can stand in a crowd and imagine being part of the noise instead of apart from it.

My phone buzzes again. The same name. Amanda watches me watch it. Her mouth softens, a small, private smile meant for me and later—if I know Amanda—weaponized for someone else's benefit.

I slide the phone back into my pocket.

"Tell Audrey we're grateful," Lucy says, wiping the counter with efficient swipes. "She keeps this place sweet."

"Yes." Pride sparks through me, quiet but fierce. "That she does." I head for the door before I stay too long or say too much. The bell jingles overhead. The cold nips my face. The dirty chai warms my palms and something in my chest I've avoided touching for years.

Next door, the bakery windows glow. Audrey will have her hair twisted up with a pencil stuck through it, lips pursed as she counts boxes, foot tapping to music only she hears. She'll roll her eyes when I hand her the chai and then drink half in one go. She'll tell me she's not a real Hidie, that she's just the whoopie pie girl, that the town humors her.

And I'll think of Eileen clapping, of Lucy's soft voice, of the way people line up for a taste of what Audrey made and leave with more than sugar on their tongues. I'll think of chowder days and cannoli whoopies and adult-store glitter, of a calendar full of appreciation for everything under the winter sun except the thing that quietly holds them together.

I'll think: *Fine. Then we'll give them a reason.*

Behind me, Eileen's laugh peals like a bell. Amanda calls my name, a question tucked inside it. I lift the cup in a wave without turning back and step into the snow with a plan I'm not ready to say out loud and a mouth that tastes faintly of peppermint and trouble.

STAGED

Audrey

The bells in the church tower chime seven when I step out into the December night, tugging my scarf tighter around my neck. The streets glimmer under strands of twinkling lights draped over awnings, wreaths wired onto shop doors. My fellow Hidies have formed groups along Main Street—laughing, knitted hats bobbing, mittens curled around steaming cups—looking woven right into the festive spirit that floats on the chilly air. And me? I feel like a Christmas cookie someone forgot in the oven—overbaked, brittle, barely held together by sugar.

It's the last Saturday before Christmas Eve, which in bakery terms is total war. The ovens never stopped, timers shrieked every three minutes, and I shuffled between trays until my calves burned like I'd run a marathon in my Crocs. By close, condensation ghosted the front case, my apron wore a map of cocoa smudges, and my hair smelled permanently of gingerbread.

Jack had been gone all day—off with Amanda at the Santa Fun Run, handing out prizes, doing whatever else celebrity-adjacent people do when they're charming a crowd. When he'd asked if I'd be fine without him, I laughed, confident in my ability to handle the bakery solo. But somewhere between the first latte order and the mid-morning rush, I realized just how much I'd started to rely on him.

He was supposed to be temporary, a guest star in my bakery life, his main job to handle the legal stuff interrupting my holiday rush. But between the sacks of flour he hauled, the floors he swept, and the way he charmed the line with that easy grin, he'd slipped into the role of partner-in-crime so smoothly that his absence today left me floundering.

And that scares me more than the cease and desist.

My mother relied on a man, and when he left, it was up to her to pick up the pieces. I've heard that story enough times to taste the bitterness. Forget my mother lamenting me leaving the Ritz for small-town Hideaway Harbor—the true metaphorical stab to her heart would be if I ended up heart-broken and with my business in trouble because of it.

I cut across Main Street toward the square where the caroling will start, my boots crunching on salted sidewalks. Every lamppost is wrapped in red ribbon and fir boughs, glittered ribbons glowing against the night. Windows fog with bodies and laughter; a lot of Main Street's shop doors still chime with customers; the scent of chowder, cocoa, and fried dough threads the air.

Normally, this walk fills me with something close to joy—my reminder that I traded Manhattan chaos for small-town magic. Tonight, the lights feel brighter than necessary, the local chatter a shade too loud. Tonight it feels like a gauntlet.

Is this what Jack meant when he described Hideaway's decorations as aggressively festive?

I pause, the thought making me wonder if, instead of small-town charm rubbing off on Jack, I've let his city edge rub off on me.

More likely, though, I'm just plain grumpy—my mood a mirror of my body. My shoulders ache from hauling the ingredient bags Jack used to grab without asking; my fingers sting from washing between piping cream and stabbing cash-register buttons—buttons he spent the past weeks tapping while I worked in rare, blissful peace.

Rolling my shoulders, I shake off the aches, along with the thoughts, and keep moving.

"Did you see them this morning? Arm in arm at the finish line." A voice floats over the wind, sharp as peppermint.

I glance left. Two women stand outside Hideaway Treasures, their shopping bags dangling like ornaments, heads bent close under knitted hats. Their voices cut through the night like gossip always does—too loud, too knowing.

"With her hair, she looked like a walking candy cane, grinning up at Amanda Willis like the celebrity had hung the moon," the taller one says. "Ridiculous, really. I always thought she was smart enough to know better."

"Mm." The other tugs her mitten. "She's just fooling herself. That actress will be gone after New Year's. They always are. And all she'll be left with is her broken heart. She should hold back—enjoy her Hollywood crush for what it is. A fling."

Their laughter bubbles into the air, light and careless.

They shift shopping bags and keep talking, already hungry for their next bite of someone else's life, but I'm frozen mid-step.

Because every word, every smug little chuckle, lands squarely in my chest.

I know they're talking about Portia—the one person I'm brave enough to call a friend here in Hideaway. And if I scroll back over the times I've seen her these hectic weeks, I realize she's never looked happier than when Amanda is near—her expressions lighting up, more chromatic than the streaks in her hair.

And Amanda, whom I've also come to know thanks to Jack, is always leaning close to her, a conspirator at the candy counter, as if the two of them share some secret. It was sweet. Lovely. The kind of happiness that makes strangers smile. And yet now, apparently, laughable to the town gossips.

But the thing is… it might as well be me they're skewering. Swap Portia's name for mine and "actress" for "lawyer," and the warning still stings. More so than my aching shoulders.

Did I get seduced by convenience? Mistake teamwork for permanence? Or did I like how smooth the day ran when Jack was around and I let that feel like a promise?

It would explain why I've been so out of sorts since that newspaper article. I believed it was because my faith in Jack's legal skills was put into question—but maybe deep down I was questioning my faith in Jack…in general.

Today made it obvious: without him, every task was doubled; every smile for customers felt stapled on; even the oven timers sounded lonely.

Hold back, the women said. *Just a fling.*

Maybe that's the smart play.

A gust ratchets down the street, turning the wreaths into

spinning halos. I pull my scarf higher and keep walking, past the bookstore with a cardboard cutout of Santa reading romances, past the Chowder House with clam-steam fogging the glass, past the bench where town teenagers practice looking bored in four layers of wool. The square opens ahead—strings of bulbs zigzagging over the gazebo, volunteers fussing with a microphone that squeals like a distressed elf.

I slow when I spot him. Jack, head tipped toward Amanda, smiling at something Portia says while she tucks a candy cane into Amanda's pocket—easy, unashamed, as if everyone in town has already agreed to their happiness. His hands are shoved into his coat pockets, shoulders loose, the light catching on the sharp line of his jaw. People keep drifting over like he's always been part of this place.

My stomach flips. Because if the gossips are right about Portia—a fling, a crush, a meteor—what does that make me? The intermission. The filler act. The one the crowd forgets once the headliner comes on.

Jack

THE SQUARE GLITTERS like a holiday movie set nobody ever struck. Bulbs strung from eave to eave cast warm halos onto brick and cobblestone. Fir garlands loop over the gazebo railing where a crooked sign reads *CAROLS AT SEVEN* in glitter-glue handwriting. Skippy has installed himself by the hot cocoa stall like security, chin on paws, tail thumping whenever a marshmallow hits the ground.

I'm early. Amanda is not because she got waylaid in The Sweetest Thing "sampling" peppermint bark with Portia—and by sampling, I mean flirting shamelessly while Portia pretended to explain crystalized sugar like it was a love language.

A dad in a down jacket hoists a kid onto his shoulders. A grandmother tugs wool hats onto reluctant teenagers who pretend they're above joy. Everywhere I look is some version of this—units, pieces that click. Family.

There's a tug in my chest I don't have a precedent or clause for.

The mayor's words from earlier in the week refuse to unhook from my ribs: me not just staying for my legalese but for the traditional small-town life—aka a family. It had landed like a compliment and a dare. The subtext was clear: not just contracts. Community. People who show up for bake sales and carols, not billable hours.

Shifting in my loafers, I wedge my hands in the pockets of my Burberry coat. I left the warmer, locally purchased one at the hotel in case any rogue reindeer decided to join tonight's fun. I look polished as Amanda's agent should but decidedly colder than I want to be.

I catch Eileen's eye from across the square, and we wave. She helped me out big time today at the Santa Fun Run, introducing me to the people I needed to talk to to get the epiphany I had during Peppermint Mocha Day up and running. It made me understand more thoroughly why Audrey was drawn to small-town life, the way neighbors rally around each other in times of celebration and in times of need.

I just hope all their work pays off in the way I'm hoping and Audrey doesn't mistake it for a gesture of gratitude instead of the truth.

As if conjured by my thoughts, my practical baker appears at the edge of the crowd, walking fast like the night air is a rope pulling her forward. Hair tucked into her scarf. Cheeks wind-bitten and gorgeous. Cocoa powder dusts the sleeve of her coat like glitter that refuses to leave after a party.

She sends me a small smile when our eyes catch, but it doesn't land. Something shuttered. Tired, yes, but more than that.

My head tilts in question, but she averts her eyes, suddenly distracted by the milling crowd.

I take a step forward, but Amanda and Portia materialize beside me in a flurry of cinnamon air and laughter. A strand of Amanda's hair snags in her lip gloss, and Portia gently frees it and tucks it behind her ear. Amanda beams like she just unwrapped Christmas.

Everyone around us notices, including Audrey.

"Get a room," I mutter, nudging Amanda with an elbow, my pretend jab sounding a little more sour than I intended.

Portia smiles, and Amanda shoots me a what-the-hell look that demands an answer I don't have.

What's wrong with me?

Seeing the mayor huddled with his family the way people who belong together can, I have a feeling I know exactly what's wrong with me. My eyes cut to Audrey once more, standing in front of the tree we both almost took down on my second day in town, and I wonder if she's already reached the same conclusion I have and she's too scared to say out loud.

But I'm not.

I may think about aesthetics before practicality when it comes to clothes, and I may overthink everything else, but if there's one thing I do well, it's act when I know the answer.

Pulling out my phone, I check the signal. The universe must be on my side because there's actual service. Not much, but enough to fire off a text.

I type one out now, focused more on speed than accuracy, trying to thread the needle as it were with my limited signal time.

"Whatcha doing?" Amanda, nosy as always, leans over my shoulder.

"Taking on a new client." And if it works out, I'll be taking on more than just a client.

"Get out." She shoves me—playfully but hard enough that I spend a few precious seconds backtracking the smear of random letters it made me type. "Really?"

"Yes, really." Though I don't want to say anything more until I hear back.

The piano on the small stage clunks a chord that sounds like it lost a fight with time—a signal the caroling festivities are about to start. A woman in a Santa hat with holly berries skewed like a crown pushes a crate of thin paper songbooks into the hands of anyone within reach.

I hit send on my text just as a book smacks my chest. I catch it on reflex.

Amanda nudges my elbow, her earlier enthusiasm dimming as she looks between me and Audrey, who's edging into an opening near us—but not *with* us, if that makes sense. "Are you sure?"

"Yes." I nod, eyes on the catalyst to my recent decision. "I'm sure."

Audrey catches us looking and tries her smile again. It still misses, but something settles in my chest.

"I spent years building my career in LA." Pulling my attention back to Amanda, I reshape my expression into its usual easygoing agent's smile. "It makes sense to—"

The mic squeals; half the town winces. The beleaguered volunteer at the keyboard clears his throat into it like he's negotiating with the machine before declaring "Twelve Days" the opening number.

Portia links arms with Amanda, either not caring or oblivious to the stares aimed their way, and Amanda forgets our conversation in favor of her first foray into public caroling.

Mine too.

Buzzing with anticipation from what I just set in motion, I find the first verse of "Twelve Days" low-stakes—everyone mumbling about a pear tree like we're unsure whether we believe in birds as gifts.

I trace the words in the booklet with my finger because the font is microscopic and the light is romantic rather than functional, wondering if I should shuffle over to Audrey since it doesn't seem like she's going to move any closer to me.

Second verse: two turtle doves, and my confidence, which was mostly distraction, is grossly misplaced.

By verse three, though, a problem surfaces.

A different problem than the one I have with the town baker.

I can't hear myself.

Or rather, I can—but I assume everyone else can't, because I am a man who has given presentations to skeptical studio heads. I project, therefore I am. I lean into it a little—pure defensive habit.

When you're not sure you're blending, you turn up the volume so you won't get swallowed by the chorus.

I attempt what I imagine to be a warm baritone. "Three French hens…"

Amanda's head turns slowly. Portia's eyebrows climb like mountaineers in need of oxygen.

I glance toward Audrey, looking for reassurance and calibration, and while she is finally looking at me, it's with wide eyes, her mitten pressed to her mouth with horror rather than affection.

This is where a wiser man might lower the dial.

I am not that man.

Verse four. A kid in a beanie pivots like a weathervane in a storm. My storm. A couple near the cocoa stall exchange the look of people who just discovered a faucet leak behind a wall: not catastrophic yet, but there's a sound—and it's me. I'm the leak.

I try to soften.

It does not soften.

What happens is that I switch keys altogether and—without consultation with the laws of music—enter a brave new place none of my fellow carolers care to visit.

"Fiiiiiive gold riiiiiiings…" I go long on the vowel like it owes me money.

Silence peels off the crowd in a flapping wave. Even the piano hesitates, like *sir?*

I look to Skippy, my lone male companion in this town,

and he gives me a long-suffering head tilt.

Embarrassment pricks the back of my neck. I see myself as they must: a man in a very nice coat thinking he can croon his way through a tradition he didn't grow up with. Because community and caroling is not me.

They see me as a power tie. A closer. The guy who finds loopholes in contracts, not high notes in a hymn.

And I am—but I can be more.

Yet just as I'm about to prove them right and invoke a caroling loophole—plead the Fifth by lip-syncing—I notice Audrey's shoulders begin to shake.

Her earlier distance cracks like sugar glass under a spoon.

If my options are her silence or her laughter at my expense—give me the guillotine and call it festive. Aggressively so.

I lean all the way in.

"On the sixth day of Christmas..." I croon, sliding a hand out of my pocket to mime an invisible microphone. The town perks up the way crowds do when a man commits publicly to a bit that might go to hell.

On "lords a-leaping" I put height under it, my loafers hovering just an inch off the ground, and the kids howl. "Maids a-milking," I pantomime, and a retiree in a tartan scarf wheezes into his cocoa.

Amanda covers her face, peeking through her fingers. Portia leans into her, shoulders shaking.

"Do the rings," a ten-year-old commands, elbowing his buddy.

I hold up a finger: one moment. Build the suspense.

He beams, front tooth missing.

The carolers vocalize about geese and swans while I vandalize the melody with good faith and poor aim. Somewhere around drummers drumming, the alchemy happens—the one I've seen in rooms where someone risks looking ridiculous without flinching. You can't boo a person offering you their whole self with nothing guarded.

By the time I unholster "five gold rings" again, a group has rotated to circle me like a cheap spotlight.

I give them everything: chin lift, shoulder roll, a slide into the note so brazen I can feel my tailor back in LA telepathically begging me not to crack a seam. "Fiiiiiive goooold riiiiings..." I belt until even those with an ironclad grip on carol tradition are hooting in amusement.

"Again!" my young tooth-gap challenger yells as a man appears with a cowbell from nowhere, raising his brows at Audrey in question.

Audrey, shaking her head in disbelief, takes a step toward me. Her nose is red and a bit shiny underneath, and her smile is half amusement, half I-can't-look-away-from-this-train-wreck.

She's adorable.

The crowd launches into another chorus, the man clanging his cowbell on "rings" like we rehearsed it. Everyone—including Audrey—roars. The volunteer pianist gives up steering me with tempo and lets me hydroplane. A teenager starts beatboxing badly; I shoot him a grateful thumbs-up.

We—the townsfolk and I—slaughter Christmas with consent.

And when the final line is sung and there are no more choruses to butcher, the crowd shifts, the volume dropping to something like reverence when the piano player begins "Silent Night."

Couples link arms. Parents gather small bodies close and

sway. Warmth stacks on warmth until I can feel it through scarf and coat. I find my way to Audrey, who holds my gaze, her eyes no longer distracted by anything.

"Well," she whispers, eyes bright as she looks up at me, "that was by far the worst singing I've ever heard."

I huff out a laugh. "I cannot object."

Her lips quirk. "I loved it."

Chest tight for reasons that have nothing to do with breath control, I choose to do both myself and humanity a favor and launch into "Silent Night" as God intended me to—by humming. Softly.

When the last chord fades, the square holds that strange, sacred quiet that happens when a lot of voices agree. On cue, it starts to snow—powder-fine, a sprinkle-sugar flurry that floats rather than falls. The lights catch it, and everything turns briefly cinematic. It dusts Audrey's hair and the bridge of her pink nose. She blinks up at it, then at me.

She's perfect.

In this moment. In this town. In the life she's building.

She deserves it all—family, roots, and a man without an expiration date buried in the fine print.

WHISKED AWAY

Audrey

"That was more fun than the time Jamie Dornan jumped off Dakota Johnson's roof into the pool. Naked." Amanda, skipping beside Portia, brushes my shoulder as I walk beside Jack.

Between the Oscar-nominated actress and the colorful candy maker, I think they downed a jug of spiked cider between them.

"I would've rather seen Dakota do that." Portia links her arm with Amanda's and grins.

"Same, girl." Amanda winks. "Same."

The carols ended on a literal high note—thankfully not Jack's—then tapered to a hush, programs and stray mittens dotting the brick like winter confetti.

Now with the moon out from behind misty snow clouds, shop windows are haloed in white lights, frosted glass winks with candy-cane reflections, and the peaceful silence settles like fresh snow threatening the skies.

Down the square, The Sweet Shop's striped awning waits at the corner like a peppermint invitation. The four of us fall in together, forming a loose blockade across the sidewalk, our boots clicking in a syncopated beat.

"Hold up." Jack points to the community board near a set of benches. "Zoning hearing." He squints in the streetlight to read. "Sale of the Harbor Clinic building." Pulling out his phone, he steps back to focus the picture. "Give me sixty seconds—Eli needs this photo."

"Ooh." Portia pulls her arm from Amanda's after spotting a flyer a college student looking for part-time hours left tacked to the board. "Let me double-check this." She veers off with him to scan the information.

Amanda, unbothered—if the soft look she sends Portia is any indication—links her now-free arm through mine. "It's too cold to stand still." She pulls me into motion. "Come on, they'll catch up."

Walking arm and arm with a movie star isn't something I thought I'd get used to, and yet here I am. "So. The movie." I tilt my chin at the town—fishing nets threaded with fairy lights, wreaths on every door, the glow of the lobster-trap tree pulsing from below the hilltop down by the harbor. "Is Hideaway giving you enough spark and inspiration?"

Her mouth quirks. "Oh, there's inspiration." She glances over my shoulder to where Portia laughs at Jack, who's just slipped on the sidewalk and grabbed a tree trunk for balance and waggles her eyebrows at me. "And definitely spark."

Warmth that has nothing to do with my coat fights its way

under my skin. I stare straight ahead at my bakery's painted door across the street.

Amanda bumps her hip against mine, conspiratorial. "And speaking of spark—you and Jack." Her tipsy smile turns knowing. "I know I stole him from you today for the Santa Fun Run, but I'll tell him I don't need him for tomorrow's library reading." Her voice dips, gentle. "Portia will be there, and I'm pretty sure if I can handle a pack of paparazzi shouting 'when did you start wanting to sleep with women and not men' outside the gate to my house, I can handle a bunch of little kids wanting me to read about Santa's eight reindeer."

I steer her out of the lamppost's path. "It's really nice how you've volunteered for so many of the town's activities. But don't underestimate little kids—" I drop my voice like I'm narrating a true-crime documentary. "They're apex predators. I've seen them pull apart a whoopie-pie tower in ten seconds flat."

"Yeah, but Portia will be there, and she's packing candy." Amanda's smile turns wry. "Besides, with Jack taking on his big new client, I want you two to have all the time you can together before he starts diving back into the Hollywood agent life."

My laugh comes out thinner than I'd like. "New client?"

"Yeah. Scott Evans. *Great* actor." She looks both ways three times before crossing over Main Street toward my shop.

Although honestly, with my brain having decided to stop working, it could've been a busy freeway and I would've followed.

"I'd love to work with him myself." Amanda veers us right to avoid an ice patch. "He's really made a name for himself in indie films, and he's poised to have a major breakthrough in mainstream films."

I pull in a breath so cold it scrapes. "Exciting."

Something in my voice must draw her attention because she pulls up short in front of the bakery. "You knew, right?" Her eyes bounce between mine, trying to read my expression like a cue card. "I mean, you two have been—"

"Having fun." I will my throat to stop strangling my voice. "Nothing serious." It doesn't listen.

Bootsteps scuff behind us. Jack and Portia reappear, cold-pink cheeks and a fresh phone photo held up like a prize.

"Triple-net with 'extraordinary maintenance.'" He says it like we should all know what he means before pocketing his phone. "Eli's going to love that little landmine."

Portia wiggles the student-hours flyer. "And I found a potential afternoon counter-helper for the shop."

Amanda—previous concern over my not-so-hidden reaction forgotten in the face of, well, Portia's—wraps her arm around her not-so-hidden love interest. "My toes are staging a coup. Let's get to your place before they defect to frostbite."

We do the goodbye shuffle at my door—hugs over puffy coats, promises to 'see you soon' while I keep my bakery-bright smile in place.

"Rest that voice, superstar," Portia calls to Jack as she and Amanda back away, already linked, wobbling and laughing.

"Hardy har-har." Jack snorts, his smile wide as the two disappear into the halo of the streetlights, their silhouettes folding into the soft, slow snow starting to sift down.

The night hushes. Jack stands beside me, hands deep in his coat pockets, eyes on the frosted glass of my door, his humor resolving into something else. Something hot but also wary.

"Go in?" His look is searching, like he's checking a pressure gauge.

My key is already in my hand. *Stop this now,* a voice suggests, the practical one that balances books and cleans mixers and knows better. Another voice—the one that still tastes cinnamon and his kiss—asks for one more night of pretend. One more hour where I don't count costs.

I turn the key. "Yeah, let's go in."

He smiles, relief flickering and heat taking its place.

Nothing wrong with having fun, I tell myself as he follows me inside.

Enjoy it while it lasts.

Jack

THE BELL over the door gives a polite jingle, and then the dark swallows it. The bakery is all silver edges and soft shadows—the glass case reflecting a sliver of moonlight from the street, stainless counters gone black, mixers hulking like quiet animals. The air smells like citrus cleaner and tastes like sugar and something warm I can't name without saying her.

Audrey doesn't flip on the lights. Her fingers find mine in the dark and squeeze once, quickly, like we're crossing a street. The lock clicks back into place behind us; the world narrows to the sound of our shoes on the mat and the hush of a building that knows her better than anyone.

She leads me through the kitchen by memory, her hip brushing against a table edge, a laugh under her breath when I stumble into a stool. My hand—flung out on cool steel for balance—finds the softer give of her waist.

I expect her to linger there, to press back. She doesn't. She keeps moving.

Up the back stairs, the wood beneath us is the only sound, creaking like it's telling secrets.

More time for my inner thoughts to amplify—like how she was quiet at the end of caroling too, a little absent in the crowd even after my attempt at a festive off-key act. And on the way back, when she wasn't intertwined with Amanda, her hands were jammed into her coat pockets so I couldn't give her mine.

Top of the stairs. She keys the apartment door by feel and pushes it open.

The living room is darker than the bakery—only the streetlamp leaking around the edges of the shade and the faint pinpricks of the Christmas tree, not lit but catching whatever light there is like a constellation that refuses to die. The soft shape of the couch. The empty hook where my scarf hung earlier. Her hand leaves mine to flick the bolt, then removes her coat.

Following her lead, I hang mine beside hers on the rack, the fabrics whispering against each other. She steps out of her boots; I slide out of my poor-choice loafers, both pairs making soft thuds on the mat. The sounds are so domestic my chest aches, Audrey's silence so loud it's deafening.

I should ask what's wrong.

Instead I replay the gathered evidence. At the square, she laughed at Amanda's joke and said all the right things and gave everyone—including me—the bakery smile she gives customers who ask if they can pay with Canadian cash. When I asked, 'Go in?' she paused half a beat too long. It was all there if you knew which lines to read.

"Hey." My whisper carries over the room. "We don't have to—"

She pivots like a dancer, a neat little half-moon that lands her in my space, and kisses me. Not cautious. Not questioning. Heat, direct and uncomplicated, like turning an oven from off to on without testing the pilot.

The sentence I was building fragments. Her hands slide up the front of my sweater and fist there, pulling me down. She tastes like winter air and the last of the snow drop taffy Portia bullied us into eating. Like a decision already made.

"Okay," I breathe against her mouth because I am a simple man with a complicated brain, and both parts are very easily convinced by this woman. My palms bracket her jaw, thumbs grazing the warm hinge of it, the place that always goes soft when I touch her. As it does now. Just like my doubts.

We take two steps sideways, shoulders brushing the coat rack, and the back of my knees find the couch. She pushes me down with both hands on my shoulders and follows, knees to either side of my hips, sweater rucking up as she moves. When her hair slides forward over my cheeks, the world reduces to the sound of her breath and the slow, patient click of snow against the window.

I let my hands memorize—again—the map I've only just started to learn. The dip at her waist. The heat where her shirt leaves skin. The tiny shiver when I thumb the notch above her hipbone. She gives me every permission in the way she moves, in the way she presses her body to mine and chases the friction she wants.

Still, a thought sits up in the back row and raises its hand. The silence. The customer-service expressions. The way she didn't turn on our Christmas tree when we first came in like she usually does. The—

She shifts her weight, lining our centers and bringing my mouth and mind back to her. Her tongue strips self-importance down to the studs. Whatever I thought I needed to ask can wait until an hour from now.

I flip us gently, a careful roll so she's on her back and I'm braced over her, one hand finding the cushion beside her head, the other palming the warm weight of her thigh. She hooks that leg at my hip, encouraging, mouth tipping into a smile I feel more than see. When I drag my teeth along her lower lip, she makes a sound that unthreads something in my chest.

"Tell me if you're too tired. We don't have—"

"Jack." My name is thick with heat as her fingers curl into the back of my neck. The sound steals the floor right out from under my second thoughts.

We undress in the piecemeal way you do when urgency outruns grace. Her sweater lifts; I chase it with my mouth over the new skin. She finds the hem of my shirt; my shoulder gets stuck; we both laugh into the fabric and then we're quiet again, focusing on the tasks at hand: buttons, zippers, the rasp of denim loosening. The thud of my belt against the rug. The sigh she can't swallow when I settle between her thighs.

I slow us on purpose, and she lets me—for a heartbeat.

Then her palm slides down my chest with intent, and I am back to being a man built of yes.

"Are you sure?" I ask, one last responsible flare.

Her answer is the arch of her hips and the way she guides me in, tight and hot and so welcoming it's almost painful. Her eyes go heavy; mine roll back. I brace and breathe and sink deep inside until I've got everything I'd been pretending I didn't need.

The first stroke is reverent. The second, less so. She meets me without hesitation, body pulling and pushing, pulling and pushing, an elegant rhythm like the tide finding shore—sure, then hungry.

I try to keep a hand on the wheel of my brain and fail gladly when her mouth finds that weak spot below my ear.

She drags her nails across my back in a line that unspools every careful argument I brought upstairs. She is doing all the right things. Saying them, too—soft YESes and my name like a secret, gratitude and greed braided together so tightly there's no telling which is which.

Maybe I read the walk home wrong. Maybe she was just cold. Maybe she's tired from a day that started before mine and hasn't ended yet. Maybe the carols were loud, and she just needed a minute of quiet to recalibrate. Maybe the only thing that's changed is I want more, and while I know how to negotiate a future on paper, I'm totally untried in asking for the kind that lives off-paper.

I put my forehead to hers and let that last thought go. She pushes my hair back with one hand, then slips her fingers into it and pulls in a way that makes me say something unholy. Snow continues to tap the window. The radiator pings once and gives up. The couch creaks a protest, and we move to the rug without breaking, her amusement caught in my mouth when I lift and she wraps around me tighter, the kind of wrap that says don't you dare stop.

We don't. We couldn't if we wanted to. She rolls us again and rides me, hands on my chest for balance, head tipped back. The reflection of moonlight off the tree's ornaments throws a few stray points of light over her—collarbone, shoulder, the soft plane of her stomach as she moves over me. I put my hands on her hips, not to steer, just to feel her power as she takes exactly what she wants. When I drag my thumbs in slow circles, her breath stutters and then evens into a deeper, more dangerous rhythm.

"Audrey." My voice is a ragged prayer.

She leans forward and kisses me. It feels like a promise and a goodbye all at once. The last thought snags; I pretend it doesn't.

I flip us again, desperate for the leverage that keeps me from coming apart too soon, and she lifts her leg higher and gives me a quiet, wrecked sound that pulls the plug on my restraint anyway.

The finish is heat and light and the kind of relief that fogs the room. She goes with me, not because I pull her there but because we built the road together, and afterward we lie there in the slow fall of our breathing, messing up the rug, my face buried where her neck meets her shoulder, her fingertips drawing lazy shapes at the base of my spine.

I remember—to my credit, however briefly—that I meant to check in. That I meant to tell her about my Los Angeles decision, about the library tomorrow, or about how I turned down three calls during caroling because the only thing I wanted to handle tonight was her. I open my mouth to start any of that, but she slides her hand into my hair and hums, a small, pleased sound that feels like permission to be happy for one unexamined minute.

I take the minute. I take another. I tell myself I'll ask in the morning, when she's not this warm and I'm not this stupid.

She shifts, and I settle deeper into the curve of her. The radiator tries again, optimistically, while below us, the bakery sleeps, saving itself for tomorrow.

"Stay," she says finally, bare and simple, drowsy at the edges.

"Yeah." I breathe the answer into her skin, into the place that smells like sweetness and soap and her, and let the rest of my doubts sit out in the hall with our coats.

BURNT EDGES

Audrey

Dawn slides under my curtains like a nosy neighbor peeking through blinds, soft and pale and way too early for a Sunday that technically opens late. My body doesn't care. Bakers are Pavlov's dogs—first hint of light, and I'm upright, already tasting cinnamon in a future that hasn't started yet.

And of course, it doesn't help that my first thought is of the bundle of heat lying heavy and comforting against my back like a weighted blanket with his arm slung over my waist, last night still warm on my skin.

Jack's breath tickles the spot where my shoulder meets my neck. I don't move. Not because I'm savoring the moment—okay, also because I'm savoring the moment—but because I promised myself I wouldn't read into it. Last night was... *God.*

Better than great. The kind of great that ruins you for mediocre. The kind that makes you grateful your bed is sturdy and your downstairs neighbor is an empty kitchen.

A different me—last year's me—would already be running a postmortem in my head, itemizing regrets and the exact cost of letting a man like Jack Lourd anywhere near my life. This me, the one dawn finds with sex hair, fuzzy socks, and an armful of man, closes her eyes for one audacious breath and admits it: I wanted it. Him. For keeps.

A minute. That dream gets one more minute.

I stare at the ceiling and count my heartbeats until one minute becomes two. Then, repeating the words *it's temporary*, I untangle myself, inch by careful inch, like defusing a bomb with a frosting knife.

Jack's arm loosens. He makes a low sound that curls down my spine. I still, breath caught halfway in my throat. His fingers flex against my stomach as if checking I'm still there, then relax.

Feeling very much a coward, I slide my legs over the side of the bed and wince at the icy kiss of floorboards. December has claws. But I welcome the pain. It helps clear my mind that's been muddied by my heart.

I tiptoe toward the dresser, hooking a finger through my bra where it dangled off the drawer pull like it tried to escape and failed. The radiator along the far wall rattles, and a bike bell chirps softly as the paper boy—another early riser—cycles past my window.

The mattress shifts.

In the mirror above the dresser, I watch Jack's hand land on the bed where my hip had been a minute ago, patting blindly.

"Come back" comes from the pillow, gravel-soft, like a rumor. The hand drifts to the warm spot I left and flattens there, possessive and unselfconscious, like it owns that square foot of cotton now. "Stay."

I bite the inside of my cheek. He's more than half asleep. Definitely not thinking clearly.

But I am. Now at least. And I don't have any more of those lazy, sticky mornings that stretch into noon if you let them.

"Go back to sleep," I whisper, already stepping into panties, already constructing the scaffolding of my day. "I have to get downstairs."

Eyes still closed, he slides his body across the sheets, his torso off the bed, held up by his tensing and drool-worthy abs as he extends his arm again, this time riding up my thigh.

His warm palm makes a lazy slide north that makes me think I'll need new panties if he drifts any higher.

"I can"—the word dissolves around a yawn—"help."

I lean over and cup his cheek, his stubble sharp just like his jawline. "Go back to sleep, Hollywood." I say the last mostly to remind myself where he's from and where he's returning to.

He wraps his hand around my thigh, pulling back until his body's back to lying on the bed, my leg up against the mattress.

His hair is a riot. His mouth is a sin. One eye slits open, heavy-lidded amusement sparking even through sleep. Heat pools low in my belly, traitorous. "You come back to sleep." He smiles into the pillow. "Or just come back and we can *not* sleep."

Amanda's voice floats back from last night, all glitter and a hundred-watt smile after caroling.

"Go help Amanda." I aim for breezy and land somewhere

near brittle. "The library thing. She mentioned it. She'll need you."

Silence. Then, muffled into the mattress, "Amanda doesn't need me."

A humorless smile pulls at my mouth. Of course she doesn't. That's not the point. The point is remembering that I *don't* need him.

How I can work the counter without him leaning there like he owns it, how to pipe buttercream without feeling eyes on me like a warm hand, how to breathe without the inhale hitching when the bell over the door rings and it's him, it's him, it's him.

Extracting myself from his grasp, I catch the corner of my sweater where it's draped over the chair. Snow white, soft from too many washes. It smells like vanilla and the ghost of smoke from our brief flirtation with my ancient oven when I forgot a pan of pecans last week because I was too busy staring at Jack's forearms peeking out from his rolled-up shirtsleeves as he worked on his laptop.

I tug it over my head and try not to get distracted now by how much more of him is peeking above my sheets or how my apartment smells different now, faint soap and cedar layered over everything like an afterthought.

"She's your client." Voice firm, I hunt for my other sock, finding it kicked halfway under the bed, and my fingers brush cold wood and a memory of his knee knocking against mine, his laugh low and shocked when I dragged him closer by the waistband.

Focus.

"That's why you came. For Amanda. For your job. In Los

Angeles." I flatten my voice to bakery-counter neutral. "So go… support her."

He rolls to his back, giving up on persuading me with a sigh. The sheet slips. I resist the instinct to look because I already know what happens if I do and I need to be standing upright with pants on if I have any hope of surviving the next five minutes.

"Speaking of Los Angeles…" The words stretch as he wakes.

I can feel him surfacing, the way a soufflé rises in the oven —slow and steady.

He scrubs a hand over his jaw. Stubble rasps. "I might have to head back soon. Take care of some things. But"—his voice tries to soften the blow with a promise—"I should be back before Christmas."

I stop breathing.

I expected this. I told myself all last night that he and I were temporary. That men like Jack don't detour into small-town bakeries and decide to stay because the croissants are good and the sex is better. Men like Jack have lives with capital letters: Deals. Clients. Deadlines. Cities that eat you alive and call it love.

And yet my sweater suddenly feels too tight. The room tilts in microscopic degrees before righting itself. I fumble into my jeans, buttoning them with fingers that don't want to work. "Don't rush." I find my voice in the same place I keep my inventory lists—practical, unsentimental. Steadying my hands, I reach for the rest of my clothes. "Don't come back on my account."

Silence again, but not sleepy now. Awake. Alert. The kind

of quiet that notices details, that puts things together. I don't look at him, but I feel his frown like a hand pressed between my shoulder blades.

"Audrey." My name, careful, whereas he usually says it like he's tasting it.

How did I not realize that until now?

I grab an elastic off my nightstand and smooth my unbrushed hair into a ponytail that would make my mother complain about proper presentation. "I have prep."

My Crocs peek out from under Jack's shirt strewn over the chair by the door, and I slide my feet in, the familiar homecoming sending a wave of bone-deep familiarity through me so strong I wobble. Cranberry red. Blue cupcake charms. Ridiculous, and mine.

Stepping into the doorway, I plant myself there like a stop sign. "Batter to mix. Cakes to cool. Frosting to whip. People will be lined up when I flip the sign."

He sits, the mattress protesting. "I can—"

"Take the morning. Sleep. Then… the library." I shrug like it doesn't matter. Like I don't care when the sudden sting behind my eyes says I care too much. "Or whatever."

He is fully awake now, I can feel it, the heat of his gaze on the back of my neck like the oven when I open the door too early. "Amanda doesn't need—"

"Go." The word comes too hard, too fast, the truth slipping out before I can dress it. "It's your life. Your work. The thing that brought you here." I half turn, too much of a coward to fully face him. "That's not a bad thing, Jack. It just… isn't mine."

He swings his legs over the side of the bed. His feet hit the floor, the sheet dragging across his thighs. I force my eyes to my Crocs, but the picture is there in my mind anyway: long lines, warm skin, the low V of muscle disappearing under the soft white cotton of my bedding.

My palms go damp.

From the corner of my eye I watch him scrub both hands through his hair and leave it standing in defiance.

Good. Be ridiculous with me for one second longer.

"What happened between last night and now?" His voice is soft, not accusing, which makes it worse. "Because six hours ago, you—"

"Weren't thinking," I cut in, because if I let him finish that sentence I'll be back in that bed and the bakery will open late and the gossip mill will spin into a cotton-candy tornado. "Which is rare for me, and probably overdue, and"—a laugh scrapes its way out of my chest—"spectacular. No regrets. But I have a business to run. And a town with very loud opinions and very short attention spans."

He stands. The room gets smaller without moving. "I don't care about the town's—"

"I do." I give him my back, my one hand squeezing the door trim like a support beam to my sense of reason. "Just… just don't come to the bakery today."

A hard breath. That's the only sound he makes.

I exhale everything I have left and stalk down the hallway, my hand grazing across the wall as I go to keep me steady.

Ignoring the Christmas tree—dark and dead-looking with the lights off and oddly mirroring my mood—I pass the photo of my mother and me at the Ritz. Younger me is smiling at her, not the camera. The early morning sun crests through the window, catching the glass and flashing it white. I don't know what to do with the sudden sting behind my eyes.

I blink hard until the room behaves. And then I get to work.

Jack

STORYTIME at the Hideaway Harbor Library looks like the holidays exploded in miniature—children's coats piled like drifts, little boots in a ring on the carpet, cocoa mustaches giving everyone the same sticky grin.

Amanda perches on a beanbag throne with a hardcover splayed like a fan, doing voices that make even the parents lean in. I'm the page-turner, the bell-ringer, the guy who says "and then?" with exactly the right amount of awe.

Outwardly: a hit. Inwardly: a dial tone that won't disconnect.

Every time the door sighs open, I glance up; every time it's not Audrey, my chest does that hollow elevator drop. A toddler offers me a half-eaten marshmallow with grave generosity. I take it because I'm not a monster. He beams like we've agreed to something important, and the lawyer in me is convinced I was hoodwinked by a kindergartner.

Amanda finishes with applause and a blizzard of construction-paper antlers. She signs a stack of programs and books while I smooth the two-piece Brioni I wear like a suit of armor, for some reason needing to feel more like the Hollywood agent I am than the small-town lawyer I've been pretending to be.

In the quiet between celebrity readers—including Hideaway born and raised model-turned-actor Brody King reading a book about a Christmas Yeti—Amanda corners me. She's got that celebrity interview smile she uses when she's about to be kind yet sadistically surgical.

"Looking charming as always." She flicks a bit of glitter from my suit sleeve. "Also distracted."

"I can do two things at once." I aim for light, trying to convince myself that the bookcase of thrillers on one side and murder mysteries on the other is completely circumstantial.

"You can." Tucking a glitter pen behind her ear, she slides a Stephen King book off the shelf and pretends to read the back. "But I meant it last night when I told Audrey I wouldn't steal you today."

That lands harder than I expect.

She looks up from the book. "You've made me into a liar."

"Wait." The image of Amanda, drunk on cider after caroling, resurfaces. "When did you talk to Audrey about this?"

"On the walk back from town square last night." She talks like she's telling me about the weather, not wielding a book about a vengeful woman soaked in pig's blood. "She asked about the movie I want to make. We talked about inspiration. I said I'd give you a pass on the library..." There's a pause like she's replaying their conversation, then a wince. "*Shit.*"

Instantly I'm on alert. "What?"

No longer looking dangerous, Amanda replaces the book on the shelf. "I also mentioned you took on Scott Evans as a client."

I blink. "You what?"

She runs a hand over her face, slightly smearing her mascara. "I might've been a bit tipsy." A grimace. "In my head, it seemed absolutely plausible she'd already know about Evans. You two have been attached at the hip for weeks." She flutters her smudged eyelashes, hopeful. "You did tell her, right? I mean, that seems like something you should tell the person you're involved with."

I picture Audrey on that sidewalk, nodding like the news didn't knock her sideways.

Amanda reads whatever expression I'm making. "Fuck."

"I'm going to the bakery." I straighten my tie, preparing for battle. "I'll fix it."

"Good." She squeezes my elbow. "And just so you know, I'm sorry." She locks eyes with me. "Really."

I bring her in for a quick hug. "Don't be. It's my fault." Pulling back, I take a moment to really look her over and—aside from the raccoon eyes— Amanda glows, just like she does on screen. But the real-life version is much warmer. I've been so busy with my own business that I haven't really appreciated all that this trip has done for my friend. "And just so you know, I'm happy that you're happy." I squeeze her shoulders. "Really."

She snorts, her eyes shining as brightly as her glossed lips. "I *am* happy." She shrugs, laughing off the sudden emotion. "Who would've thought, huh?"

We share another hug before Amanda pushes back, thumbing behind her toward the door. "Go." She runs her fingers under her eyes, looking picture perfect once more. "I can survive a town's worth of five-year-olds without your legal counsel."

Portia spots us and starts walking over. If possible, Amanda shines brighter.

Leaving my friend in her girlfriend's capable hands, I weave through the library crowd until I make it outside. The day is a quiet, pale bowl compared to the vibrant interior of the children's section of the library. Snow does that soft sifting thing that turns everything so pristine it almost hurts to look at.

Hands jammed in my pockets and my heart doing its worst version of a pre-workout warm-up, I'm about to cut across Lobstah Lane when a vintage pickup pulls up in front of me—two-tone paint, chrome grinning, breath clouding from the exhaust like an old dragon.

Eli leans across and rolls down the passenger side window looking straight out of an L.L. Bean catalog in a red and black flannel over a thermal Henley. There's a duffel in the passenger seat and what looks suspiciously like a pair of ice skates tossed in the back.

"Counselor!" He thumbs the brim of his honest-to-goodness local hardware store trucker hat. "Heading to the bakery?"

"That's the plan." I make a show of looking him over. "You heading to the lumberjack competition?"

He laughs. "I'm heading from hockey practice over to my sister's to grab my niece." He glances at the clock on his dashboard. "She volunteered to help with the Woolen Sock Run over at Locke Reserve."

I nod, impressed. "I guess even teenagers are wholesome enough to volunteer in the community when they live in a small town."

He drops his chin. "*Or* small-town teenagers have heard that a local heartthrob by the name of Brody King will be in attendance and want a shot at an autograph and picture." He tilts his head as if looking behind me. "Did Amanda volunteer as tribute to this event as well?" Eli's truck ticks as it cools, smelling like old leather and pine and looking like a Hallmark Christmas special.

I'm suddenly very conscious of how much I paid for my suit. "Not this one."

Looking over the roof of his truck toward Main Street, I catch the edge of Audrey's chalkboard sign set up on the sidewalk advertising all the new flavors I've seen her spend hours creating.

Dropping my gaze, I catch Eli squinting at me like I'm a puzzle with three pieces missing.

He scratches his jaw, the universal sign for I-left-something-on-your-desk-you-didn't-mean-to-show-me. "I've been going through the relocation listings you sent—clinic space looks promising. Also, uh..." He lifts his chin, as if assessing me as I did him. "Found a couple of house listings mixed in. Fenced yards. Bonus rooms labeled 'kids' playroom' in the realtor photos." He drapes one arm on the steering wheel, deceptively casual. "You not billing enough hours? Trying to branch into residential real estate?"

Heat blooms under my coat. "Those were mine." I clear my throat. "Must've mixed those in with your file by mistake."

He lets the words sit there between us, the corner of his mouth lifting. "Huh."

I shove my hands deeper in my pockets. "Don't make it a thing."

His smile is full-blown now, not letting me off the hook. "It feels like a thing." He follows my gaze across the corner of town square toward the bakery then back. "You thinking about making Hideaway more permanent?"

I open my mouth to say something clever and land on nothing. The truth is a spinning coin, and I can't tell which side is up. "I don't know."

His phone chirps. "That'll be my niece." Looking at the screen, he winces. "Apparently I'm late, and her whole world will end if I don't get her there before Missy Whitehall, her high school nemesis." He rolls his eyes, but they stay kind. "Let's talk later." With a clunk, he releases the parking brake. "About the clinic." A wink. "And houses with fenced-in yards."

"Go." I wave him off. "Save yourself." *And me.*

He rolls the window up, drops the truck into gear, and pulls away with a honk that echoes off the brick like a warning.

I stand there for a beat too long in the gentle snow, watching the taillights disappear toward family obligation, toward domestic life, toward pick-up times and someone in the back seat complaining about the playlist.

I wanted to walk to Audrey's door and say the thing that terrifies me. I wanted to knock and hand her all the messy parts and ask if she'll take them anyway.

Instead, watching the kind of man I'm not drive his truck around the corner toward things that Audrey gave up to move here for, I pivot.

Sliding my BMW SUV rental key out of my pocket, I head toward the library parking lot.

I catch my reflection in the driver's side window—polished and tailored, not a plaid or flannel in sight. Ten minutes out of town, I turn onto The Haven Resort drive, tossing the keys at a bell boy like the well-practiced Hollywood cliché I am.

Tomorrow, I tell myself when I reach my room and shrug out of my suit coat. Tomorrow I'll find Audrey, clear the air, and make things right.

Powering up my laptop, I pretend not to hear how much that sounds like a lie.

CUT!

Audrey

Monday is for maintenance.

No more tree cutting, Winter Market, or other distractions no matter how handsome or festive they might be.

The CLOSED sign sits in the window while I'm in the back—calibrating, testing, perfecting. Sheet pans dry in formation. The mixer bowl gleams because I made it gleam. "Day off" means margins and measurements.

I like it this way.

Parchment slides. A bench scraper whispers. The oven ticks a satisfied cooldown.

A shadow crosses the front glass.

Knuckles, three measured taps. Not tentative. As if sure that the owner is just on the other side despite the sign.

I should ignore it. I don't. Habit has me wiping my hands as I walk past the counter toward the door.

Jack.

He's forsaken his sleek cashmere trench for his reindeer bait coat again.

He never came to the bakery yesterday. Just as I asked. Just as I wanted.

But the way my heart double-times makes me wonder if I should've been more final. Should've put a stop to all distractions sooner.

Turning the lock, I step back, the bell above the door giving a guilty jingle as Jack steps inside, snow glittering off his shoulders.

"Hey." He smiles—if you can call it that— before looking behind me at the spotless front case, then past it to the kitchen's military order, and something in his face softens before it steels.

His greeting feels ominous and a lot more serious than what our holiday fling calls for. "Hey."

I flip the lock again before leading the way through the swinging door, feeling the need to be surrounded by my kitchen equipment— the things I know how to work and run with elite proficiency.

The small kitchen swallows us: stainless and tile and the faint bite of cleaner. I set the spatula down and flatten both palms on the prep table to keep them from doing anything embarrassing. "So how was the library reading—"

"I was going to tell you about the client." His voice lands sharp and careful on the tile between us. "I meant to. I was going to explain—"

"There's nothing to explain." I shift a tray a half inch like proximity is a math problem. "But congratulations." I stare into my wavering reflection in the steel prep table. "Scott Evans. That's huge."

Out of the corner of my eye, I see him studying me, like he's cross-examining a witness who won't sit.

"Congratulations?" He's leading the witness.

"You seem to think I'd be angry." I force myself to meet his eyes. "I'm not angry, Jack." My tone, like my smile, comes out laminated—bakery-counter smooth. "I went into this knowing it wasn't permanent."

He opens his mouth then closes it. The sentence he had dies without a sound.

"I was always honest about what I wanted." I drop my eyes to the seam in the steel so I won't have to see his. "And you were honest about who you are." The smile I paste on is glassy and wrong. "And we both know a Hollywood agent-lawyer isn't part of the life I moved here for or want."

I glance at the oven door to my left, its reflection clear enough to see the muscles in Jack's jaw moving like a storm under his skin.

He looks around like the room might help him like it does me, inventorying the racks, the scales, the lined-up spoons.

"An imaginary life. With an imaginary man." His voice is too gentle for how sharp it lands. His eyes flick back to me like he already regrets the words but can't pull them back. "That's what you moved here for. A postcard husband in flannel with a moral compass that always points to your door."

Heat prickles under my skin, rising in a rush that feels like tormenting goosebumps. I grab the towel draped over the counter, twisting it hard enough to wring out water that isn't there.

"Two years ago you moved here, Audrey. And how far along is that dream?" He drags a hand through his hair, leaving it mussed, the clean-cut Hollywood polish slipping. His mouth twists as if the words taste bitter. "That carefully laid out plan with no room for negotiation or deviation?"

The words lodge in my throat. I press the towel flat against the counter, trying to smooth away the sting of them, but my fingers tremble too much.

"And with the way you work"—a breath, a wince—"with how much of a perfectionist you are, do you think you'll ever find it? Him?"

It's hard to swallow.

His eyes catch mine, steady and unblinking, daring me to argue. "Even if he's right in front of you, I doubt you'll see it."

We stare at each other for a beat with nothing but the hum of the refrigerator and my own pulse.

"Maybe I won't." My voice floats out, light as powdered sugar so he won't hear the crack in it. "Maybe I never will." I set the towel aside with deliberate care, like the gesture alone can prove I'm steady. "But not wanting to build a life around flight times and clients isn't a flaw. It's a boundary."

"I wasn't calling it a flaw." He breaks his stare, scrubbing a hand over his mouth. "I just..." He leaves his thought unfinished. Like us.

Reaching for a cooling rack I don't need, I slide it between us like a shield. "Neither of us are wrong. We're just wrong for where we're headed."

He leans on the opposite side of the table, palms braced,

the two of us bookending a battlefield we built together. "I could—"

"Don't." It's sharp enough that he goes still. "Don't offer to flip your life to make me feel safe about mine."

His eyes narrow, the lawyer seeing the weakness in the opposition's argument. "So you're scared."

"Of course I'm scared." The truth of it is hot and humiliating. "I have a business that works because I work it until my feet go numb. A town that can't whisper. A mother whose spreadsheets are a love language. I don't have room for a man who leaves."

He takes that without flinching. "I haven't left."

"Yet." I aim for kind and hit honest. "And I'm not mad. I'm grateful. I—" The words stop as my heart stumbles. "It was great while it lasted."

"Was." He tastes the past tense, grimacing like it's a bad drink. His gaze flicks to the wall clock, to the door, back to me. "So this is what, audit day? You close the books and write me down as a seasonal expense?"

"That's unkind." My words lack the vehemence of truth.

"I'm trying not to be." He closes his eyes, his voice fraying on an exhale. "I'm trying very hard not to be."

We hang there in the quiet kitchen, two people pretending not to collapse.

Finally, Jack straightens, moving the way a man does when the punch he didn't block has landed. His eyes flick to the immaculate sink, the knives in their slots, the neat parade of cooling shells. "It seems you have your picture, and I'm not in it."

The echo of my words—spoken without venom—is somehow worse.

All I can do is nod.

He obliges by pushing off the table. Not angry. Tidy. Moving through my kitchen with confident, careful steps, pausing only when he reaches the door.

I wait for him to say something. Something brave. Something stupid. Maybe both.

Instead, the moment of silence passes like a final farewell before he unlocks the door and the cold comes in and carries him out.

I stand where he left me, in a kitchen so clean it feels sterile—and just as empty. The table gleams—no flour dust, no stray sprinkle, no proof I didn't imagine him with his sleeves rolled up and his hand on my lower back telling me I'm out of parchment when I'm not.

The timer for our relationship that I never set goes off in my head.

I hit it with the heels of my palms, rubbing them into my eyes until the burn subsides. Until I can count the week's orders I memorized in my head. Until I'm positive that I won't be adding extra salt to my treats with my tears.

Getting to work, I line up a row of whoopie pie shells so straight it hurts. Then I line up another.

Perfect little halves, waiting for someone to put them together.

Jack

. . .

THE HAVEN'S room key is heavier than it needs to be. It thunks the desk when I drop it, an accusatory little paperweight beside my laptop and a glass of water I forgot to drink.

I drop my shapeless-but-warm coat over the chair and stare at myself in the full-length mirror on the wall. No tie, no Brioni—just a hand-knit scarf and the kind of fatigue that makes even good decisions look guilty.

I pull out my phone and draft a text: *I took on Evans as a client because—*

Stop. Delete.

I try again: *I didn't go into this thinking it was temporary—*

Stop. Delete slower.

"I went into this knowing it wasn't permanent."

What's the point on explaining when she already made it clear I'm not what-who she wants?

Dropping onto the bed, I check my inbox. Three messages from LA, one from a studio attorney with a subject line that reads like a threat dressed as a favor. I flag them all and answer none before crunching up off the bed to move to the desk and open my laptop.

When you can't fix a problem, open a spreadsheet. Tabs march across the bottom like good intentions: Permits. Budget. Contacts. Listings. I open the spreadsheet labeled HH —Vet Relocation.

I've never been remotely interested in real estate as a profession, and yet I built this file under the guise of helping a friend. Clicking Listings, I find the real reason I started this file in the three houses I flagged for my personal what-if project. Fenced yards. A swing set in one photo. A mudroom that looks like it could survive a childhood of hockey players.

I drag the "Houses" tab toward the trash icon, hover, let it go—then pull it back like a coward and rename it "Misc." Congratulations, me. I've rebranded denial.

A calendar reminder pops up: *WPAD— schedule posts (pre-set).* I already did that, but I check anyway. The social media captions are still there, cheerful and as unassailable as Eileen was when she helped me with them.

Buy one, gift one to help the Harbor Veterinary Clinic move!

Try the Peppermint Bark Whoopie—Love at First Sip staff favorite!

Nothing says holidays in Maine like Making Whoopie.

I close the laptop like it burned me.

Suitcase on the bed. I toss shirts in like I'm mad at them. The Brioni folds crisply, almost smug about it. On the dresser, a Haven boutique bag I forgot I bought—flannel, impulse purchase when I bought the coat. It's the kind of thing you wear when you've decided to look like you belong here. I pull it out and hold it up. Could be a twin for the one Eli was wearing earlier.

I hate it. But I pack it anyway.

Phone buzz.

Amanda: *How'd it go?*

I type: *Fine.*

She types back immediately: *Liar.* The bubbles tell me she isn't done. *If that were true you'd be in town right now and not sulking at the hotel.*

I turn it off, not understanding why I get cell service when I don't want it but can't when I do.

All part of Hideaway's charm, I guess.

No phone. No laptop. No work. Just the kind of silence that lets you replay the recent gut-wrenching transcript line by line.

"...a Hollywood agent-lawyer isn't part of the life I moved here for or want." Audrey said it calmly, like she'd lived with the verdict long enough to make peace with the sentence.

What if she's right? What if everything she said was what I refused to accept the whole time I was playing the part of a local and doing my best impression of a forever family guy? What if leaving now makes her life lighter? Easier? More complete?

I can live with the weight of missing her if it means she gets her happily-ever-after.

Even if it means I don't.

It takes a night of tossing and turning in my Haven bed, all high-thread-count sheets and downy quilts wasted on a man too restless to sleep, before I finally call time of death on my future in Hideaway.

Gathering the rest of my things, I zip up my suitcase and pocket the key. I don't even check airline departure times. I'll wait for whatever flight is next when I get there.

Killing the room lights, I shoulder my coat and head downstairs. The lobby smells like fir and patchouli, and when I check out early, the clerk gives me a sympathetic nod I pretend not to understand.

Outside, the BMW chirps. Snowbanks wear Sunday's storm like heavy collars, and the plows have since carved the road into a narrow, patient lane. I point the rental toward the airport and let caution set the pace.

Ten under the limit. Wipers metronoming. Headlights stitching a tunnel through the gray.

I keep my phone dark so I don't get Amanda's earful and because there's nothing I can say that won't make this harder for Audrey— or myself.

Plenty of time, then, for the rerun. And not the heartbreak.

I replay her laugh during my cloven-crush disaster at the farm. The constant sprinkle of flour or cocoa powder on her cheek. How her brow pinches in concentration over the smallest details when she bakes. And the way she looked past me to the life she's building and didn't blink.

Okay, a little of the heartbreak.

The road curves, slow and sure.

Tightening my hands on the steering wheel, I drive it the same way.

OVERBAKED

Audrey

The bell falls silent after the lunch crowd drifts back to their offices and errands. A lull. Normally, I'd savor this time to catch up on dishes, prep a new batch without tripping over myself.

But today the quiet presses heavier than the rush. My body aches like I've worked a double shift, though it's only midday. Saturday and Sunday I managed alone, steady as ever, but this —this hollow Tuesday—has wrung me out more than both of those days combined.

Behind me, Jack's corner is empty. No low, masculine rumble of a laugh while he takes orders on the phone. No moments of heated friction when he grazes me as he passes by, even though there's plenty of space for us both.

Now it's just me.

Flour. Sugar. Cocoa. Salt.

I measure carefully, like maybe I can keep the rest of my life from spilling.

Whisk, fold, scrape, pour.

Leaning against the counter, I breathe in the whisper of cocoa and cinnamon, waiting for it to soothe me. It doesn't. The mixer hums like a loyal hound and the ovens tick softly as the cakes cool, but the kitchen feels wrong. Stretched thin. Unfamiliar.

The bell jingles, and I snap upright, a smile plastered on like over-whisked meringue—so stiff I'm shocked it holds.

Lumi Snowe, the postmistress, breezes in on a puff of cold air, her wine-red hair pulled back in a casual ponytail, a paper sack tucked under her arm. "Afternoon, Audrey." She nods at the display case. "Came for a peppermint whoopie."

"Of course." I pull a square of parchment paper from the box. "Your timing's perfect. They've just been filled." I grab one from the line on the tray and drop it into a light blue paper bag stamped with Making Whoopie's logo.

I ring her up, and she takes the bag with a nod of thanks, resting the bundle under her arm on the counter. "Thought I'd bring your mail while I was at it."

"Thanks." Normally not one for small talk, I find myself willing Lumi to linger. "How's business at the post office? Holiday rush started yet?"

She huffs, eyes crinkling. "Started? Honey, it never stopped. People think Santa lives at my counter this time of year."

I grin, a little thinner than usual but real. "Then you've definitely earned the sugar hit."

Her gaze drifts to the corner behind the counter. Jack's table. "Where's your lawyer? Haven't seen him in a bit."

Smile still in place but tighter, I force a swallow. "He's gone home." True enough—Portia heard it straight from Amanda—but it still catches like a crumb in my throat.

"Ah. Too bad. I liked him." She takes a bite of pie, pushing it to the side of her mouth. "He was a nice guy."

He was. Is. Will be—for someone else.

That last thought does the opposite of cheer me up.

"When did you meet Jack?" The question is out before I can think better of it.

Lumi tilts her head. "Last week. Came into the post office, had me notarize something."

My brows shoot up. "He did?"

She swallows, pausing before taking another bite. "For your trademark application." At my expression, she frowns. "The one for 'Making Whoopie'? The final step to secure the rights statewide by filing them nationally?"

"Oh." I stare at the empty space in the display case where Lumi's pie used to be.

"Did someone try to take your name?" she asks, voice curious, not nosy.

"Yeah. I..."—my throat tightens—"...hired Jack to figure it out."

"Well then." Lumi beams, easy as you please, and takes another large bite of dark chocolate cake and pink and white striped peppermint cream. "Looks like he did his job." It comes out muffled but understandable.

With a wave, she's gone, the bell chiming cheerfully in her wake.

Yeah, he did his job.

He handled the cease-and-desist. He filed the paperwork. He protected me the way he knew how. Exactly as promised. And then some.

I smooth an errant piece of parchment flat against the counter, hands steady though my chest is not.

Shouldn't I feel relieved?

The threat to my business was supposed to be the thing keeping me up at night. Step one of attaining my dream. So knowing Jack went above and beyond to protect it for any future threats should make me relieved. Happy.

I'm not.

Standing in my too-quiet kitchen, the truth presses down on me like snow on a sagging roof. I don't miss Jack's legal skills. I just miss him.

I miss the way he leaned against the counter like he belonged here. The way his grin made the room feel less small-town and more like possibility. The way he made me feel seen.

The bell jingles again, bright and merry. I keep my eyes fixed on the counter, refusing to glance at Jack's corner.

But the emptiness settles in anyway.

And it clings to me the rest of the day.

Jack

SINCE YESTERDAY, I've watched flights out of Maine die slow deaths on the departures board while I outlasted them in a vinyl airport chair.

One point for Los Angeles. At least in the land of palm trees and bikinis I never spent a night at the airport courtesy of cancellations and delays due to "inclement weather." And yet as the points are stacked pretty high against Hideaway, I still can't summon up anything close to excitement for my return trip home.

Whenever that will be.

At six a.m., the terminal hums like Audrey's double refrigerators. A pair of guys dressed like me—lawyer me—park themselves at the bar. The bartender slides a rocks glass toward the nearest one. There's a healthy splash of orange juice on top, just enough to make drinking before noon look respectable.

The suit laughs too loudly at nothing, and I wonder if that's me in a few years. I shift in the hard-cushioned seat, my body feeling twenty years older, and wonder if it might be me in a few minutes.

The windows shift from black to pewter, and I try to place Audrey in her morning routine. She'd be up by now having already pulled her hair into a tight bun that won't make it to noon, no matter how ruthless she is with those chestnut strands. Her socked feet are wearing Crocs bedecked with a plethora of ridiculous bakery-holiday-themed charms. She's probably squeak-squishing down the back stairs, arriving to more than just her usual pristine kitchen.

Will she be relieved when she figures out what I've done? Or will it be one more tally mark in the column labeled Reasons Jack's Not Right for Me?

My phone vibrates in my pocket like it has opinions. I turned it on earlier to keep track of the weather. News flash—no change.

I thumb it awake to check the rebookings I already know don't exist. FaceTime tries to ambush me with Felix's face. I sigh and let it.

He's in a kitchen with marble and morning light. Sofia leans in at his shoulder, robe tied, hair up, no lipstick. For a Portuguese woman of a certain age to be seen without makeup, it usually means Armageddon has arrived.

Surprise wins over manners. "Why the hell are you both awake?"

"Language." Sofia's voice is gentle yet brooks no argument.

Felix winces.

"Sorry, Sofia" falls out automatically. "Morning."

Then, as if she hasn't just made me feel like the ten-year-old she once took in, she smiles. "Bom dia, meu filho."

Felix does a very poor job of hiding his amusement at my scolding. "Amanda was my wake-up call. She gave me the rundown on everything you've managed to screw up while allegedly on vacation."

I mentally roll my eyes at my interfering client-slash-friend-slash-sister stand-in. "Of course she did."

"Come to New York," Felix orders like it's the part of this conversation that matters most. "Skip LA. Spend the holidays with us."

Something sore in my chest feels a tug at his invitation. "Thanks, but I don't want to intrude on your new family traditions."

Felix looks confused, while Sofia's eyes gloss, fast and bright.

"Meu filho." She presses a hand to her chest. "Did I fail you?"

Instantly, both Felix and I are on high alert.

"No, Sofia." I lean forward, the words rushing out. "Never." Our conversation replay in my head. "Why would you say that?"

Just as quickly as the tears came, they disappear, Sofia's mouth setting in a hard line that says if I was within arm's range the back of my head might just be smacked into next week. "Then why do you think you are not a part of the family? Why do you keep yourself away?"

"Oh." I sit back, not prepared for the questions. "I just, uh..."

She shakes her head. "While I never wanted you to think I was replacing your mother when you came to us, it doesn't mean that I'm not your *mãe.*" The word lands exactly where it always lands—behind my ribs, where breath gets complicated.

"Yeah, man." Felix nods, sidling closer to Sofia, a clear two-against-one stance. "You're my brother and—" He jumps up with a curse, shouting, "Damn it, Mike!"

He moves off screen completely. "Elizabeth! Come get Mike Hunt!"

Sofia rolls her teary eyes. "I have two sons—one stupid about cats and one stupid about love."

I expel a tired laugh. "Amanda really did tell you everything."

"Not everything." Her ramrod posture speaks to the formidable woman Sofia Jones is. "But I am your mãe. I infer." She makes a come-here gesture, like she's been waiting years rather than minutes for me to explain. "So tell me, meu filho —what is she like?"

I rub the sleep from my eye. "She owns a bakery in town."

"That's what she does." Sofia tilts her head. "But who is she?"

I laugh, though the sound isn't cheerful. "Funny you should say that, because if you asked her that same question, she'd probably give you the same answer." My voice softens. "She has trouble separating the job from the person." I manage a small shrug that I hope distracts from my cracking composure.

Not falling for it, Sofia waits.

Sighing, I poke at the wound that hasn't yet stopped bleeding. "Audrey Nouel is one of the most stubborn people I know. She's beautiful and hardworking—but too much so." I cross the arm not holding my phone across my chest, sulking. "She's a perfectionist who doesn't have an off switch. It's like she wants to be chained to her kitchen."

An airplane moves across the tarmac for the first time since I arrived. I barely notice it, my thoughts on a woman who leaves scarce times for laughter but who gives her heart freely to a community she isn't even sure has accepted her as their own.

Unbidden, my lips tug upward. "But she's also the first to help others without any expectation of a return." Both my grin and my wound pull wide. "And when she lights up, it feels like you're the only one she's shining on."

Sofia's eyes soften. "She sounds like you."

That pulls me up short.

Remembering Audrey's words about not wanting a lawyer in her life, I clear my throat and force the wistfulness away. "I don't meet her dream-man qualifications."

One eyebrow arches as imperious as her tone. "And just what qualifications are those?"

"Simple." I lay it out like the closing argument. "She wants a family man." I swallow past the hurt. "And I don't know how to be that."

"Are you kidding me?" Felix reappears and doesn't even try to sit on his reaction. "You are the best family man I know."

I smile at his vehemence on my behalf. "Hate to break it to you, bro"—Felix smiles at the word—"but I'm not the Casanova you think I am. No secret kids running around I'm paying tuition for."

With a laugh, Felix rolls his eyes. "That is *not* what makes a family man."

"Sim." Sofia nods once in hard agreement. "Being a family man is being responsible. Thinking of others before yourself."

"Showing up for the big things and most of the dumb little ones, too." Felix leans back, expression uncharacteristically earnest. "You switched law focuses because of me. And don't think I don't know that every time you start to wonder about moving on and I get a new job offer or Amanda gets a salacious article written about her, you park your plans to make ours easier." He tips his head toward the screen. "Just like you're doing now."

Sofia pats his cheek. "You're not so stupid after all, meu amor."

Felix smiles toward her, surprised and pleased. "Thanks, mãe."

They lapse into soft bickering, which buys me a minute to absorb the indictment disguised as a love letter.

Elizabeth slides into frame behind them like a stage whisper, holding Mike Hunt under the armpits. He looks like attempted homicide in an elf costume. "Question," she says, letting it be known that she's been eavesdropping on our conversation this whole time. "Amanda said you took on a new client. If you were thinking about leaving the business, why do that?"

I rub my hand down my face and try to line up the thought I had before everything went sideways. "Pre-breakup me had the idea that instead of *poaching* Scott Evans from his agent, I'd bring both him and his agent over. Mentor the agent so I could build out some infrastructure. Enough so that I could step back from the agent side and focus on law."

Felix nods, not even pretending to be surprised. "You were always telling me you needed an assistant."

The moments he means line up in my head, sharp and clear. "Exactly. I could introduce Evan's agent to the right people, give her a bigger foothold, and we'd all win." I meet his eyes through the glass of the phone. "But I'd never finalize anything without talking to you and Amanda first."

Felix's expression flattens. "Seeing as Amanda's exact *early-morning* words to me were, 'Stop our asshat lawyer friend from doing what he thinks is noble but is actually self-sabotage, or I'm leaking Elizabeth's nude sketches of you—'"

Elizabeth coughs. "They were studies." She juggles the hairless cat closer to her chest, his jingle-bell hat jingling. "And nobody is passing anything around."

"Point is"—Felix pinches the bridge of his nose, needing a minute. Whether that minute is due to potential nude art of him being passed around to the paparazzi or the fact that he has to deal with the woman he loves dangling a Christmas-costumed cat, I'm not sure—"we both think you stepping back is a great idea. We fully support it."

"Me too," Sofia adds.

"Us three and four." Elizabeth raises Mike's hand.

He hisses.

Ignoring the cat in favor of my doubts, I close my eyes and replay the last conversation Audrey and I had in the bakery. "Yeah, but Audrey doesn't think I'm—"

"Then show her," Sofia cuts in, throwing her hands up with theatrical despair. "Be a man, meu filho. All this talking of feelings is exhausting."

Felix bites his lip to keep from laughing. Elizabeth turns herself—and Mike Hunt's murderous stare—away from the camera, shoulders shaking.

"Because if she doesn't think you are the right man, then she is also stupid," Sofia declares with finality.

Felix snorts.

"Therefore, you two are perfect for each other." She flicks her fingers like she's shooing a fly. "Go, meu filho. Bring me a new daughter."

Everything I've been trying not to feel rises like a tide, but heaven forbid I exhaust the woman who helped raise me any more than I already have. "Sim, mãe."

Her face softens. "Boa sorte."

We say our goodbyes, and as the screen goes dark, another power-suited clone nearby lifts his phone to a small face on his screen. "I'll be home soon, buddy. Very soon." His voice is steady in the way a trustworthy man needs to be, lighting up the child's smile.

I look out the window at the plane readying to take off. At the gate information a board where the flights that will eventually go west are listed. At the coat in my lap that smells like pine and horny reindeer and the Italian loafers on my feet that look as impractical as they are expensive. Closing my eyes from all distractions I think of everything Sofia, Felix, Elizabeth, and Amanda—*my family*—just said.

Turns out I don't need flannel and thermals to become the man Audrey needs. I've been him the whole time.

Standing, I grab my roller bag.

Time to prove it.

SHOWSTOPPER

Audrey

By nine o'clock the next day, I'm officially losing it. The ovens have been running since dawn. The counters are lined with neat rows of fresh whoopies, buttercream fluff piped with ridiculous precision, boxes stacked and waiting by the register. Business as usual—except it isn't.

Because not a single customer has walked through my door.

Not Mrs. Wexler with her cranberry scone order. Not the electrician who usually grabs a gingerbread whoopie on his way to the office. Not even Skippy, who tends to wander in to nap across my stoop like an unpaid security guard with selective hearing. The bell hasn't jingled once.

I wipe the case glass anyway—slow circles that squeak like I'm trying to buff out a bad mood—then straighten the stacks of napkins that are already straight.

My reflection in the metal trim looks like I lost a fight with sleep and then decided to double down.

I glance outside to appraise the weather (no storm), flip through my copy of *The Almanac* to check for today's town events (nothing listed), and check my pulse (present, erratic).

"Okay." I slouch over my prep table, head in hands, and talk to the various-sized whisks all neatly hung on hooks on the wall. "If you know something, now would be the time."

The bell jingles.

I straighten. But before I even take two steps toward the counter, it jingles again. And again. Until I'm standing there, watching my door become a turnstile that spits out bodies like confetti.

A veritable flood of coats, boots, and laughter. The sound ricochets off stainless steel and tile like a marching band discovered sugar.

Mia is one of the first to reach the counter, camera already up, ponytail swinging. "Look alive, whoopie girl." The camera clicks and flashes before she slides sideways to make room for the tide of customers—neighbors, friends—all leaning over the display case and calling out orders.

"What is happening?" I manage even as I pop the register and grab a stack of boxes by instinct. Because if there's one thing the holidays have taught me, it's to keep moving when the universe tries to bowl you over.

Mia snaps the crowd, checks her screen, then points her lens at me again. "Community event." Her mouth curves, and I pray she doesn't use whatever picture she just took of me. "Trust me, you're going to love this."

One by one, people I know step forward, bearing offerings like it's some kind of whoopie coronation.

The owner of The Perfect Package glides up first, a discreet little display cradled in her arms like a newborn. She sets it on my counter with reverence. "Our newest: whoopie pie–flavored lube." A wink. "Two for one if you promise not to ask me how we nailed the flavor profile."

"Uh, thank you." But she's already gone before I can finish, Portia sliding in with her own contribution.

"Whoopie pie taffy." She sets her tray next to the lube. "Swirled chocolate and vanilla cream." She assesses her goods like the candy pro she is. "Chewy but soft enough not to pull a filling."

"Thank—"

"Make way!"

The crowd parts to reveal the crew from Chowder House Rules muscling a tray that takes three people to carry. "Cornbread bundt cakes, sliced, slathered with honey butter, stacked into whoopie pies."

Whoopie pies the size of hubcaps.

Collectively, the town inhales. The smell alone could start a religion.

And from next door, Eileen bustles in, fireman Hudson hot on her heels with a large coffee urn he plants beside the lube display.

"Limited-run whoopie pie coffee," Eileen announces, addressing the crowd like a mistress of ceremonies. "And there's more where that came from."

"This'll be my workout for the day," Hudson mutters, shaking out his arms.

I blink, brain still struggling to catch up. "Thank you?"

Amanda, somehow beside me now, leans in. "What do you think?"

"It's amazing." And it is. It *so* is. Emotions I've been wrestling for days surge up for an entirely different reason. "But, uh… *what* is it?"

"Whoopie Pie Appreciation Day!" Eileen and Amanda shout, complete with jazz hands as if they rehearsed ahead of time.

And knowing the two of them, they probably did.

"Whoopie pie what?"

"Appreciation Day," Eileen repeats, already steering the crowd into an orderly line.

Portia materializes again, snapping like a paparazzo on a sugar bender. "Chin down, eyes up—yes, sell me the frosting."

Amanda obliges, tray of Fa-La-La-Filled balanced like a couture clutch.

"When did this happen?" I ask Mia as she hovers at the front of the line. "It wasn't in *The Almanac.*"

"It wouldn't have been a surprise if it was." She grins, pointing at a stack of Naughty List Nibbles. "A dozen for the newsroom, please."

Hands on autopilot, I pack her order.

Amanda pauses her photo shoot just long enough to chime in. "And Jack said if you knew, you'd spend so much time prepping you wouldn't enjoy it."

"Jack?" His name slips out of me, sharp and startled.

"This was his idea." Eileen smiles, steadying the urn as she fills paper cups.

A warm weight presses at my elbow. Lucy slides in, cheeks pink, hair in a businesslike knot, planting a to-go cup in my hand. "Chai latte. Extra dirty." Her grin is so wide her eyes nearly disappear. "Can't believe we kept this under wraps for almost a week."

"A week?" My heart stutters.

"Carb reinforcement!" Eli Bennett pushes through, tall and unbothered by the storm of people. He sets a paper bag that smells like bagels on the counter and surveys the chaos like he's seen stranger. "Wasn't sure what the Vet Clinic could contribute to Whoopie Pie Appreciation Day, so I figured breakfast."

"Oh." My voice snags. "Thanks."

He waves it off. "No—thank *you*. Those dog-safe cookies and cake crumbs you send over?" He gives the counter a happy knock. "My patients barely notice the shots. Or the thermometers up the rear."

"Glad to be of service," I murmur, stunned.

Eli leans closer. "By the way, where's your guy? There's a bagel for him too. Wanted to thank him for the help with my lease contract and the clinic relocation advice."

"Oh, um." I glance toward the empty corner where Jack usually parked himself. "He left."

"Left?"

"For the airport. Yesterday morning." My throat tightens.

Eli frowns. "Well, he better get back quick. The realtor he put me in touch with said those houses he was looking at already have offers. Fenced-in yards don't stay on the market long in Hideaway."

The room tilts. It doesn't fall—I've glued this place together with willpower and powdered sugar too many times for that—but it tilts. "Houses?"

But Eli's already waylaid by a pet owner with questions.

The line trundles on, people laughing and buying more than I'm sure they meant to because this is Hideaway and restraint is for January. I run out of Jingle My Berries and

Sleigh Me Softly and nobody complains; they simply pivot, as if joy were a menu with options.

"Uh, you okay?" Portia asks, apparently having taken enough pictures for Amanda's social media accounts. "You haven't moved for over a minute."

I manage to nod. "Uh huh." But the room is buzzing, not only around me, but inside my head.

People keep stepping forward—customers who became regulars who somehow became friends—dropping dollar bills in the tip jar like they're investing in stock that always pays dividends. Neighbors salute me with their purchased whoopie pies and say the things you don't expect to hear in public: *Your whoopies got me through chemo. Your cookies are what my kids think Christmas tastes like. Your Maple Me Moans saved my marriage—don't ask.*

I don't. I never do. Never found the time to.

But Hideaway Harbor has made time for me.

Before me is everything I thought I wanted: a bakery alive with joy, a town that loves me, proof I belong.

And yet it isn't enough.

Because a dream isn't just ovens and sugar and steady business. It isn't even a Christmas tree farmer.

Not anymore.

Where I once imagined flannel shirts and a man who could build me a bookshelf without a level, I see cashmere and loafers. A man not deft with a saw but with legal jargon sharp enough to carve out security and space for me—and for us.

I see Jack.

All of this—the love, the laughter, the community—means nothing without him beside me.

"Um, just so you know." Amanda slides up to the counter,

Sharpie poised to sign a customer's Making Whoopie bag like she's an A-lister at Comic-Con—which, honestly, she kind of is. "Jack's still here."

I whip my head toward her so fast my neck twinges. "I'm sorry—what?" Slightly whiplashed, I steady my hands on the display case. "But you said he left."

"He did." She scribbles her name with a flourish. "But the LA flight was canceled because of weather. He's been stuck at the airport ever since, waiting for them to reschedule." She grabs the customer's phone, holds it high, and takes a practiced selfie. "Which they did. For noon." Her head bows just enough for her eyes to angle up, sly and unblinking. "Today."

My eyes shoot to the clock. My pulse barrels in triple time.

I swivel to Eileen still handing out coffee by the register. "Eileen!"

She startles, sending a few drops of coffee splattering on my clean floor. "Yes?"

"I need your help." I dig into the pocket of my apron.

Her brows lift. "Of course."

Yanking the key to the shop out of my apron pocket, I toss it to her. "Close the store."

Eileen fumbles the catch, staring at the key like I just handed her a live grenade. "Now? You want to close *now*?" She sweeps her eyes over the line snaking to the door and down the street, customers chattering and laughing, fully expecting their sweet tooth to be soothed.

"Yes!" I whip off my apron, toss it over a bowl of icing, and jog toward the back door. "Thank you!"

I don't look back. I can't. My body is already moving, set on one singular mission: get to Jack before his plane leaves. Tell him I'm sorry. That I'm an idiot. That while my head convinced me we were temporary, my heart always knew he was the forever I didn't dare plan for.

Bursting into the back lot reserved for shop owners, I nearly collide with someone standing there.

"Mom?" I skid, breath fogging in the cold.

She looks up, startled. "Audrey! Sorry I'm late. The roads around town are fine, but right outside—icy." She brushes frost from her camel coat. "Took me longer than I thought to get here."

For a beat, all I can do is gape. "But *why* are you here?"

As if realizing not is all right with me, she drops her hands. "Jack invited me." Her words slow as her eyes travel the length of me, trying to figure out what's wrong.

Of course he did.

Inside, the bell rings and voices swell, muffled but insistent. My mother's gaze cuts to the back door still ajar then back to me. "Where are you off to?"

My words tumble out just as sharp as the air is cold. "To leave work in the middle of the day, let go of a week's worth of money, all so I can go beg the man I love to stay with me in a small town where I'll probably always worry about my bakery's bottom line but I'll be happy to do so."

She blinks, then nods once, as if that's exactly the answer she expected. "I see." Digging into her bag, she pulls out her key fob and presses it into my palm. "Take my SUV. It's safer on the roads than your delivery van."

For a heartbeat, everything inside me swells with words—gratitude, fear, love, the kind of confessions you only think of when you know you'll regret it if you don't say them. But instead I just wrap my arms around her tightly.

She squeezes back, warm and fierce.

Then I slip away, running across the icy lot in my Crocs, praying my socks don't soak through before I even make it to the driver's side. I throw myself into the seat, crank the ignition, and grip the wheel.

Jack

THE TRUCK FISHTAILS—TIRES skidding across a patch of ice that might as well be greased glass. I wrestle the wheel, jaw tight, muttering curses that fog up the windshield.

Whoever plows Hideaway Harbor's local roads should be promoted straight to state level—hell, *national* level. Because if the drive from the airport through the mountains is any indication, the rest of Maine must be limping along on sled dogs and prayer.

At this rate, I'll miss Whoopie Pie Appreciation Day altogether.

I smack the heel of my hand against the steering wheel, the thud echoing in the barely insulated cab.

Nice move, Lourd—waste time at the airport after Felix and Sofia finally talked sense into you because clearly you're a glutton for punishment.

And why? Because I had to change. Literally change. Into flannel, jeans, and boots—a costume straight out of central casting for "small-town boyfriend." After all that big self-talk about it not mattering if I wore suits or not, that I'd show Audrey I was the right man for her without the Hallmark vision she has her heart set on—I caved.

Years of lurking on movie sets taught me one thing: Costumes sell the story. So if Audrey Nouel wants a Christmas-tree-farmer fantasy, fine. I'll play the role long enough to deliver my closing argument—that while she thinks she wants flannel and firewood, what she really needs is me: legal pads, contracts, all of it.

And just to be extra—because apparently that's what Audrey Nouel does to me—when I couldn't find a vintage truck at the rental counter to complete the scene, I bought the desk worker's. Cash. For the price of a brand-new BMW.

The big red monstrosity better be worth it.

'Cause here I am, bouncing on a bench seat older than I am, wrapped in a wardrobe I have no business wearing, and praying I don't end up in a ditch before I make it back to Hideaway.

I glance down at myself—rolled-up flannel sleeves of my unbuttoned shirt that reveals the Henley underneath. My denim stiff. My boots scuffed from exactly thirty minutes of ownership. All this and I am still wondering if I look like a man who belongs in small-town America or just a lawyer in disguise.

God, I hope she knows. I hope Audrey sees past all this. That it isn't about the props. It's about her. About *us*.

Because if Audrey doesn't believe me when I show up looking the part and declaring that I'm here to stay, then maybe I deserve every pothole this road throws at me.

In the distance, I spot headlights cutting through the trees

—an SUV barreling toward me, faster than any sane person should drive on these roads.

I ease the wheel, trying to hug the side and give them space, but the old truck jolts too far right, tires crunching over a frozen rut. My hands yank left by instinct—right into the SUV's path.

"Fuck." I wrench the wheel back the other way to avoid clipping them—

Snow sprays across the hood. The bench seat bucks under me. The engine sputters in protest as the tires spin uselessly against ice and mud.

My breathing huffs in time with the tick of the cooling engine.

Fucking figures.

Figures I'd end up in the one place I swore I wouldn't—the literal ditch I'd been mentally cursing for the last ten miles.

And like the universe thought I needed a cherry on top of my wild mountain Oldsmobile adventure, an avalanche of snow slides off the towering evergreen above me, burying the cab of the truck under a wet, heavy sheet of white.

Perfect. Just perfect.

Audrey

WHAT THE ACTUAL?

I'm idling, heater blasting against my frozen ankles, staring through the windshield in stunned silence.

I just watched an ancient truck—one that looks like it bribed its way through state inspection—skid sideways until its front right tire disappeared into a ditch.

For a second, I can't quite believe it happened. My brain needs an extra beat to catch up. Then the shock fades, and reality creeps in.

If I stop, I could miss Jack.

And if I miss Jack, that's it. Next stop: LAX, where I'll be the pathetic woman camped outside his celebrity compound, begging for him to talk to me like one of those reality TV reruns that make me cringe.

Blurry movement stirs behind the frosted glass—the driver.

They wouldn't be moving if they were hurt. Right? And while I have no faith in that truck's tires—as evidenced by their ice-skating demonstration—I'm sure he can reverse out of that ditch and be on his way without me.

Right?

I grip the wheel tighter and consider just driving past.

But then the pine above the truck shrugs off its load, dumping an avalanche of snow over the cab, burying the thing like a frosted cupcake.

"Son of a..."

With a sigh heavier than a snowbank, I throw the gearshift into Park, grab the ice scraper off the passenger seat, and shove the door open with a curse about vintage trucks and their drivers. Cold slaps me in the face, the kind that instantly chaps your lips and stings your nose.

One step and my Crocs sink into the snow, socks soaked through immediately.

I can't. I just can't.

But I do.

Stomping up to the half-entombed truck, I flip the scraper and use it like a shovel, attacking the driver's side door with all the vehemence of someone who was just personally wronged by snow. Which, frankly, I feel like I was.

My arms burn, my forehead beads with sweat, and my mouth mutters words that would've gotten me grounded for weeks as a teenager. A flash of plaid appears through the ice-crusted window, a shoulder shoving against the door until the hinges give way with a groan—like even the metal knows this is a bad idea.

I step back, breathless, snow dripping down my wrist, Croc charms sacrificed to the snow gods.

The door swings wider.

And then—because fate has a wicked sense of humor—Jack unfolds himself from the cab. Except it can't be Jack. Jack doesn't wear oversized flannel button-downs, worn Levi's, or boots scuffed like he's worked with something other than movie stars and subsidy clauses.

"Audrey?" Jack blinks at me, confusion knotting his features.

Holy crap.

I stumble back, right into a pile of slush. Cold seeps through my Crocs, but I barely feel it. Because it's him.

The man I've been chasing down the mountain, desperate to catch before his plane left. The man I pushed away when I should've pulled him close. The man I swore I could live without—only to find every day since hollow and aching.

His coat is dusted with snow, his hair mussed like he's fought the same storm I have. But it's his eyes that undo me. Steady. Searching. Like I'm the thing he came here for all along.

My throat tightens, my breath snagging in the icy air. My heart slams against my ribs, louder than the ticking engine, louder than the scrape of snow slipping from the branches above. Louder than the voice in my head that still whispers I don't deserve him after sending him away.

I toss the ice scraper—and every bit of caution in my body—aside, then launch myself at him, lips crashing onto his.

THAT'S A WRAP

Jack

The impact knocks the breath out of me, not from her weight but from the fact that Audrey Nouel just threw herself at me in the middle of a snowbank like we're reenacting a holiday rom-com stunt gone wrong.

Her lips are on mine—hot, frantic, desperate—and I don't care that I'm half-buried in a ditch with a truck older than disco. I kiss her back, one hand cupping her frozen cheek, the other anchoring around her waist like she might slip away if I don't hold tight.

When we finally break for air, she's panting, eyes wild, hair stuck to her damp cheeks. "You idiot," she breathes, voice muffled against my collar. "You absolute, flannel-wearing idiot."

I huff out a laugh, forehead against hers. "That's fair. But for the record, I'm only in flannel because I thought you wanted a lumberjack."

Her brows knit. "A lumberjack?"

I nod, already bracing for impact. "Yeah, I figured you wanted plaid and sawdust. Big guy with an axe."

She blinks at me, then shakes her head, snowflakes scattering from her hair. "Jack, I don't need a lumberjack."

I open my mouth to argue, but she silences me with a hard, fast kiss that robs every smart-ass rebuttal from my throat. When she pulls back, breath warm against my skin, she adds, "And no, not a Christmas tree farmer either."

Her hands fist tighter in my shirt, her eyes burning into mine. "I need someone by my side. Someone who makes me slow down and actually notice the world instead of racing through it. Someone caring enough to worry over a stray dog's limp and look after a neighbor's lawn gnome rights. Someone who organizes a surprise celebration of sexual-innuendo pastries because the owner of the store is too blind to see what's right in front of her."

My chest tightens. The air steams between us. I should kiss her—agree with her—but the only thing that comes out is, "But what about your dream of small-town life—"

"That was made when *I* was an idiot. Before I met you." She huddles closer as if afraid I might slip away.

Which is ridiculous. I'm not going anywhere. Not anymore.

Her fists tighten around my flannel. "*You're* all that matters."

I've always been a man of considerable vocabulary. It's imperative to persuasiveness, which is key in my line of work.

And yet on top of a mountain, on the side of a road, a foot from a ditch, all I can think to say is, "Yeah?"

"Yeah," she parrots, my stupidity apparently making her smile. "And forget small-town life if you don't want it. Eli told me about the house listings." Still smiling, she shakes her head. "Thank you, Jack, but you don't need to move or buy a house. I know your work is in LA."

The lawyer in me—the part that always hunts for the rebuttal—snaps to attention. "But yours is in Hideaway." My counter comes out as more plea than argument.

"Yes, but thanks to you"—she flutters her lashes, a stray flake catching like a rhinestone—"I can open a Making Whoopie anywhere in the country."

My brain flashes to the trademark application I drew up; the idea fits in my head like a puzzle piece turned the right way.

Her arms wrap around me, warm and fierce. "Even the diet-driven citizens of LA need a whoopie pie now and then."

"You'd do that?" My voice reads less like a lawyer and more like a kid who's just been offered his favorite thing.

She regards me like I've declared both the most outrageous idea and the most obvious truth. "Jack," she says—no drama, only steadiness—"I just closed the bakery in the middle of a holiday sales rush for you."

My jaw drops. I glance at my watch over her shoulder; she's right—she should be cash-register deep in Whoopie celebrations. "Wow. You really do love me."

She pauses, as if the sound of it surprises her, then the shock melts into a smile. "I do, Jack. I do love you."

"I love you, too." The words come out raw and certain.

"I know." She kisses me again—a real, deep kiss. Not that

the ones before weren't real, but this one is different: not an experiment, not a dare. This kiss folds in everything—apology and forgiveness, danger and promise, half-forgotten jokes and serious plans. It lands like a promise, a vow, a private treaty: whatever comes next, we choose each other.

I hold her until the world resumes—engine ticking, snow settling, the truck cooling—until the scent of wet wool and buttercream fills my senses, and for the first time in weeks, maybe months, I am exactly where I'm supposed to be.

Audrey

BY THE TIME Jack and I roll back into town in my mom's SUV, my toes are finally thawing courtesy of Jack's dress socks unearthed from his suitcase. I wedge my bundled feet into my dried-off Crocs—not exactly what Armani had in mind, but it works for me.

The rest of his luggage came in handy, too. Because when we finally stopped kissing long enough to realize certain vital parts of our anatomy were courting frostbite—my fingers and toes, Jack's cold bits more centrally located—the look he gave me as he peeled off my wet clothes before wrapping me like a present in his dry ones was enough to save me from hypothermia.

We left his new-old truck by the side of the road, one of

his white Calvin Klein undershirts flapping in the driver's side window like a surrender flag. Probably not the official way to mark an abandoned vehicle but close enough.

As the SUV noses into Main Street, my heart, already fit to burst, stutters at the sight: Making Whoopie is glowing like a lantern, spilling warm light onto the snow-packed sidewalk. People are coming and going, their arms full of boxes.

I sit forward. "It's still open?"

Jack glances at me, brow arched. "Didn't you say you gave the keys to Eileen?"

"I did." I squint down the road, spotting the line of bundled coats outside my door. "Told her to close it."

But she didn't.

We park around back, the rear light above my back door cutting a weak circle into the night, steam curling from the vents like the place itself is breathing. Jack and I, fingers laced, slip inside.

The noise hits first—the hum of chatter, bursts of laughter, the steady ding of the register. Then the smell: chocolate, peppermint, sugar, and coffee.

From the shadow of the kitchen doorway, I take it all in.

Portia is boxing orders, ribbon between her teeth as she ties bows with the speed of someone who knows how to pull taffy. Amanda has commandeered a piping bag, cream swirling on cakes like she was born for it rather than the stage. Even Mia is juggling her camera and trays, snapping candids between shoving more whoopies into the display case.

And at the cash register—my mom.

The line stretches out the door, coats and scarves trailing behind. Steam curls from cups of coffee Eileen is doling out with the gravitas of a maître d'. "Next! Keep it moving, darlings, these whoopies won't eat themselves."

Jack leans close, his breath warm at my ear. "Looks like they've got it handled."

I can't speak. My throat's too tight, heart too full.

"Thank you for shopping at Making Whoopie," Mom says brightly, handing a customer their change—then casually tossing a bottle of lube into their bag. "Where every craving deserves a happy ending."

The customer snorts. Someone in line laughs so hard they nearly drop their box, and the whole place ripples with it.

It might be my bakery. But tonight, it's also Hideaway's.

Jack shifts beside me, his body tense like he's about to step forward, announce us, let the whole town see we're here and we're together.

But I catch his sleeve, fingers curling tightly into the flannel. A quick shake of my head.

His brows lift in question, but I tip my chin toward the narrow door at the back, the one that leads to my apartment. His gaze softens, understanding reflecting in the warm light filling the shop.

We move together, silent as guilty teenagers, slipping over the threshold and shutting the door behind us with a quiet click that muffles the laughter and clatter on the other side.

Our footsteps creak, hushed by the thick hum of adrenaline in my ears. Halfway up, his hand slides against mine, rough and steady, and I squeeze back, eager for harder touches.

By the time we reach my apartment, my breath is already ragged. We tumble inside, the door nudging shut on a room washed in soft lamplight and the faint scent of pine from the Christmas tree.

Our Christmas tree.

There are no words left to argue, no doubts left to wrestle. Just his mouth finding mine, the weight of his body pressing me back against the door, the heat of him chasing away every chill the day tried to carve into me.

Jack bends, strong arms sliding beneath me. I gasp as he lifts me clean off the floor, my legs wrapping around his waist by instinct.

My world sways as he carries me down the narrow hall, each step creaking beneath his boots. His lips never leave mine, kissing me through the stumble and sway until we reach my bedroom. The lamp on the nightstand throws a soft, golden glow, the quilt on my bed rumpled from this morning's hasty exit.

He lays me down like I'm breakable, but his eyes—dark, hungry, reverent—tell me otherwise. I tug him over me, pulling his weight, his heat, wanting every inch of him pressed to every inch of me.

Clothes scatter in our wake—his flannel sliding from my shoulders, his jeans pushed down with impatient hands, my borrowed socks flung aside one by one. His body covers mine, hot skin to hot skin, and when he finally presses inside, slow and deep, I arch into him with a cry.

He moves carefully at first, like he's savoring, memorizing, until my nails drag down his back and his restraint breaks. The rhythm builds, steady and consuming, until the room is full of the sounds of us—breathless gasps, low groans, the squeak of the mattress beneath our bodies.

I cling to him, every thrust driving away the cold, every

kiss sealing something permanent between us. When I come apart beneath him, it feels like falling and being caught all at once. He follows, shuddering, whispering my name against my skin like a prayer.

Afterward, he collapses beside me, pulling me against his chest, his heartbeat pounding against my ear, his arm heavy and sure around me.

I burrow closer, wrapped in a quiet, steady happiness I never knew existed. Not something to chase. Not something to win. Just a place to rest. With Jack.

He presses a kiss behind my ear, his voice dropping to a rumble. "I want you to know one thing, Audrey."

I smile against his chest. "That you love me?"

"Well, yeah." Lips brush my hair. "But also, freezing my balls off for whoopie?" He leans back, eyes locking on mine, his grin wicked and tender all at once. "Smartest move I ever made."

ENCORE

Jack

The Zoom window freezes, and Sloane Mercer, my partner of almost two years, is caught looking like she's mid-sneeze.

A second later, she vanishes completely, along with the Hollywood skyline behind her, as my signal stutters into pixel confetti before the app gives up altogether.

I check my phone, finding that, oddly, I have cell signal while my hardline Wi-Fi malfunctions. With an eye roll for small-town quirks, I fire off a text to Sloane that I'll see her in person next week and close the laptop.

Leaning back in my desk chair, I listen to Hideaway Harbor breathing through the open window of Audrey's old apartment.

Gulls cry, a porch swing creaks, and kids shriek in sprinkler arcs down by the docks. My second summer here smells like salt and sunshine and something sugary that's permanently embedded in the walls.

Probably marshmallow fluff from Audrey's upcoming Fourth of July s'more whoopie pies—decorated with a sparkler on top.

The door at the bottom of the steep apartment stairs pops. Footsteps. The kind I know better than my own pulse.

"Absolutely not." I stand as the apartment/office door opens.

Audrey pauses on the landing, a bakery box in hand, the other resting on the five-month swell of a bump under her sundress. She tilts her head, giving me a look that says 'Hi, darling' and also 'Explain yourself.'

I point down the stairs, scowling like they're a sworn enemy. "You're not doing those again."

One brow lifts. A dangerous angle. "Those?"

"*Those*." I point at the staircase as if it personally offended me.

With a roll of her eyes, Audrey toes off her sandals and pads inside, sunlight glancing auburn off her dark tresses. Her little blue dress has strawberries printed all over it, like she's trying to tempt fate into inventing cravings.

Not that I mind. Cravings mean more sweets, which means more of my favorite new morning cardio program.

My wife sets the box on my desk and breathes out buttercream. I swear even the floorboards get a little aroused.

On her tiptoes, she kisses my cheek. "You're being dramatic."

I hold her to me. "It's not dramatic to insist the mother of my child stop climbing the Death Stairs of Doom."

She rolls her lips. "Is that the official municipal designation?"

Jokingly puffing out my chest as I do whenever the mayor asks me to consult on town meetings, I adopt my most haughty look. "Pending council review."

Head shaking, she slides out of my grasp and opens the lid on the bakery box. Chocolate, cranberry, maple, pistachio. Sinners in a lineup, all of them.

Plucking out a Jingle My Berries and taking a bite like Christmas came to taunt me in July, she leaves a swipe of cream on her lower lip that qualifies as cruel and unusual punishment.

I thumb the sugar from her mouth and pop it in mine. "We're putting in an elevator."

She snorts, loud and lovely. "I've had enough of contractors, haven't you?"

She's referring to the ten months of renovations it took for the farmhouse I bought just outside of town to be dragged into modernity.

"No," I lie, cleanly and with purpose.

She narrows her eyes. "You already called someone."

"Maybe." I tap the desk, the old wood warm under my fingers, and run through the plan I'm definitely not telling her about yet: construction starts while we're in LA next week; preliminary inspection passed; the lift cab big enough for Audrey and a stroller.

Outside, a truck backfires, and the gulls swear about it. Seaside Maine is loud in the most charming way imaginable.

"Jack." Audrey's chin drops, her eyes lasering in on me.

"Mm?" I pause mid-thought, already cataloguing how to

spin this into "responsible husband" instead of "overbearing lunatic."

She points back toward the door. "You do realize I made it up those steps every day for years."

I level her a look right back. "Not while incubating." My hand slides to her belly, an instinct I didn't know existed until three weeks ago when the first flutter hit my palm and my skull turned to stardust.

Her mouth tilts into something that warms me behind my ribs.

"Who was on the call?" Audrey's hip bumps my knee. Her hand settles on the curve under her dress, the absent, proprietary touch making my throat burn.

"Sloane." I scratch my jaw, buying a second to shove myself back into work mode. "Studio wants us both in person next week."

Since pulling Sloane on board as the first agent in Lourd & Co. LLC, she's been handling the talent while I handle the paper. Bi-coastal lawyering has turned into an entertaining challenge. I love it.

Audrey hums approval, already a card-carrying member of the Sloane Mercer Fan Club. "Any more clients tell you your voice sounds like a 'contract in cashmere'?"

Having my wife repeat a client's flirty soundbite back to me is infinitely more mortifying than when it happened in the first place. "Who told you?"

"Elizabeth." Audrey smiles. "After hearing about it from Felix." Her nostrils flare as if trying not to laugh. "Who got it from Amanda, who got it from Sloane."

I wince at the reminder that the rumor mill needs no

middleman when family and clients are one and the same. "I assure you, wife, my cashmere remains strictly for you."

Audrey licks the last of the cream from her lip slowly and smugly. "Mmm."

The sound slides under my skin like heat rising off her whoopie pies.

As if reading my mind, she opens the box again, pulling out a smaller, pale green cake from the corner. "Maya's."

I bite. Pistachio, chocolate, a whisper of something citrus that shouldn't work and absolutely does. "Damn."

"I know." Pride slides through her words like butter over hot toast. "She built it off my almond base, then switched it for pistachio and cut the sweetness with dark chocolate."

When the trademark paperwork I filed came through, Audrey made quick use of it, setting up a bakery in LA just like she said she would that day on the mountain. Making Whoopie is now a two-store chain, with plans in the works for a third located inside Moore's Department Store in Manhattan this Christmas.

A Christmas we'll spend with both our families—born and chosen.

"When you check on the LA store next week, make sure to tell Maya I'm a fan. You chose your employee well."

She tips her head as if still surprised how the woman who once shouldered a whole town's worth of expectations by herself is no longer carrying them alone. "Turns out hiring competent people and delegating doesn't make me lazy."

"There are many things I would call you—" I lick pistachio from my thumb. "But lazy is not one of them."

Eyebrows lifted, she arches a challenge. "And what things would you call me?"

I lean closer, nuzzling the skin just under her jaw. "Glowing."

"It's the first of July and ninety degrees outside." Her voice is flat enough for me to feel the eye roll. "I'm not glowing, I'm sweating."

I nuzzle her neck anyway. "It's a wet glow."

Pulling back, she swipes her finger across the cream of a pastry. "Can you think of anything else less... damp?" Heat dances in her eyes.

My pulse trips, the air shifting from sweet to something decidedly hungry. "Alluring."

Smiling, she smears my bottom lip with cream. "Better."

Watching her watch me, I tongue it off, the sweetness melting into something far more decadent. "And tempting."

A slow smile unfurls, heat tucked in the corners. "Oh, I like that." She braces her arms behind her on the desk, her breasts straining against the thin fabric of her sundress. "Anything else?"

"Yeah." I place my hands on either side of her, caging her in. "*Mine.*"

Against the July heat she just complained about, she shivers.

But just as I'm about to claim what's mine, a knock on the half-open door interrupts the entirely appropriate plan I was forming to test the craftsmanship of my desk—Felix's idea of an office warming gift for a small-town lawyer.

The knock drags a growl out of me while Audrey slips off the desk with infuriating grace, smoothing her dress like she hasn't just weaponized strawberry print and buttercream.

"Come in," she calls because apparently I work in a commune.

Eli Bennett fills the doorway, cap tugged low, a clipboard tucked under his arm, a grease-stained paper bag in the other. Hideaway's vet looks freshly scrubbed from whatever barnyard emergency he's just handled, smelling faintly of cedar chips and horse liniment.

"Sorry to interrupt." His gaze bounces from me to Audrey and back, like he walked in on exactly what he did. He waves the clipboard. "But since I was nearby—Jack, I could use your take on something legal." Noting my less-than-thrilled expression, he lifts the bag. "Fish and Chips from Chowder House as a retainer."

This time it's my stomach that growls. With one last glance at Audrey, I nod, albeit reluctantly. "Acceptable."

Audrey tries to hide her smile. She's never said it out loud, but I know she's happy about my friendship with Eli. I think she was worried that if I moved away from Los Angeles where Felix and Sofia are based that I'd regret moving.

She has no idea the lengths I'd go to for her.

And I would have given her ample evidence of my current length if said friend hadn't shown up.

My new 'bestie,' as Amanda—another recent Los Angeles transplant—likes to call Eli, drops the bag of unhealthy and delicious food on the island before turning his clipboard toward us like it's a smoking gun. "It's about my neighbor. The one next to the new clinic property you helped me close on. She's been..." He hesitates, then blurts out, "Antagonizing me to no end."

"Antagonizing?" I cross my arms, wondering what could flap the unflappable Eli Bennet. "What did she do?"

"So much." Heaving a long-suffering sigh, he points to a picture of what looks like tree branches and something vaguely metallic. "First there was the windchimes." He closes his eyes as if to relive the horror. "So many wind chimes."

"I see." I don't see.

Eli, as if sensing my skepticism, flips the page on his clipboard. "Now she's set up an above ground pool and sunbathes at all times of the day while listening to music, totally distracting to the clients coming and going from the clinic."

The look Audrey and I share asks the obvious question: *Clients or you?*

Not wanting to outright dismiss his complaints, I ask, "Is the music loud enough to be considered a noise violation?"

He lowers his evidence, muttering something like "setting the wrong tone for my clients," which gives me the sense that no, his neighbor's music is not a noise violation.

Straightening, he changes tactics. "She's gone and planted butterfly bushes all along our shared property line."

"Butterfly bushes." I'm not seeing how such a pleasant-sounding plant can be so offensive.

"They attract *bees*." He says the last as if it's damning evidence that should send me reaching for legal paperwork.

"Aren't honeybees endangered?" Audrey asks, not realizing she's trying to reason with an unreasonable man. "I just read about how planting butterfly bushes can help restore the population, improve pollination, and boost food production."

Eli deflates like a popped balloon, his next words as weak as his argument. "They could sting my patients."

"Oh." Audrey looks at me for help.

I've got nothing. While bees could be a legitimate problem if someone or some animals were allergic, I happen to know, thanks to handling the paperwork of his clinic's purchase, that

Eli has at least an acre between him and his neighbor's supposed bee-sting death traps.

Rallying once more, Eli flips to yet another photo on his clipboard. "And now she's gone and strung lights across her back fence." He taps the picture that's mostly black with a few golden spots.

I blink. "Lights."

"Yeah." He nods fast, gearing up. "Big, twinkly ones." He scoffs. "It looks like a carnival over there."

I'm seriously concerned that all Eli's 'evidence' does is give his new neighbor grounds for a peeping-Tom case against my usually laid-back and easygoing friend.

"That sounds..."—Audrey's mouth quirks, but she keeps her voice diplomatic—"...aggressively festive."

I shoot her a look while also trying to keep my expression neutral.

"Festive," Eli mutters. "It's disruptive is what it is."

Me thinks the vet doth protest too much.

Clearing my throat, I attempt to scrub all amusement from my voice. "Sorry, Eli. Lights are not a legal issue. As long as it doesn't encroach on your property or go against township regulations, she can decorate her property as she likes—that includes lights and shrubbery."

Eli's expression reminds me of a child being told he has to eat his vegetables before he can have his dessert.

Rolling my lips in an attempt to remain professional, I offer, "If it bothers you, you can always put up blinds." I rethink my peeping-Tom concern. "In fact, I *strongly* suggest you put up blinds."

"Right. Yeah." He sighs, his eyes flicking to Audrey as if just noticing her rounding stomach. Expression softening, he suddenly looks a lot more his usual calm, mature self than he did a second ago. "Congratulations, by the way."

Audrey beams. "Thanks."

My hand slides over Audrey's bump, staking a claim I don't need to make but want to. "Thanks, man."

Eli tips his cap and makes for the door, muttering something about checking on a colicky mare—and maybe buying a decibel meter just in case.

Audrey waits until the door clicks shut before turning to me, amusement dancing in her eyes. "What was that about?"

I kiss the corner of her mouth. "About how an extravagant display of twinkle light décor can make any calm, logical man spiral into Grinch territory."

"Grinching in July?"

"Hey, Christmas in July." I point to her Jingle My Berries Whoopie Pie. "It's a thing."

Her laugh spills out, warm and wicked. "You're ridiculous."

Maybe. But I know an over-invested man when I see one —and Eli Bennett just found his plotline.

Meanwhile—I re-cage my wife against my desk—it's time to get back to mine.

Her laugh is still warm on my mouth when she whispers something about buttercream smudges on important legal briefs, but I don't care. Not when she's here, soft and sharp all at once, strawberry dress bunched under my palms.

I traded skyscrapers for salt air, contracts for cookie sheets, and somewhere along the line, the town I swore I'd never belong in became the only place I want to be. The only place *we'll* ever want to be.

Audrey tilts her head, smiling that smile that ruined me from day one. "Happy?"

Happier than I've ever been. Happier than I thought I'd get to be.

I kiss her slowly, savoring everything—her, this town, the life we're building, the baby kicking under my hand like he wants in on the joke.

"Happy doesn't even begin to cover it," I murmur against her lips. "You?"

She answers with a sexy grin before pulling me close and giving me more of my hard-earned and well-used lifetime supply of whoopie.

Ready for more holiday fun in Hideaway Harbor? Next up...

This single mom's sudden gloom during the *hap, hap, happiest* time of the year is turned upside down when a globe-trotting toy industry mogul is stranded in her small harbor town and needs a place to stay. Finding room in her heart for the silver fox hadn't been on her Christmas list, but there is something magical about this mysterious stranger. Something that makes her wish he could stay forever.

Read Now!

Christmas at Hideaway Harbor series

- The Holiday Hate-Off by Angela Casella
- The Holiday Fakers by Evie Alexander
- The Holiday Whoopie by Sara L. Hudson
- The Holiday Post by L.B. Dunbar
- The Holiday Clause by Lydia Michaels
- The Holiday Grump by Enni Amanda

Hideaway Harbor books are interconnected standalones and can be read in any order.

Want more Sara L Hudson?

Scan below for a FREE novella when you sign up for my bi-weekly newsletter. Freebies, Amusing Anecdotes, Book Recs & more!

ALSO BY SARA L HUDSON

SPACE SERIES

Smart, sexy, and a little outrageous—NASA's women have it all, and the men who love them are along for the wild ride. Strap in for laugh-out-loud banter, panty-melting romance, and happily-ever-afters hotter than rocket fuel.

ANYONE BUT YOU SERIES

What happens when three Moore siblings—heirs to a luxury retail empire in New York—fall headfirst into love? Expect laugh-out-loud banter, panty-melting chemistry, over-the-top family drama, and one very inappropriately named cat.

ABOUT THE AUTHOR

I'm an author and mother driven by anxiety and a perverse sense of humor all while being fueled by coffee and ADHD medication.

It's a wonderful, wild ride of a life made possible by my supportive (but cheap) husband, my incredible (but too far away) parents and my amazing kiddos Holly and Adam.

I love to make people laugh and hope to continue to do so in the genre that always guarantees a happy ending ;)

xxx, Sara

www.ingramcontent.com/pod-product-compliance
Lightning Source LLC
Chambersburg PA
CBHW011133190726
48289CB00012B/3023

* 9 7 8 1 9 5 4 6 0 2 8 1 6 *